# THE FOUR ARROWS

## A NOVEL BY
## RANDALL BETH PLATT

CATBIRD PRESS

**Library of Congress Cataloging-in-Publication Data**

Platt, Randall Beth
The Four Arrows Fe-As-Ko: a novel
by Randall Beth Platt.
p.  cm.
ISBN 0-945774-14-1 (alk. paper)
I. Title.
PS3566.L293F6  1991
813'.54—dc20          90-28802

To Christopher Booth Platt

*S*et down, son. Set down. I don't mind saying I was in a transport of delight when I got your letter asking me, ol' Royal R. Leckner hisself, to talk about his favorite subject . . . myownself.

Here, have some lemonade. Cookie?

Now you be sure to make a note I said to tell ol' FDR he's doing fine and it's gooda him to come up with that Federal Writers thing so's you young folks can work and all. I want you to know I've been thinking on the past, just like you suggested, and I think I come up with a jim dandy story for you.

Hell, my whole life has been a jim dandy story, and it took me a whole day just to settle on which episode to give you. Plus, you'll be happy to know I got a right good memory. But old folks like me, well, somehows we get thought of as spellbinders. You know: tall-tellers, leather-stretchers. And pretty soon nobody believes a thing you say and then, well, they just stop asking or, worse still, they just set there and nod kindly-like. They're smiling, they're nodding, but they're thinking, "Oh sure, Gramps."

Shucks, son, don't look so scared. I promise to you here and now this, what I shall now tell you, is the truth, the whole truth, and nothing but the truth, so help me Aunt Agnes.

# Part One

## o n e

*H*ell, I reckon most stories oughta start right off with a humdinger, so you'll be glad to know this story begins with a end: the overdue demise of one Samuel J. Perrault.

I can't say as I was overly wrung-out when Ol' Man Perrault died. Can't say I was even upset in a passing, polite sorta way. I can say, though, I had to laugh when word got out that his own horse had shot him; I sure as hell reckon there's better ways of dying. Couldn't happen again in a million years, Sheriff Agnew said. As near as we could figure it, a rattler worried Perrault's horse and, being a consummate snake hater, the old man cocked his rifle to blast the poor reptile on back to the devil. The horse reared; Perrault fell off and dropped his rifle; the horse, also being a consummate snake hater, thrashed about as horses do and stepped on the rifle. The stock was broke clean in half and the snake was, in a literal way of speaking, quite beside hisself. And Perrault, he had a bullet smack dab between his eyes which, they said, had one of them *Et tu Brute* looks in 'em.

At the inquiry, some joker wanted to hang the horse. Even though the critter had a guilty look about him, I came to his defense. I showed Sheriff Agnew the spur scars on the beast's flanks which quickly brought in a verdict of innocent-based-on-justifiable-homicide with a tinge of temporary insanity tossed in onaccounta we all wanted this case sealed up tighter than Wondrous Wilhelmina of Winnemucca's corset (which I can tell you first hand is damn tight).

Folks came from miles around for Ol' Man Perrault's funeral, but mostly just to hear Pastor Dennison's piece. He managed to find a few good things to say about Perrault, but when it came time to reconcile how he died (which was sometimes the highlight of funerals in those parts), well mosta us liked to have bust a gut trying not to laugh. Womenfolk was lucky: they had hankies and veils to hide their smiling tears. Ol' Perrault's horse never even let on, though. He just stood there, his back foot hipshot kinda casual-like, swatting flies with his skimpy, Cayuse tail. I was the one saddle-broke that horse, so I knew there was a grin behind those dozy eyes of his. But other folks made comment to me they thought the horse held up just fine and with remorse befitting a horse in his position. Naturally, I kept my quiet.

Nope, can't say as Perrault's death bothered me much. But I did commence to worry about where all this left me and the other boys who worked Four Arrows. Naturally, as foreman of the ranch everyone looked to me for answers, as though just being ranahan made me privy to Perrault's personal affairs.

*O*h, now there I go, getting aheada myself. You're looking a little adrift, son. Maybe I'd best back up a piece so's you can understand just how things stood back then, the summer of 1892.

The only reason I'd gotten the dang job as ranch foreman in the first place—let's see, that was in '84—was I was the first range hand that Perrault ever set eyes on that had him some education beyond first or second grade. I could write and cipher, so even though I was only twenty

4

and considerable younger than the rest of the crew, Perrault gave me the job. Well, what with me being a tall and scrawny stretcha water and having a voice that never quite finished pubertating, I remember me having one awful time riding roughshod in those early days.

Anyway, Samuel J. Perrault was what we nowadays marvel at and tend to elevate in our conversations: the self-made man that somehow is only available in these United States. I know right now you're thinking about them Morgan, Weyerhaeuser, Rockefeller, and Carnegie boys. Well, drop down a few dozen pegs and then you might stub your toe on ol' Perrault. I've seen me plenty of them moving pictures, and them folks in Hollywood these days seem to have a good bead on the likes of ol' Perrault: short, cocky, bull-faced, and mad as hell about it. Kinda like . . . what's that kid's name? Cagney, Jimmy Cagney.

Perrault's story wasn't so special in the early years, 'cept when he told it in the later years. He woulda told you he led a wagon train along the Oregon Trail (he was a cook for some eastern nymphs du prairie heading west to share their wares), that he fought the Indians with his bare hands to lay claim to his land (he stole it plain and simple), and that he built his empire with hard work (of other men), honest sweat (he sweat only when he drank), and constant prayer (that his competition would fail). Hell, the way he told things, no doubt he's setting 'round heaven to this day waiting to be offered a shot at sainthood. That is, if he hasn't stole the title by now.

Well, whether you take in his story or mine, what you gotta remember is his kingdom, Four Arrows, was one of Oregon's largest and finest spreads. Even his brand—four arrows all pointing to face each other—was a good example of his power and conceit. Like he was center of everything. Yep, that's what it was: conceit. Just remember the Four Arrows brand and that's all you need remember about Perrault.

So if I was so smart, having got through eight grades and all, what was I doing under Perrault's stubby, little thumb? Well, I was only twenty when I signed on, don't forget, and ol' Perrault seemed to me like God Almighty Hisself. Oh, we had us a few years of lean back then, when nobody had nothing and Perrault was always borrowing it. But mostly we did just fine, onaccounta ol' Perrault was damn shrewd. Too shrewd. I reckon that's why it didn't take me long to cultivate me a strong dislike for him, and I always planned to move on. But things got mighty confusing by '87 and . . . well one thing led to another, and before I knew it that dang horse shot Perrault before I could ever tell the old fart where to go.

*I* remember that first night after the funeral. We alla us rode back to the house at Four Arrows. At first us wranglers was quiet, just watching our horses' feet and listening to our saddles crunch and our bridles jingle, which was music, pure and simple, to any cowboy's ear. Zeb Hardy started first with that damn contagious chuckle of his. Then Jay, the kid, started in. Well, before you knew it, we was all laughing so hard that ol' Perrault probably heard us from his grave down by the Walla Walla River. Cripes, by the time we got back to the bunk house, we'd decided to pull the shoes off Perrault's horse and retire him to the greenest pasture we could find at Four Arrows. Saint Cayuse, we'd call him, Redeemer of O-pressed Cowhands.

Yes sir, we all concluded that was one redeeming horse.

We passed the bottle and, though I never held much with me and my men all drinking together, I allowed it onaccounta it was a special occasion. After several rounds of the bottle, talk got kinda serious, as whiskey-talk eventually does.

"Come on, Roy," Jay—he was our youngest hand— prodded. "You gotta know what's gonna happen."

I looked acrost at him through our feet on the table and said, "What am I, a swami or something? I can't see the future. Your guess is good as mine."

Hardy said, "Yeah, but Roy, you're the foreman. It's your job to know these things," Hardy added as though saying it made it so.

"All I know is the boss died on Tuesday, today is Thursday, and Monday is payday," said I. I declined another shot outa the bottle, which was looking a little blurrish by then.

Then another hand leaned outa his bunk and asked me, "You mean you can set there and tell us Perrault never told you what would happen if he kicked off?"

I unfolded my legs down from the table top and stood up. "Meaning no unintentional disrespect for the dead," I began, "Perrault never planned on dying. Ever. Leastwise he never talked about it to me. I reckon he planned to go on just about as long as the Columbia River herself." My voice cracked even more than usual under the effects of the coffin-varnish we called whiskey in those days, and I remembered why I never drank to impress women.

"But what happens to Four Arrows? Everyone knows Perrault don't have any living relation," Young Jay persisted, a very sincere look of concern spreading over his fuzzy, sunburned face.

I unplucked my starched collar to let my Adam's Apple settle back down some and replied, "I'm not so sure he has a *dead* relation." I tried to hold in a smile. Then, more seriously, I lied: "Hell, for all I care, Four Arrows can go back to the Indians."

Well, Hardy took a immediate exception to that and shot me with a: "I'd sooner die!"

"Careful now, Zeb," I cautioned, hoping my smile would put him at ease as I added, "think I heard ol' Perrault say that same thing just last week." Hardy straightened up some and said, "Yeah, but *my* horse loves me."

Well, we all laughed, and then I reminded the men that work the next day would be as usual and I advised them to save some whiskey for the reading of the will in the next coupla days. There was no doubt in my mind that we would all need a stiff belt that day.

I had me a set of rooms that Perrault had built off the main house. I could come and go as I pleased, yet at the same time I was at Perrault's constant beck and call, which over the eight years of my service at Four Arrows had proved to be annoying, taxing, and a damn nuisance. But Lord, since he'd died, it'd been a blissful kinda quiet. I had the whole house to myownself, with only Anita, our plump Mexican cook, to run into now and then, which, depending on how long it'd been since I'd been to town, wasn't a altogether displeasurable experience.

Looking back on that night, the night after we buried ol' Perrault, I guess I thought I was a pretty big gun. I sat in the burgundy leather chair and ran my fingers down the fine brass tacks. A painting, some ten feet long and six wide, graced the mantle. It was of a fine herda Four Arrows cattle as they made their way down to the Walla Walla River, which paraded through our land. And as near as I can recall, it was about as pretty a artwork as I ever saw, including those I seen in a Portland museum.

Am I talking too fast? 'Cause if I am, I can slow down some.

Yep, I sure as hell thought that horse had sealed my future . . . me, Royal R. Leckner, cattle baron at age 28. Maybe after all those loyal years, me, the meek, had a right smart chance of inheriting the earth or at least a damn nice chunk of it.

I took a snort of Perrault's finest brandy, tidied up his desk a bit, and went to bed, thinking on how glad I was I'd stuck it out long as I had.

# two

Course, now I'd be the first to admit that back then I was a arrogant sonovabitch. And I suppose if I have to admit that, then I'd also have to admit that back then I'da been the last one to admit it. I knew I had a certain measure of good looks and I was never too far from a mirror just to make sure my blue eyes still sparkled and my smile still had a dazzling quality about it. Like firinstance, that evening after the funeral I spent a whole hour in front of my bedroom mirror, practicing looks of overwhelming surprise for when I would hear my name called out as sole heir to the Perrault holdings. I guess even now my face gets kinda red when I thinka myself back then. I guess maybe we all turn red, nowanthen.

Yes sir, inheriting Four Arrows seemed like a foregone conclusion: it oughta come to me by good rights. As far as I knew, Perrault didn't have any silent partners. Though I didn't do all the fancy-financing bookwork, I'd looked over enough shoulders to know Four Arrows was one man's domain . . . all thirty-thousand, six-hundred and forty-one acres, 2,469 heada cattle, not counting the one hanging on the beef wheel, and 234 horses, and them nearly all shod . . . hell, that's over 900 horseshoes and a small fortune in iron alone.

I sure do like to set back nowanthen and think on Four Arrows. Lord God, it was a pretty speck of land all right. Mostly good, rolling hills for grazing land, you know, lotsa hills so shade was easy. Then we had timber in the higher sections that reached clear into the foothills of the Blue Mountains. We had lotsa water from the Walla Walla River and we was conveniently nestled into the Northeast corner of Oregon State, with Washington and Idaho for neighbors. Walla Walla Wash was the closest big town, or we could always go down to Pendleton, but the whiskey was just as scorching and the women was just as risky in our own little town of (so help me, God) Idlehour.

Idlehour had been the name of the saloon. It was the first establishment erected at the cattle crossing and that's how the town got named. Only town I know of named after its saloon. I always thought that was sorta telling . . . you know, either the townfolks thought alota the saloon or maybe they just didn't think much of the little town that grew around it. I'll never know, I guess. Leastwise, it don't matter now, 'cause you won't find Idlehour on any map nowadays. It dried up and blew away by '22, so what I tell you about Idlehour is most likely all anyone will ever have to say about it.

So there was I, making plans for Four Arrows and carrying on sorta prideful-like inside for a few days, yet trying to pretend to the boys that I didn't care just what became of Four Arrows. I remember thinking I didn't want any of the boys to think I'd planned it all along . . . that Perrault's horse and me'd been in cahoots or something and we'd both end up in the calaboose. 'Course, no way a man could plan such a act of God. Nope. Only Perrault, his horse, and that rattler knew for sure what happened that day, and most likely the horse had forgot by sundown.

*I*t took the circuit judge a extra week to get to Idlehour onaccounta there was a hung jury up in Milton. Anyway, story went, after the judge explained how the term 'hung jury' got its name, them boys just exchanged glances and came right back with a guilty verdict, then hung 'em some horse thief so's the judge could get hisself over to Idlehour for more important things, like what the devil was gonna happen to Four Arrows. 'Course, by then the whole county was on tenderhooks. I reckon every merchant started looking up accounts to see if Perrault owed 'em any money so's they could lien on the land. I even reckon every bastard in the state pleaded with his momma on the chance ol' Perrault was his daddy. But since no one came forward with any claims against the land, I thought I had a better and better chance, the closer the will-reading got.

Just one man had me fretful: Silas Terwilliger Burnbaum. Now let me take a moment to ask you: what would you suppose anyone with that name might do for a living? If his momma didn't plan on him being a banker from the day she hung that handle on him, then Teddy Roosevelt never rode a dang horse. Ol' Silas T. owned the bank in Idlehour and, I don't mind admitting, he had me plenty worried.

He and Perrault had lots in common, that's sure. And it was sure when they had their two heads together, someone was about to get Scrooged outa something. I watched Silas T. real close at the funeral and I just prayed that the grin under his handlebar was about the snake and the horse and not that he reckoned he was in line for Four Arrows. He'd been kinda quiet about the will that following week. In fact, he just carried on like nothing was outa the ordinary, 'cept for that he'd miss Perrault and all. But Silas T. wasn't a smiling man and it was like, ever since Perrault died, he needed the corners of his mouth to hold up his handlebar, and I was mighty worried.

Maybe Perrault had the goods on him and Silas T. was glad to be rid of him. Although it seemed to me that if Perrault had it on Silas T. then Silas T. had it on Perrault. Like when they'd do a grange convention, they'd get all lickered up on cheap booze and divvy up the services of a whore and come back to Idlehour all wrapped up in scandal. I just didn't know. 'Course, I know now.

Let's see, it was Tuesday morning, July 14th, 1892, when Zeb Hardy asked me, "What time you riding in?" Like alla us at Four Arrows, he too was kinda anxiety-struck.

I fumbled with that long, black, damn tie, ripped out the knot for the third time, and snapped, "Maybe never, if I can't tie this blasted noose!"

Hardy swirled me 'round and I reckon it must've looked kinda odd, one man tying another man's tie like he was my momma sending me off to Bible School. But he tied it fine and I looked right handsome with my starched white collar up against my tanned, clean-shaved face and with my strawberry roan hair all slicked back.

"Eleven o'clock," I finally answered, looking myownself over in the mirror and smiling onaccounta I thought I looked just about as pretty as Custer on his wedding day.

Then Hardy asked, kinda hopeful-like, "Want me to ride in with you?"

"Twenty horses yet to be broke by Saturday," said I, "and you want to lollygag 'round the courthouse? Why, I'm only going onaccounta I was demanded upon by Armentrout." I straightened out the rim of my Montana Pinch, which I had laborishly chose over my good Stetson, and I wondered if Hardy had a notion that I wouldn't've missed the will-reading for the world.

Hardy walked me out to my horse and said, "Don't know why they have to make such a ballyhoo."

"Oh, lawyers and bankers and such, it's what they live for," I replied, untying my horse from the post. "They's all just frustrated actors, Hardy. How come a old smooth-mouth like you lived past forty and never come to know that?"

Hardy just shrugged his thick, rounding shoulders and said back, "Yeah, but it ain't no burlesque they're playing, Royal. It's our jobs on the line, I figure." As I pulled myself into the saddle, he hung onto my horse's bridle, which is something I always held as a gesture of respect, helping a man mount his horse.

I looked down on Hardy's rugged face and knew he didn't have any idea how wonderful things was gonna turn out. How he'd become foreman with me new owner and I'd pay him more money and give him his choice of any horse and offer him the chance that Perrault never did. At fortyish, Hardy was going down the Western slope and shoulda sold his saddle years back, but like me, he'd held in. In that moment of good feelings, I damn near thought I'd even give him a few hundred acres of his own. I came damn close to telling him not to worry, that things was gonna be great then on, but I kept quiet, which I reckon was one of the smarter things I ever did.

And, up to that point, I'd been pretty duncical.

# three

*H*ow the hell can you read them short-handed scrib-
bles, boy? Thought only women could write and read them
notes. Let's see. Where was I?

Oh, I know. I let my horse find his own way into Idlehour that morning. I was too busy looking 'round in every
direction, surveying Four Arrows land and making plans
for the future and all. I reckoned it was a good time to start
courting some woman since there wouldn't be no question
as to my ability to afford one now. As a wife, that is.

We passed a good herda mares and my horse stumbled
whilst he stared down into the meadow. He glared at the
stud with all his ladies in attendance, but since my horse
was gelded I suppose he was more curious than jealous.
It always bothered me not knowing for sure if a gelding
knows what he's missing, both on him and with the gal
horses.

The main street of Idlehour was choking with Oklahoma
Rain and hotter than Anita's tortillas, which I shall leave
for you to imagine. Folks knew it was the day for the
reading of the will and that's why the town was so busy
and fulla life that morning. As I rode by the Idlehour Glass
(they added Glass to the joint's name so as not to be
confused with the mail and the phone and all, and by and
by we alla us just called it the Glass), I could see lotsa men
standing up to the bar, which was never the case till noon
or so when the free lunch-spread came out.

I nodded politely to the folks that recognized me in my

fancy, will-reading duds and I guess you could say, from atopt that big black gelding of mine, I thought I was a fife riding through my fifedom . . . 'Prince Royal the Loyal' I kinda joked to myself. I hadn't felt so mighty since the time I was elected grand marshal of the Fourtha July Parade a few years back. I reckon I'd forgotten the only reason I was grand marshal was my horse was the only critter with enough calm to pull that blasted, lily-covered float toting Mrs. Burnbaum dressed like that new Statue of Liberty them Frenchmen built. As I recall, even that ol' gelding of mine took some exception to Mrs. Burnbaum at first, which seemed normal enough to me.

So there we was again, that gelding and me, only without the Burnbaum of Liberty, heading toward the courthouse to go a will-reading. We looked mighty fine all feathered-out, that black gelding and me.

The road widened in front of the courthouse, where there was a turnaround of sorts. The town fathers had spared some large alders when they'd laid out Idlehour, and there they stood (the alders, not the fathers) offering shade and a place for dogs to visit. Under the alders was hitching posts and troughs for the horses and even a few chairs for folks to lollygag on. I guess someone wanted to put up a statue there like them fancier towns back east and call it a town square. But things in Idlehour never calmed down enough to be setting up any statues. No two folks could ever agree on who to have a statue of, anyhow. Sure as hell wasn't gonna be Mrs. Burnbaum.

But that morning at the turnaround there wasn't no place to hitch a jack rabbit, let alone a horse. There was horses at every tie-up and buggies and wagons clogging things up proper. 'Course, nowadays parking problems is normal in some places, but back then I was right roiled no one had saved me a spot, being as I was the guesta honor and all. So I rode 'round back of the courthouse, tied my horse to a buggy and, since I was so close, visited the outhouse before going up the back steps to hear all about my future.

Since I'd never been to a will-reading before, I just thought all the folks that'd scrounged theirselves into the courthouse was gonna be the audience, sorta. As soon as I appeared, talk stopped and folks turned to me, bringing a flush of roses to my face.

Some man in the crowd hollered out, "Where the hell you been?" I forget who he was, but he made me know the whole shebang was waiting on me.

"It ain't even noon yet," I said, defensive-like. I took my hat off, which is a indoors habit with me.

"Well, they said everyone's there 'cept you," he went on, and then he ushered me to the judge's chambers.

I paused at the door, just staring at the brass door knob, feeling my pulse tapping in my fingertips. I looked behind me and there was half the town watching, smiling, and wishing I'd get on in there.

I opened the door and went in. I guess I've relived that moment a million times, and I know now my hand was trembling when I shook hands with the men in the room, even though I'd known most for a good long time. There was the circuit judge, James Blaylock; Perrault's lawyer, Julius Armentrout; and, of course, ol' Silas T. Burnbaum. Sheriff Agnew was there too, and so was Pastor Dennison. Now what them two had to do with a will-reading, I didn't know. I just figured they was invited outa consideration for their professions and being as how they'd serviced Perrault's death and all. After all, Agnew had done a right good job investigating and Pastor Dennison would be immortalized in those parts as the only sinbuster who coulda kept a straight face at the funeral.

After we shook hands all 'round, they offered me a puffy leather chair in the center of the room. I eased down my six-foot-four and tried not to look too uncomfortable as the cushion let out air, like as to protest under my weight. I

knew if there'd been younguns in the room, they'da snick-
ered at the chair-fart, but as it was, no one said nothing.
We all just waited for me to finish sinking and for the chair
to expire. So uncomfortable was I that under less formal
circumstances I woulda been tempted to pull out my gun
and put that blasted chair outa its misery.

"Well, gentlemen," Judge Blaylock finally began, after
I'd settled down and balanced my hat on my knees, which
was pretty near level with my nose, "everyone is here who
needs to be, so I see no reason to wait until one o'clock.
We might as well get a jump on things and maybe we can
still get out in time for the lunch-spread over at the Glass."

We all agreed that would be nice . . . and deep down
inside I knew I would be buying the drinks.

When Judge Blaylock picked up a large envelope, I
could feel my heart slam against my chest. "As you all
know," he continued, "Samuel James Perrault was a very
thorough man. He ran his ranch, Four Arrows, precisely
and with great calculation. Unfortunately, his sudden and
no doubt unexpected demise may have left his estate on
quavering ground. . ."

Why the hell can't these yahoos just say what they mean,
I was wondering as I tried to take apart what he was
orating about. I glanced about the room and noticed right
away that no one was smiling any longer.

Perrault's lawyer, setting next to the judge at the long
desk, looked at us and said, "Even though I have been the
deceased's lawyer for a good many years, I'm afraid that I
was never able to advise him about his will. Rather than
allow me to draw one up, he insisted on writing his own.
For two years I've kept this will locked in my safe and,
upon his request, it has remained sealed until now." He
held up the envelope for alla us to see. "Judge Blaylock
and I have agreed that any will, as long as it was witnessed,
is legal and binding, although it is perhaps rather unor-
thodox and we furthermore agree it is certainly not advis-

able not to seek professional legal assistance when dealing with an estate the size of Four Arrows." He sighed a little here-goes-like and glanced to the judge.

He was talking legal, but I didn't want to appear overly anxious or stupid, so I just nodded like I knew what was going on. Like I said, I hadn't never been to a will-reading.

Judge Blaylock took the will outa the envelope, set his spectacles upon his nose, and cleared his throat. "Let me read," he began.

I thought that would be best and leaned back in my chair to hear what ol' Perrault had to say.

" 'I, Samuel James Perrault, Bosmab. . .' "

"Bosmab?" asked I, startled outa my skin by such a foreign-sounding word. "What's a bosmab?" I sure did hate to let my ignorance on legal matters show its ugly head, but a bosmab!

Judge Blaylock smiled at me over his tiny Ben Franklins and answered with, "I'm terribly sorry. Bosmab is an acronym, Mr. Leckner."

I know my face didn't change much at his explanation. I was afraid to look over to Agnew or Dennison to see if they knew what the judge was talking about.

Julius Armentrout leaned over to me and said slowly, "Being of Sound Mind and Body . . . Bosmab. Typical will jargon, Royal."

"Typical to lawyers, I reckon," I said, feeling a gush of embarrassment. That sure wasn't the place to put my ignorance on display.

The judge smiled to Silas T. and started over. " 'I, Samuel James Perrault, Being of Sound Mind and Body, do hereby declare this to be my Last Will and Testament. I've been a thorough man, but not a complicated one, so let it be with this last document. There are benefits in death, for there are no explanations. All you have is this, my word and my will, and all I have to do now is relax.

" 'A successful man is a secretive man.' " The judge took

a pause to see how that struck us, then continued. " 'Here are my secrets: I married long ago. My wife bore me a girl which, being the first, she named Genesis. The baby died. Next came Exodus, a son who also died. My wife wanted many children and, being a woman devoted to God, she picked names from the books of the Bible. But on the third try, the baby lived and it was my wife that died, so there's no use talking about her. She gets nothing. That was in 1872, before I came West. I cared for the child for one year, until I realized the boy was not right in his head. A man starting to build his name and raise a baby at the same time, that's hard enough, but a child that will never be right in his head was too much. I gave the baby to a Christian home to be fostered in Spokane. That was back when I thought I might settle in the Washington Territory. Well, it pains me to confess I forgot about the child for eighteen years. Out of sight, out of mind, I suppose. I had always planned on another family to erase my error, but that never came. Then, two years ago, after I nearly died battling the grip, I began to realize that I won't last on this earth forever. A man begins to realize his transgressions while lying sick. I began looking 'round for the boy, but he was no longer in Spokane. It took money and pay-offs, but I finally found him up in Pasco in an asylum for the deranged. Fact is, I had hoped the boy had died somewhere along the way. But to my surprise, they had actually taught him a few things. He can take care of his personal needs, talk, and even sit a horse. But as a man, he will never be more than a small child.' "

I felt the blood leave my head and settle into my boots where it seemed to pull me down even lower into that man-eating chair.

" 'Some folks in the county and even the state think I'm a ruthless man without a conscience. Well, through this will, I intend to prove them wrong. I hereby bequeath my entire estate, all of the land and holdings known as Four Arrows, to my son, Leviticus James Perrault.' "

Judge Blaylock looked 'round the room at our astonished faces. He and Armentrout exchanged glances onct again. I looked over to Silas T. If I looked faint, he looked dead. His eye dots was kinda tiny and maybe it was his tight-fitting vest, but he didn't appear to be breathing too much.

"There's more," the judge said, almost like he loved tugging the rug out from under our chairs. " 'But, I have also been a man of practicality. I would never rest thinking that all I have worked so hard for would go fallow for the guilt over one son. And this is where I address you, Royal Leckner.' "

My heart tried to call back some of the blood from my boots at the mention of my name.

" 'I have arranged a trust fund for you at a bank in Boston (no offense, Silas T.) in the amount of twenty-five thousand dollars. The trust matures exactly five-hundred days from the reading of this will. What you must do to collect that trust is this: Bring my son down to Four Arrows and give him a chance at ranching. Teach him all you know, Royal. Five-hundred days for twenty-five thousand. That's fifty dollars a day to make my son a rancher. With this sum, I buy back my conscience to rest easier and give you the job of raising the man from his child's mind. For this purpose, I name you executor of this will. You are to have complete control of Four Arrows, including my finances and investments, which Silas T. will tell you about. I choose the awkward period of five-hundred days for a reason. Not knowing now the season of my demise, I want more than an entire year to pass with Four Arrows in my son's hands. As all who read this know, Four Arrows, like any ranch of its kind, is only as successful as its cattle sales.' "

Judge Blaylock took another pause, like he had to swallow the words a little. I tried to set up a piece straighter, wondering what all this was building up to.

" 'If, after a complete audit of the books—to be done by an independent accounting firm out of Portland—it appears that my son has made a profit, then I grant everything to him. Now Royal, your duty is to instruct, advise, and then let Leviticus do his best. I know this will be hard, knowing your loyalty. This is why I've been so generous with the money I've left you. But the accounting firm which I have retained will be assessing and auditing and watching with care the entire five-hundred-day period.

" 'Should Leviticus not be able to take on these responsibilities, I request that Four Arrows be sold, with one-third of the money going in trust for my son here in Idlehour (that's you, Silas T.) and the other two-thirds going to the town of Idlehour for general betterment, such as sanitation, libraries, hospitals, and parks. It is my last desire that my son will take his rightful place as my sole, living heir. In the event he should precede me in death, then none of this counts. Just tear down the fences at Four Arrows and let the cattle go free. Burn the house, discharge the men, and give the rest to charity. It doesn't matter to me, Samuel J. Perrault, apparently quite deceased.' "

The judge took off his glasses, rubbed his nose, and looked over to Julius. But before Julius could say a thing, the judge said, "There's a postscript."

Julius looked a little like he'd been insulted and said, "A postscript? In a will? I never. . ."

The judge began reading again. " 'P.S. I've enclosed another sealed letter, to be opened by my son, Leviticus Perrault, upon the completion of the five-hundred-day period.' " He held it up, looked at it, and said, "Hmmm. Well, now I know why he wanted this will kept sealed. Too bad he wouldn't take any of your legal advice."

To which Armentrout answered, kinda bland-like, "No one advised Perrault of anything with much success."

"Amen to that," Silas T. joined in.

Then Sheriff Agnew asked the judge, "That thing legal?"

"As long as the conditions are met, he could have left the whole dang place to his horse," the judge replied.

"Now wouldn't that have been ironic?" Pastor Dennison asked, his hands folded prayful-like in his lap.

I hadn't been able to say nothing. Then I realized they was all looking at me. So long, Four Arrows, I was thinking.

"Well," Julius asked me. "What do you think?"

I swallowed hard, stared at my hat in front of me, and tried to bring my thoughts back onto the trail. Sinking ever deeper into a slough of despond, all I could say was, "Any man who'd name his son Leviticus couldn't be bosmab."

# four

*C*ourse, you're young and so I should tell you that what I know now and what I knowed then is two entirely different things. I have the luxury now of knowing how this all turns out, but I sure as hell was a confused sonovagun back then, in '92. I had no idea what a precious mess I'd stepped in. If you get as old as me, son, I reckon you'll know what I mean. Seventy years living: that's all it takes to sort things out. So if you ever want to make heads or tails outa life, just keep waking up every morning and one day it'll all be clear as gin.

Anyway, I can remember I was in a state of shock or

something. I made that crack about the name: Leviticus. No wonder the youngun weren't right in his head. Then just when I was about to ask the judge to read the part in the will again that talked about me, he looked at me with kind cow eyes and asked, "You understand what all this says, Mr. Leckner?"

I wisht I was outa there and on the range somewheres. They was all looking at me and waiting for a gusha gratitude, I think. But I chewed my words good before I spoke 'em out and I nodded my head slowly like old men do whilst looking over a ticklish situation. "Nothing in that will says I'm bound to Four Arrows," I finally said.

Silas T. scooted his chair closer in toward me. My, his blue suit sure was fine. For a older gentleman, he looked real good. He looked at me and said, "I think that's asking alota any man, taking on an insane asylum idiot."

There was something eager in his blue eyes, and his face was commencing to glow from behind his white handlebar, which, like I said before, wasn't really in his nature. His wheels was turning all right, but I tried not to worry about it just then.

So I replied slowly, "Yes, but twenty-five thousand is right equitable." Then, it all came home to me, so I asked, "You mean, all I gotta do to collect that money is to be a nursemaid to this so-called son of Perrault's?"

"To agree with your statement means I have to agree with your wording," Armentrout said, lawyer-like.

"Then go over it with me in your own wording," said I, knowing I clipped my words a little sarcastic-like.

The lawyer rose, cleared his throat like as to address a jury, and stuffed his fingers into the tiny pockets of his vest. He sorta leaned back some and I knew a oratory was looming. "I think we all have to look at this will and determine its impact on the town as well as the whole county," he said.

I didn't recollect him running for any office that year so

I said, "Well, beg pardon, but I didn't hear the town or the county being mentioned in the will, 'cept if. . ."—then my eighth-grade education started kicking—". . .'cept if his idea fails. Then the money all goes to the town, and you, Silas T., you get a thirda Four Arrows in your bank." And since I was holding the room silent, I added, "Is that the impact you was referring to, Julius?"

"But Royal," he answers, "you get twenty-five thousand even if Perrault's son . . . this Levi . . . Levit . . . Leviticus can't run Four Arrows. You have it made, boy. And what's five-hundred days to a lad your age?"

To which I replied, "So you're saying that, as executioner of this will, I. . ."

"Executor," Judge Blaylock corrected.

"Okay, that too," I continued, kinda annoyed, for I was beginning to roll. "Anyhow, if I just walk through the steps Perrault laid down there, you know, not even work at it, I get twenty-five thousand, the community gets two-thirds of Four Arrows, and you get the other third?" I shook my head and said, "Now, I'll allow as alota this is above my bent, but I'm not so sure that's what ol' Perrault woulda preferred. Sounds to me like he wants his son to just be given a chance to succeed, like any other man." I looked 'round the room and saw faces of confoundment. Since no one was saying anything, I added, "Or did I hear wrong?"

They was still silent and I knew right then they was going in one direction whilst I was going in another. Most likely you're thinking, for a man just lost the entire spread, I was acting good and calm. Well, I always took responsibility real serious and it looked to me, just because ol' Perrault was dead and gone, that he intended for me to keep right on running things at Four Arrows. The notion of this Leviticus feller was a new cog in a old wheel. But the thing that bothered me most was, why ol' Perrault wanted *me* to break him in. Why the hell didn't he bring his boy down hisself and teach him Four Arrows *his* way?

That was a question that surely did occupy my mind back then.

But I always held with a son is a son, entitled to his daddy's land, no matter what. Besides, with twenty-five thou, I could build me my own Four Arrows someday. Maybe even six.

Finally, Judge Blaylock said, "No, no, you heard right." He put his specs back on whilst he glanced over the document and sighed, "You seem to have grasped the concept."

Silas T. grumbled, "The whole idea of an imbecile running Four Arrows! It's . . . it's . . . imbecilic!" Now there was the Silas T. Burnbaum I knew.

"Now I take exception to that, Silas T.," said I, trying to lean forward in my chair to look at him. I knew he was talking about this so-called Leviticus, but how I loved to bait that man.

"I'm talking about Perrault's son, not you!" said Silas T.

"Oh," I nodded, figuring I looked half-imbecilic myownself folded up in that chair like that.

At that point, Pastor Dennison rose. I don't believe he had moved that whole time, for his hands was still folded in front of him, even as he walked around. He looked real wise and we all waited for him to say something God-like. He stood next to the judge's desk and looked directly at me. "Son," he said, "I think you have been charged with a momentous task."

If it weren't for the fact that he spoke so softly, I woulda thought he was running for office too. But Pastor Dennison was a good, humble man, and I knew he was talking the way he thought he should, considering who was in the room and all.

I looked down at my hands, I guess outa the habit of just hearing his slick, preaching voice. I noticed my fingernails coulda used a trim.

Pastor Dennison went on: "Can you imagine what it will

be like to take a man who has spent his entire life in an institution for the mentally retarded and try to teach him how to run a ranch?"

Well, he had me there. I couldn't even imagine, so I said, "No, but I reckon I'll find out soon enough."

That wasn't good enough for him, so he asked, "Have you ever been around a . . . a, well, someone who's . . . mentally deficient?"

I couldn't keep the grin offa my face. "Why, you only need half a brain to punch cattle, Pastor Dennison," I replied. "In fact," I added, sharing my grin 'round the room, "I think only half a brain is a damn good asset."

But before I could get my laugh, Silas T. broke in with, "Yes, but we're not talking about just punching cattle. Perrault wants his boy to run Four Arrows. Now there's a laugh. It's bound to be a total failure."

"Well then, sounds like you got nothing to lose but five-hundred days," said I. Then I turned to the judge and said, "Now tell me about this here independent accounting firm."

He flipped through the papers and said, "Here it is: Howell, Powell and Gallucci, Accountants, Portland, Oregon. Here's a receipt for their retaining fee and a note requesting me to inform them of Perrault's demise and of Perrault's boy arriving at Four Arrows. Apparently, they'll send someone over to inspect the books and see if a profit is turned after the cattle sale." He turned to Silas T. and said, a little lower in voice, "I assume they'll be calling on you as well, Silas T."

"But I thought the will said *I* was the executor," I asked, getting suspicious.

"Well, you look over Howell, Powell and Gallucci's shoulders and they'll look over yours," Blaylock said, trying to be funny, I guess.

Things was sure turning out more confusing than I'd planned on.

"Howell, Powell and Gallucci?" I asked. I knew I'd never heard of 'em before and I wondered how the hell ol' Perrault had dug 'em up.

We all just sat in silence for a spell. Then I said, looking at each man, "Now, it seems to me like Idlehour sure has a lot to gain if this high-faluting plan fails." I could see a new jail in Sheriff Agnew's eyes and a new church in Pastor Dennison's face. I could see ol' Silas T. expanding his bank vault and filling it with Four Arrows money, and I could see the lawyer and the judge serving as Presidents of the Park, Hospital, and Library Boards of Managers, maybe even naming the place Perraultville or something.

They all looked at me kinda hopeful-like and I reckoned they was wondering which side of the rail I'd step.

I asked, "Five-hundred days, eh?"

The judge nodded.

I asked, "Mentally retarded, eh?"

The lawyer nodded.

I asked, "Twenty-five thousand dollars?"

Silas T. nodded.

I asked, "City improvements?"

The pastor and the sheriff both nodded.

"A independent accounting firm," I said, piecing it all together.

"It's asking too much, son," Pastor Dennison said, holy-like. To which Sheriff Agnew agreed by saying, "It's crazy, if you ask me."

"Far be it from me to forecast failure, my boy, but. . ." Julius Armentrout said, sadly shaking his legal head.

Then Silas T. broke in with, "I'll tell you this, Royal: Howell, Powell and Gallucci can all be blind, deaf, and dumb, but all of us here know how this will turn out. You don't have a Chinaman's chance. So just don't go getting your hopes up. I don't see why you'd care, anyhow. You're set for life no matter how this turns out."

Well, I looked at each man and made my decision. Like

I said, I'd always been a man of great loyalty. And any man tells me I can't do something, well, sure as hell I'll set out to prove him wrong.


## five

*T*hings'd got so all-fired up at the will-reading that I'd kinda forgotten half the town was on the other side of the door, waiting for us to come on out. I'd always been on the friendly side with mosta the folks, but I thought it then and I'll say it now: I sure as hell wisht they wasn't all waiting out there. 'Course, it wasn't a matter of keeping ol' Perrault's last will and testament quiet or anything like that, 'cause I knew it would be printed, word for word, complete with editorial comment and odds against my success, in the next edition of the *Idle Gazette,* our little weekly bladder, which just ached for news of any sort.

So I waited for everyone in the judge's chambers to file on out and I just remained setting like I was in deep thought, and turning over and over the sealed letter addressed to Leviticus Perrault. Fact was, I was a little concerned about getting outa that chair in a dignified manner. I looked 'round the room to see if I was alone, then stretched my legs forward and slid out. I quickly got up and, well . . . I know it wasn't sporting . . . but I climbed out the back window.

When I got to my horse, I was sorta annoyed he'd gotten

all twisted 'round like horses do when they're bored. I could hear the judge and Silas T. and Julius talking all at onct to the folks inside, which made me work all the faster to free my horse. As I pulled up into the saddle, I noticed my gelding had backed up against Julius Armentrout's buggy and had let go on the floorboards. Now normally a man takes full responsibility for his horse's transgressions, but being as I wanted outa there and that Julius wasn't no real friend to me, I just smiled a little as I rode out. I know my horse wasn't any smarter than any other critter in those parts, but I thought he acted real symbolic-like, so I didn't chew him out or anything.

I don't mind telling you, the ride back out to Four Arrows was a entirely different story from my ride in. Things was going 'round so fast in my head, I reckon it was a good thing my horse knew the way. All I wanted to do was set at my desk and write things down to see on paper how they stood. Can't nothing take the place of good ol' American black and white to figure things out some. I'd make me a good and bad list, that's what I'd do.

Lucky for me, all the boys was down at the breaking corral working in the new horses, so I went straight to work thinking things out. Perrault had a better desk for working out these sorta things, so I borrowed it. I figured I'd lean me back in his grand leather chair and put my feet up on the desk like I'd seen him do a million times when he was sorting and thinking and writing. It worked real good, like the good-thinking blood that had abandoned me at the will-reading finally returned to my head or something. I made my list and I had to try hard to keep my eyes from staring at the big $25,000.00 I'd written at the top of the paper.

Before long, I was making lists of what twenty-five thousand could buy. I figured I could live to the age of 752 at my current level of spending, or 432 with some whimsical little distractions, or 213 with some mild extravagances, like wine, women, and God knows how many songs. I settled on shooting for the more respectable age of 93 and living the life of Riley eacha my remaining days.

I crumpled up that page and cursed myself for letting my mind wander so, when there was Four Arrows to think about. I coulda tossed the paper into the fireplace acrost the room, but instead I uncrumpled it and stuffed it into my pants' pocket. I think I still have it somewheres but I'm not gonna look for it now, so please don't go asking to see it, son.

Five-hundred days. I commenced to calculating the days and, even though I had to cheat by reciting the thirty-days-hath-September bit, I deduced five-hundred days landed on Friday, October 27th, 1893. Five-hundred days exactly. I wrote the date on my desk blotter, though it was doubtful I would forget that day. Then I just stood there, staring at it and letting my mind wander again and trying to imagine what this Leviticus feller would be like.

*I* heard some heavy scrambling of boots on the front porch and looked out the window. Hardy and Jay had seen my horse tied up out front and they was both trying to get through the door at the same time. 'Course, they'd never seen 'em, but looking back I'm reminded of those two greats, Laurel and Hardy—always together, but one always working against the other. Maybe that's why I see alla their movies—they remind me of ol' Hardy and Jay. And I sure've come to miss 'em.

When they finally broke through the door, they just stood there, staring at me like they was demanding a explanation. I leaned back against the desk, folded my arms in fronta me, and thought I'd have me some fun.

Jay asked, "It's bad news, ain't it? Else you'da come on down to tell us."

Hardy came closer, fixed me glareful-like, and just

demanded, "Well?" He was older, so I reckon that's why he talked to me that way.

"Well what?" I asked right back.

"You know well what!" Hardy barked. Even though I was foreman and his boss, I had respect for him and I always flinched when he barked.

"Oh, you must be referring to the will," I answered, like a half-witted chawbacon.

"Come on now, Roy," Jay chipped in, impatient like all kids. "What happened?"

I was trying to thinka something wild to tell 'em, like Perrault had left the land to the Indians or, worst yet, the Mormons or something like that. Then I realized that the dang truth of the matter was: the way Perrault had worked it, it was downright ridiculous standing on its own. So I looked at the boys and said, "Ol' Perrault left Four Arrows to his son, who lives up to Pasco."

Hardy took a bow-legged stance and said, "What son? He don't have no son!"

"He does now," said I. "Wait, here's the lollapalooza: the son is nuts." I ran my pointing finger 'round my ear to make my meaning clear.

"Huh?" both Jay and Hardy asked together.

"This son of Perrault is in a home for the mentally out-of-sorts up to Pasco. Let's get something to eat and I'll tell you all about it." And I started for the kitchen.

Hardy pulled me back 'round. His face was half smiling like he was waiting for the rest of the joke. "Come on, Roy. What really happened?"

"*That* really happened," I said. "Come on, I'm hungry." I kept on heading toward the kitchen, knowing they'd follow and our appetites would get taken care of.

Anita was working on a kettle of chili. I reckon she was always working on chili. When we walked in she stopped her kettle-stirring. She was just as worried as the boys was about Perrault's will. She plopped the lid down on the kettle and looked at me for the news, whilst I dove into the cornbread.

I could feel their eyes on my back, so I said, "All right, this is the way things is: Perrault left Four Arrows to his son. That's surprise number one. This son ain't right in his head, which is surprise number two. He lives in Pasco—that's number three—and I got five-hundred days to teach him ranching." I took a pause, leaned backwards theatrical-like in my chair, and said, "Surprise!"

Whereupon Anita said, "You're yoking," Never could get her to pronounce a 'j'.

"Yeah. You're making this up, Roy," Jay said, and he gave me a teaseful push.

I took another bite and I'm afraid I kinda sprayed out some cornbread crumbs when I spoke. "Ain't no one could make this up."

"He never talked about a son! He never even talked about a wife!" Hardy said, like he was Perrault's bosom friend or something.

I came back with: "So he could keep a secret. Besides, if you had a yack for a son, maybe you'd keep your mouth shut too." I retrieved some crumbs from the table by stomping 'em with my finger.

"So what does this mean?" Anita asked, and she calmly stirred the chili again. Ol' Anita only got herself riled over two things: her cooking not being appreciated and snakes.

"It means we got us a little over a year to make us a new owner of Four Arrows," I replied, cringing at the thought of their next question.

It was Hardy got to it first. "And what happens after five-hundred days?"

"Well," said I, "according to the will there's this here accountant feller from Portland to come in and kinda see if this boy does all right. He's to be the one to decide if the numbers is all looking good and how this boy can run the ranch, I reckon. If the boy can't pull it off, then . . . now don't get too excited . . . if he can't . . . well, Four Arrows will be sold and the money will go to Idlehour for fixing things up and the like."

I remember looking real careful at Hardy and Jay, then over to Anita. I wondered if it made any sense to 'em. The whole idea still had my head a-spinning. They just stood there in the middle of the kitchen and looked at me like they was hoping I'd jump up and say April Fool or something.

Well, we all agreed it was a right tangled mess and not even my story of how my horse had flowered Julius' buggy, or the thought of my twenty-five thousand dollars brought much joy to us that night. As I recollect, we three boys sat around and got mighty roostered as we tried to make some sense of it all. I remember the three of us setting 'round the kitchen table, chowing down Anita's chili, staring at the bottle of bug juice and watching it slowly disappear.

# six

Course there was no way on God's green earth or Hell's half acre that I had any idea just what I was getting myself into. I look back and wonder if I coulda seen it all unravel ahead of me, would I have broke for high timber and forgotten all about the twenty-five thou? Well, I'm the first one to admit that twenty-five thousand now, in the middle of the Depression, sounds like heaven on earth, and I reckon it did back then too. And then, there was this pride-and-honor thing. Four Arrows meant a whole lot to me and, hell, I wasn't more'n a kid myownself, so I thought I could endure all sorts of hell for five-hundred days. Cripes, I'll bet I was younger than you, kid, and like I said, I was a bit arrogant and blatherskitish, which is a affliction you get when you're too fulla yourself.

As you might expect, the three of us—me, Hardy, and Jay—we didn't get a whole lota problem-solving done that night. Anita just worked around us, fed us more when it looked like we was going to pass out, and then booted us out when it looked like we was gonna puke on her tiled kitchen floor.

When I woke up the next morning, my first thought was I only had four-hundred and ninety-nine days left and, hung over or not, it made good sense to get on with things.

Pasco was some piece away and, believe you me, I had no plans on riding all the way up there. So whilst I packed a satchel, I set off to wondering which railroad ran where and which stage lines I'd sworn I'd never ride again. I just generally put together my traveling plans, thinking how much food I should take and how much money I should draw out. I thought about taking Hardy or Jay with me for company, then I said 'company, hell!' I might need one of 'em just to help me with this Leviticus feller. Jay seemed like the most logical choice. I'd need Hardy to ramrod things whilst I was gone, and besides, Jay and me, being closer in age, we might have us some fun in the big cities of Walla Walla Wash and Pasco. I began to think, as his boss, it was my responsibility to teach Jay about city things. Walla Walla Wash was upwards to several thousand people; now if that wasn't bigger'n any damn city Jay'd seen, I was prepared to eat my hat.

So I said, "Pack your things, kid. You're coming with me." Jay and his horse was leading each other outa the stock barn. I could tell, just one look at him, that he'd had a rough night, with the effects of the whiskey and Anita's chili and all. He kinda looked past me, came to a halt, then tried to get his foot in his stirrup. Well, he was moving real slow and I started to laugh whilst I watched him miss the swaying stirrup. His horse seemed to be playing right along too. That critter would move just far enough away from Jay so's the boy couldn't quite swing on up. I reckon Four Arrows horses always had a reputation for their senses of humor.

I told Jay the news again. This time he heard me.

"Huh?" he mumbled, kinda tortured-like.

"I said, I decided you're coming with me up to Pasco to help fetch that boy." I took the reins outa his hand and tied his horse back up.

He looked at me with his eyes kinda squinting, like to focus on anything smaller than the horizon hurt him real bad.

Well, I couldn't help grinning some. I reckoned I'd been real familiar with that kinda headache a few times myownself. Poor ol' Jay's hands was shaking and his face was almost as grey as his dappled horse's rump. How he'd figured on staying on his horse, I'll never know.

Then I said, gentle-like, "Go put your grip together, boy. It's time for you to see the big city." I pointed him in the direction of the bunk house.

"Stop shouting," said he, holding his head.

"Go pack," whispers I.

"No whiskey," he mumbles, like we all do the day after.

"Not a drop," says I, soothful-like.

"And no chili," he pleads, starting to move some.

Well, now I just couldn't promise him that, but I smiled kindly, like his pa woulda done, and told him he'd feel better as the day wore on. Leastwise, I sure as hell hoped he would. I didn't have the heart to tell him we'd be buckboarding to Idlehour within the hour. Sick like he was, you just take things one thought at a time, in the order they come along.

Nextly, I found Hardy and told him all I thought he needed to know about the Four Arrows business the next coupla days. Not knowing how long we'd be gone, I talked about bringing down the last of the spring calves and for him to commence to branding and ear-notching and nut-lopping. Ol' Hardy, he knew what had to be done. Hell, he'd been top wrangler for almost five years. But I was foreman and saw the need to keep the puncher protocol, and I knew it looked good to the rest of the boys that I was still in charge even though I was two counties away from Four Arrows.

*U*nless you're a crow, getting to Pasco from Four Arrows was a mite tricky. To be factual about it, even if you was a crow it'd be tough going, seeing as crows like to stop and eat onct in a while. Actually, I reckon a buzzard would do hisself better than any other bird, but I'll leave the final verdict about that to them Audobon folks. Anyways, for us humble, two-legged land critters, getting to Pasco meant one, buckboard it from Idlehour to Milton; two, stage it to Walla Walla Wash; three, a few hazardous miles of train riding to Wallula; four, stage it up to Hackley; five, steamer acrost the Snake River to Pasco; and six, plenty of patience and a helluva lota prayer. Oh, and seven, a few bottles of Golden Rule Whiskey never hurt none, for medicinal purposes, which, if you've ever ridden in a stagecoach, you'd understand right away.

Now to you greenhorns and city dwellers, I reckon all this antique kinda travel probably sounds real intriguing. But let me tell you, after only a few hours of this, a man is apt to wonder how the basic wheel can take on all sorts of proportions and imperfections. Now, no two horses is gaited the same way, but legs is legs and you always know what to expect from atopt a horse. Wheels, now they's different. At least a horse has the common courtesy to trip or stumble before giving out. Wheels just bounce you 'round and then, without so much as one of them 'by-your-leave squires,' they give out, pop off, or refuse to turn one more revolution, and there you are, high and dry, staring at a harnessed-up horse who probably coulda told you before you left the barn that there'd be a breakdown exactly halfway up the first steep hill.

Wheels on tracks, now that's different, and I'll commence soap-boxing about them later.

Well, there was no way poor, young, hungover Jay coulda sat in the buckboard that morning. He chose to ride his horse, which followed the wagon like a dutiful critter. I swear that horse knew the condition of poor ol' Jay, cause it seemed to me he stepped like he was walking on rattlesnake eggs. And Jay's horse smiled kinda knowing-like. Now, I know you think I'm being generous to that horse's very nature, but when I tell you he smiled, he smiled. I guess now I'd better explain about Jay's horse.

We called him Hero the Harelipped Horse, but not to

his face, of course. Well, it all happened two, three years previous when Hero the Harelipped Horse wasn't no more'n a yearling. Some fool, might even've been me, thought a coupla Texas Longhorns might spruce up the pasture a little, onaccounta they sure looked mighty with them horns and all. Well, hell, no way a Longhorn could stand a Northern winter, so you know they was just for show. Besides, we'd been using railroads to ship cattle for years and them damn, arrogant horns just cause all sortsa havoc the way they sprout all this way and that.

Anyway, Hero'd been set out to graze in the same field as one of them Longhorns. Well, youngblood horses have a way of being right curious and Longhorns have a way of being downright sourful. After a somewhat one-sided altercation between the yearling and the Longhorn, Hero ended up getting his upper lip caught on the tip of the bull's horn. Ripped that lip clean up his snout.

I don't recollect who was madder, the bull, the horse, or Jay. When things finally calmed down, Hero had to be stitched up by Hardy. My eyes still water thinking on how much that had to hurt. Well, Hardy wasn't no surgeon, but he did his best. Like most folks know, a horse can't graze without proper lip-work so, in a way, we was saving Hero's life, although I doubt the horse thought so at the time.

Well, Hero eventually developed the most fetching, rabbit-like smile, although he also took on a most agonizing fear of cows, which proved to be rather annoying, considering the line of work we was in.

The Longhorn didn't fare so well in the wake of Jay's anger, but it did make a fine chair for the house. And, I suppose, that's a more lasting tribute than most cattle come to expect. Almost everyone who sets in that chair makes a nice comment on how comfortable it is.

Anyway, there Jay was, riding Hero the Harelipped Horse. I'd look back on the boy every now and then and I'd chuckle to see him holding on the saddle horn with both hands like he'd never ridden a day in his life. He'd stop nowanthen to mark his trail and, having been in that sick-like condition myownself a few miserable times, I could commiserate with him. I reckon he woulda had to get a whole lot better just so he'd feel good enough to die.

Onct, I stopped the wagon to allow him to catch up and I started thinking maybe he was a lot sicker than he oughta be. I thought, considering all that came outa him, he would do well to put some water into hisself. When his horse caught up, Jay looked over to me like he'd just as soon slip off and cash in his chips right there on the trail.

"Why are you doing this to me?" he whispered, like I was that Marquis de torture or something.

I handed him the canteen and smiled whilst I said, "Here kid. Put something wet in your body."

"I can put it in, but it won't stay in," he said.

"Why don't you just pony up and lie yourself down in the buckboard?" I asked, watching him drink.

He scowled at me from under his hat and said, "My momma'd shoot you in the knee if she could see how drunk you and Hardy got me."

Jay was always threatening his momma and her shotgun on me onaccounta him being just a kid and like nothing was ever his own fault.

I took back the canteen and said, "I ain't afraida your momma. Never have been, never will be."

Jay swelled up some and said, "Oh yeah? Half of Umitilla County is. . ."

In mid-sentence, he leaned over Hero the Harelipped Horse and proceeded to air the paunch onct again. Seeing how miserable he was made me feel just about as bad. You know how contagious those things can be. I just turned my head and left him some privacy.

Then, when he'd emptied, I climbed down off the wagon, led his horse 'round to the back, and helped Jay unmount. When I got the boy all warm and comfortable amongst the bed rolls and tent, I unsaddled Hero and tied him off the wagon, telling him he'd been acting real good to Jay, even though, as you know, a horse can't be sympathetic about puking onaccounta onct they eat something, they's more or less stuck with it.

Hoping to hell Jay was just sick from whiskey or maybe Anita's chili and not setting out with the diphtheria or grip or influenza or black death or anything else he could buck out from that his momma would shoot me for, I drove as careful as I could to Idlehour. Even if it meant a extra day or two's delay, I wasn't going one step outa Idlehour till poor Jay was fixed.

I drove directly to Doc Rumson's, whereupon he took Jay's temperature and offically declared his malady as a champion, world-class hangover, complicated perhaps by Anita's chili. Well, I was relieved Jay wasn't spreading typhus all around the county. Doc Rumson gave poor Jay a dose of Gingerine or Styllinger or something. Anyhow, it hardly matters onaccounta it just came back up with a vengeance. Finally, we gave the boy a sturdy dose of Globe Flower, which is primarily for coughs. Well, Doc Rumson knew and I knew and most likely you know too that, when you get right down to it, the best thing for a hangover is the hair of the dog. If Jay'd've known the better part of the cough syrup was alcohol, he wouldn't've touched it. I reckon to this day he thought it was a miracle drug or something, 'cause he commenced to feeling much better. I paid Croaker Rumson cash, thereby insuring that word of Jay's illness and subsequent cure would not get back to his momma, and we left. Jay was weak all right, but smiling a little and able to at least endure the tickling sound the jingle-bobs on his spurs made as he walked Spanish back to his horse.

We bought some supplies for our trip and hung around Idlehour just long enough to fill up on the free lunch over at the Glass. I had a beer, but Jay drank soda. Folks wanted to talk about Perrault's will and all, but we kept to ourselves and got out fast, taking a coupla extra sandwiches for the road.

So with Jay feeling a whole lot better and with a long road ahead of us, we lit outa Idlehour to fetch us back that Leviticus feller.

## seven

*T*he way I see it, when God set out creating Northeast Oregon, He wasn't quite sure exactly what kinda landscape we'd be needing, so he put in just about everything. There's cool valleys holding in the Walla Walla River, low grassy plains sneaking up on velvet-like foothills. There's wheatlands, sandlands, forestlands, and boglands and, of course, there's mountains called Blue, Black, Bald, and Bally scattered all around just to keep us mortals humble. We can dam up the rivers, chop down the forests, fence in the plains, and water the deserts, but them mountains . . . well, I reckon there's not much we can do to change those.

So there we was, Jay and me, following the road to Milton, looking 'round and admiring the views, and enjoying the cool breeze off the Walla Walla. It was good to see Jay with color back in his cheeks, even though it made his freckles pop out more. It was good he had those freckles though 'cause, as I recall, he was having real trouble with pimples, and I told him as long as he had so many freckles, no one would know which was which, unless they got up real close. But Jay, he had the promise of real beauty, even at sixteen; pretty soon he'd stop growing and fill out some, and with practice he'd learn how to grease his hair so's it didn't stick out like a porcupine's tail, and them pimples, well, we was always telling him they'd go away onct he got hisself laid.

It kinda always made me laugh, and I reckon I was the same way too when I was a cub: Jay was a real man in the saddle. Hell, he'd earned his spurs when he was only twelve. Why, he could ride, rope, and shoot as good as any man and I reckon he'd forgotten all I'd ever know about horses, but onct his boots touched the ground, he was all legs, arms, and glands.

"Feeling better are you?" I asked him.

And he answered, "Least I can set a horse. May the Lord strike me dead with lightning if'n I ever eat chili with whiskey."

Well, I know my shoulders kinda cringed when he said that, onaccounta we had terrible thunderclappers in those parts and I figured the Lord didn't need any more encouragement to blast us around, starting range fires, crisping cattle and all.

"I don't think it's a good idea to suggest that sorta thing out here in the open, Jay," I said, and I wisht I had some salt to toss over my left shoulder. "Besides, I don't think it was chili and whiskey did you under." I hadn't planned on telling him till he mighta seen some humor to it, but hell, he was growing and had a right to know.

Jay's fluffy eyebrows kinda grew together-like and he asks me, "What're you saying, Royal?"

"Well, I'm just saying maybe it was something else made you sick."

"Like?" he asked.

Well, I clucked some enthusiasm into the team of horses and said, "Like king snake."

"Like heck!" Jay said. "What's a king snake gotta do with it? I drank too much of that nose paint you pass off for whiskey. I tell you, Roy, my momma ever finds out. . ."

Then I came back with, "Well, I ain't saying you didn't drink too much, 'cause you did, just like me and Hardy did. But me and Hardy, well, we're kinda used to Anita's chili."

"So what's a king snake have to do. . ."

"Well," I interrupted, "you know how we always keep a kinger 'round the house to keep the rattlers away?"

Jay was looking at me real suspicious-like whilst he answered, "Yeah."

"Well, Anita . . . well, every so often, after she's been scared more'n her share by the kinger. . ." I just couldn't say it, myownself not deciding whether it was comedy or tragedy.

Jay's face was going back to its previous shade of grey and he said a long, "Royalllll."

Whereupon I smiled and said, "Some folks think it adds a whole new worlda texture to chili." And I clucked some life into the team.

Jay stopped his horse and barked, "You mean that woman served us snake meat?"

When it was obvious I didn't think the issue was important enough to stop for, Jay sprang his horse back up. Well, I just looked over to him and smiled like my nature calls for and said, "Means, of course, I gotta go out and get us another king snake and break him in. This one lasted almost six months. I reckon that's some kinda Four Arrows record."

I never did know why Jay got so frothy about it. He chucked down that chili same as the rest of us. But I suppose he had a right to know what probably made him so sick. It hit me the same way the first time too. 'Course, the whiskey didn't help none. Maybe them Mexicans know best when they drink tequila with their king snake chili.

$\mathcal{M}$ilton was just another hopeful little speck on the map in the Land Grant Office. As far as a town goes, I've seen better and, to tell you the truth, I don't think Jay was all that impressed either, even after I told him they was still hanging rustlers in Milton. Walla Walla Wash and Wallula up in Washington held more promise, I told him.

We boarded the horses and the buckboard with the livery man and booked our passage on the stage. Even though riding in the coach was a torture all to itself, I was glad to have another man do the driving. Jay and me, being the only two passengers, stretched out best we could. I knew Jay was still holding a grudge about the snake in the chili, which set me off to wondering if sometimes a man just ain't better off not knowing some things. Whereas I can see it's beneficial for a man to know a few things, I did wonder about a man knowing alota things.

I laid down and poked my legs outa the window of the coach, pulled my hat down over my eyes, and tried to pull off some sleep. It took some doing, but I finally nodded off and didn't wake up till the driver shouted we was there: Walla Walla Wash.

Jay bounded outa the coach like he'd just had a hour's set in church but, when I unfolded my legs, I knew I'd been riding in a stagecoach for four hours. I knew there was a good reason I hadn't brought along ol' Hardy; with his advancing age and ailing knee, no telling how long it woulda taken that ol' grissard to undo hisself.

I did my best to show Jay a good time without showing him 'everything,' figuring we had a long ways ahead and plenty of time for that.

So, instead of 'everything,' we ate steak, bought us a hour at a bath house, rode on one of them horse-drawn trollies, and ended up listening to a brass band and some political folk taking turns ripping apart Harrison and Cleveland, who, as you may recall, was jousting for president.

Somehows we ended up at the reading room at the YMCA, which I myself found a little boring, but Jay found real relaxing. That's 'cause he didn't know 'everything' he was missing.

It was getting pretty late when we left the YMCA and we ended up at the telephone and telegraph office. We just hung around there for a while, staring in through the window at the night clerk and waiting for something electrical to happen. It didn't and, even though Jay was disappointed, we wandered back over to the hotel and turned in.

*I* reckon right after God created our corner of Oregon, He set out to have Him some fun, so He turned right around and created the railroad man. Now, I have nothing against railroads or men who want to get ahead in life, but somehow, when you put them two together, you get all sortsa misery. By then, you see (and it was to get worlds worse later), every Tom, Dick, and Harry was trying to get rich off the railroads. There was short lines, long lines, unfinished lines, dream lines, abandoned lines, cattle lines, timber lines, passenger lines, and God knows what other kinda lines I never even heard of. Rates was sky high, of course, being as those railroad men had a built-in stubborn streak regarding passage rates and monopolies. It musta been worse on the East Coast, with all those places to go, but it was downright amusing in our own little corner. I never bothered remembering which line was which for, sure as shooting, things would change next time I got back to town. I guess maybe that's why God finally ended up inventing the airplane: it just got plumb too hard to keep track of all those tracks crisscrossing the land.

Jay was all worked up for getting to ride a train, and I guess I stretched the leather a little bit on telling him how comfortable and posh it was. Well, wheat traffic was considerable more than passenger traffic in those days, and it was clear which got the better accommodations. The car, probably a Pullman that had been bought scrap-cheap, was loaded past the windows with sacks of commodities, leaving only about seven rows for passengers.

Jay tossed his satchel onto the corduroy seat and a puff of dust burped up. Jay sneezed, fanned the air, and glared down at me. Then he dusted the sand off the seat and grumbled something like: "You call this posh?"

Well, to tell you the truth, I'd been expecting a little more comfort and pampering myownself, but, being the adult, I didn't let on to Jay, so I said, "Your daddy crossing the plains back in the sixties woulda thought this was a chariot of salvation, son."

We pulled outa the station with no one to wave goodbye to 'cept the ticket agent, who just stared back, supporting his head on his hand like he was real bored with the whole affair.

They got this thing now they call the 'whiplash,' the concept of which became popular when they started driving automobiles all over and colliding 'em up. Well, I guess you could say we had whiplash even then, 'cause when that train jounced forward, our heads jerked back, and even Jay, stretchable as he was, complained of pain in his neck for several days, which I said was only good and equitable turnabout and fairplay, since he was a pain in the neck to me sometimes.

About the time the train had cleared the station, the conductor came through the wobbling door at the front of the car. He kinda eased from side to side whilst he walked and took our tickets, like his legs was a part of the train itself. Well, being a avid reader, I'd heard all about sea legs and I guess that what I'd seen there was track knees.

He said, "If it gets too hot in here, you can open the windows." But before I could answer, he added sad-like, "But then you'd have the dust and the sand."

"How fast does this train punch the breeze?" Jay asked, like the fascination for speed was inbred in all young men, even then, before speed became something to get hopped up about.

The conductor set his little cap back and you could tell that he'd been sweating. "Well, ordinarily this trip takes only a hour and a half. But we had some trouble with the regular engine, so we're working the old engine today. You boys can catch up on some sleep." He smiled like he thought that was a real bargain and we had all the time in the world. He waddled his way to the back of the car and disappeared out the door.

Well, Walla Walla Wash wasn't disappearing 'round us real fast and, onct again, I could tell Jay was sorely disappointed about going so slow. I can see him now, glaring sideways at me like it was all my fault.

Cripes, I reckon I knew it would be a long day myownself when I looked outa the window and saw the conductor walking alongside the track on his way back to the engine. Without even putting a push into it, he passed us, smiled friendly-like, and waved at us as he moseyed on by. Seeing a man overhaul a train sure riled ol' Jay; he just slumped down into the seat and crost his arms on his chest like he'd been hornswoggled right proper.

It was only a thirty-mile trek from Walla Walla Wash to Wallula, and it didn't take a genius to see that we had passed outa God's corner and into the desert. Even with the advances that folks was making with irrigation, that little strip of land was mighty dry and alkaline, and I always did wonder what God was thinking about when He invented sand.

Well, Jay grumbled and I read the latest Sherlock Holmes episode in a magazine, but that thirty miles seemed like forever, and I have to look back and say, that old rattler of a engine musta had a big hand in inventing the expression 'hell on wheels,' 'cause that's what it was and I don't remember Jay ever letting me forget it.

# eight

Course, the folks that settled Wallula most likely thought they was founding a major city. I think most settlers have dreams like that. You just can't fault its location: setting right where the Columbia and Walla Walla Rivers come together. Then, not far away, just a few miles north, the Snake River takes off, I mean comes in. Well, no matter which direction the water flows, Wallula seemed like a right ideal location to set a city down. And the place has served its purpose over the years. But major city it wasn't. I don't know, somehow I think that any city name that forces your lips into a fish-face position just ain't destined for glory. But that being neither here nor there, Wallula was, as them English folks say, one jolly kick in the jodphurs, back in '92. It was the closest thing to a cattle town as I ever recalled, only without the cattle. It was a starting and ending point, a place to jump off, just like Jay and me did, and the town was real friendly to alla us travelers.

It was in Wallula Jay and me did the 'everything' of which I have previously alluded. By then, the spell of his momma's revenge had worn off and I knew a healthy colt like Jay oughta do 'everything,' since he already thought he knowed everything. Now don't go getting all righteous and slam me down or anything like that. Those whores had a good reputation . . . well, as good as coulda been expected. I mean, the church elders didn't endorse 'em or nothing. But I had connections and we both had a larruping good time, and the girls said they'd look forward to entertaining us on our return trip. I said we'd have to wait and see.

Well, Jay stopped grumbling about the discomforts of the rest of the trip, which consisted of another stage ride up to Hackley and then a steamer acrost the Snake to Pasco. I'd like to tell you the boy became a man, but that wasn't so, even though he sure did commence to swagger 'round like Hardy and the other boys at the ranch. Oh, he got laid all right, but he still was a kid. Even so, his smile was crinklier and he swore his pimples shriveled up and died that night, which always struck me as something those boys over to the Harvard Medical School might wanna look into.

$\mathcal{B}$eing the county seat, Pasco was as thriving a farming community as you could expect, sorta like Pendleton down in Oregon. It was alota desert, but they was working hard on irrigation ideas and the wheat grew just fine there.

"Jay, you go on over and get us a room," I said whilst I got out the instructions telling me how to find Perrault's boy. I had to admit, I was getting real nervous about things, even though I sorta put the Four Arrows issue to the high desert of my mind during our trip to Pasco.

After hearing the place was a piece outside of town, I rented a buggy and, to be on the wise side, I left Jay in town whilst I took the next step in securing my twenty-five thousand.

It was easy finding the place: a large house on a hill, setting all alone. And you know, my first impression was a pleasant one. Mind you, I wasn't sure what I was expecting, but any time you mention a feeble mind you get to thinking about all them places of horror you hear and read about. Insane asylums and prisons and such. But this was just a house outside of town. Right pretty too. I mean, it had a garden and a white picket fence and cheery curtains blowing outa the upstairs windows and a wishing-type well in the yard. It was a place just like you see on postcards or like one of the places them English ladies write about in their diaries.

I looked at the directions again and, sure enough, I had the right place. I climbed outa the buggy and tied the horse to the fence and we both, the horse and me, looked around. I think I felt the skin on my neck itch a bit, 'cause all 'round it was quiet and deserted. The horse snorted like he was clearing the dust outa his nose, but I wondered if he was trying to tell me something. It was a peaceful place, but as still as a bone orchard, and right then I wisht I hadn't made that comparison. I noticed my heart was thumping a little harder'n usual. Now you know about these involuntary reflexes, such as breathing and swallering and all, well they don't take kindly to being thought about too much, so I reckon the more I heard my heart thunk, the louder my heart did thunk.

The horse looked at me like he heard my ticker, and I think I heard his some too. Anyway, I pet his nose for luck and mumbled something to him like, "don't get too relaxed," and then I opened the gate. All gates creak, I don't care what kinda grease you use on 'em, but I'm here to tell you, that gate downright moaned "go away" as I opened it. I swung it back and forth a few times, relistening to the creak, like as to reconsider things. As I walked the stone steps to the porch, I wisht to hell I hadn't been reading so much Sherlock Holmes of late.

"Hello?" I calls out. Cripes, my voice creaked almost as bad as the gate.

As you mighta guessed, there wasn't no answer. I

walked up the steps and onto the porch. My eyes pulled me to a small and shiny brass plaque next to the door. I etched up to it, and when I read it I damn near fell through my boots. It read, "The Samuel J. Perrault Home for the Mentally Retarded, Founded 1890." The first thing that struck me was, he didn't have just one son in this condition, he had a whole houseful of 'em!

There's this feeling you get when you're riding between two large boulders. We hands call it riding down a draw and you can't see nothing but rock, but you know, and your horse knows, that something's 'round the bend, maybe looking at you and planning your demise. Well, that's how I felt just then. So I wasn't surprised when the door opened just before I was set to knock on it.

We talk a lot nowadays about the hearty pioneer woman, and there she was, gushing bosoms held up by a dirty apron, sleeves rolled up on John L. Sullivan arms, and hair pulled back so tight that it was a wonder the woman could blink.

Now, I'm gonna interject right here, that you should write down two exclamation points after everything that woman said, even though, grammatically speaking, it ain't correct.Anyways, you should at least think double when she speals.

This woman bellowed at me, "Thank God you're here!!" Then she wiped what looked like thick, sticky bread dough from her hands. She reached out, yanked me through the door, and added, "I thought you'd never get here!!"

"You did?" I asked. Now I have to tell you, I was confused, and damn, I hate to admit it, I guess you could say I was scared. "Then you was expecting me," I stammered. "My name is. . ."

"Simon Buffley!!" she said for me, taking my hand for a hefty shake. "And it's about time, I don't mind saying!!"

Well, right then I knew *she* was the confused one. "Pardon me, ma'am," I said, or maybe stammered, "but I'm not

Simon Buffley. My name is Royal Leckner and I'm here to fetch Leviticus Perrault."

I reckon it musta been hard for a stone-chiseled face like hers to go blank, but hers did it all right. She stared at me like I had some nerve being me and not that other Buffley feller. She fixed me a glare and demanded, "I beg your pardon!! Aren't you from Olympia?!"

I answered, "No ma'am."

"Then what are you doing here?!" asks she.

"Like I said," I says, getting annoyed how she didn't let a man finish his sentence, "I'm here to take Leviticus Perrault to his daddy's ranch down in. . ."

Well, she hollered, "Perrault!! *He's* the one that got me into this mess!!"

Now it was my turn to beg her pardon and I did, only I took a little step back when I spoke. Ain't nothing cowardly in the use of a little caution.

"Sit down sonny and let me fill you in!!" she ordered, and she pointed to a nice settee, but I took a highback chair instead. Now, it had been a long time since anyone called me sonny, but since she was offering to tell me what the hell was going on, I didn't take no offense.

"I had a feeling he was the type to do something like this!!" she began, like I knew exactly what she was talking about.

Since it still was hanging in my mind that maybe this woman was one of the inmates, I asks carefully, "Like what, ma'am?"

"Up and die, that worm!! Leave me stranded with all them . . . all them. . ."—she whirled her chubby hands 'round her head like she was referring to the upper portions of the house—". . .them *people!!*" The way she contorted her mouth when she said "people" made me realize she wasn't referring to normal people.

I scooted to the edge of my chair in case I had to make a run for it and said, cautious-like, "You'll have to forgive me, but I don't reckon I have the slightest idea what you're talking about. Is this where I can find Leviticus Perrault or not?"

"Oh, he's around all right!!" she answered. "Come supper time, you can't miss him!! Do you want to hear this story or not?!"

Well, you know what I wanted and that was outa the whole kittankabootle. But I was in it then and I just replied, "Oh yes. Go on, Misus. . . ?"

She glared at me like I oughta of known she was a maidenlady. "*Miss* Wintermute!!" she said, watching my reaction real close, like if I had anything to say about her maidenhood, it would cost me my manhood.

So I tried to smile and said, "Go on, Miss Wintermute."

"Well," she went on, "a few years ago Samuel Perrault bought this place, fixed it up, hired me, and put a coconut in each room!!"

That pretty much explained things. Leastwise, it took care of the brass plaque out front.

"He provided this home for his son, you mean?" I thought that was a safe question.

"And three of his. . ."—again, her mouth made fun of the word—". . .*colleagues!!*"

"Well, that sounds right charitable," said I, wondering what other sides of ol' Perrault I might be running into.

"Indeed?!" she hollers. "So then I read he's dead!! And two months behind on my pay to boot!! So what am I gonna do with this place?! How am I gonna live?!" I suppose the water is always clearest at its source.

"You mean, he financially supported this place?" I asked, and I tried to imagine what expense column that woulda fallen under in the ranch account books. It didn't seem like a dumb question, but Miss Wintermute looked at me like I was one of the coconut colleagues.

"Well, how do you think we keep this place running?!" she asked me. "Weave baskets and huck 'em to the Indians?! The folks here can hardly do for themselves, so how would you expect they could do for me?!"

I wondered why they'd want to but, of course, I just smiled like I was sorry for asking such a stupid question. And then I said, "Well, I can see your predicament, Miss Wintermute. But if you'd be kind enough to fetch Leviticus, I'll lighten your load some."

"So what is it *you* have to do with Perrault?!" she asked, ignoring my request.

"I'm his ranch foreman and, well, his will wanted me to work with Leviticus down to Four Arrows." I smelled something burning in the kitchen, but I wanted to stick to the subject at hand.

"How could that old man have been so stupid not to think of us when he died?! The bills are just piling up!!" I think she was starting to get weepy, which woulda just about made it a perfect afternoon.

"I suppose he musta overlooked you," I answered. I was noticing a bitty stream of smoke coming from the kitchen. "Excuse me, but I think you have something burning."

She sat upright, gave the air a bear-like sniff, leaped up, and shouted, "Piss!!" Then she stomped to the kitchen, setting some plates on the sideboard a-rattling.

Well, I'll tell you, I ain't never before heard a woman say 'Piss!' in my whole life and I wasn't sure whether to laugh or what. I heard alota clattering and banging and shouting in the kitchen and I thought maybe twenty-five thousand wasn't so much money after all.

Then Miss Wintermute came back in and picked up the conversation just where she'd left off. "Overlook indeed!! Well, I can tell you one thing, mister: as soon as this Buffley joker gets here from Olympia and takes them other three simpletons, I can get outa this place and wear on with my life!! A single, eligible girl like myself has no business being locked away in this house with a bunch of coconuts!!"

Well, there was lots I thought about saying, but I had to

ask, "If that's the way you felt, why did you take this job in the first place?"

Again, she shot me a look of disbelief in my not recognizing the perfectly obvious whilst she barked, "Well, I had reason to believe Perrault had marital intentions towards me, that's why!!"

I closed my eyes at the very thought and, even though ol' Perrault and me had our differences, I thanked the Lord this Miss Wintermute hadn't come into my life under any other set of circumstances. I had a brief glimpse of Anita and Miss Wintermute squaring off and duking it out in the Four Arrows kitchen. Sullivan versus Corbett comes to mind but, of course, you're way too young to know about them boxers.

"Well then, I understand your annoyment," I says weakly. I could see outa the corner of my eyes that some of the folks that lived there was sneaking a peek at me from the kitchen, but I forced my eyes on Miss Wintermute, which I thought might always be mandatory in her case.

"A fine thing, him dying!! I hope it was a painful death!!" she puffed on, shoving up her sleeves, which you could tell was just a nervous habit of some sort.

I thought of the horse and Perrault and the rattlesnake and replied, keeping my smile to myownself, "I'm sure it was a painful experience. Well, maybe you could call in Leviticus so's we can get on our way." I stood up and fingered my hat some. I wanted outa there in the worst way.

Miss Wintermute pointed to the long, velvet window curtains behind me and said, "Don't have to!! He's been here all along!!"

I looked over my shoulder and I was immediately struck by the blood-red color of the curtains. They was exactly like the bordelo curtains over to Wallula. I followed the velvet down till I saw two large boots poking out. Then, ever so slowly, the curtains parted to reveal his face.

*L*ike I said before, I didn't know what I was expecting, maybe some deformed nondescript, kinda like ol' Quasimodo or Frankenstein. I reckon it's hard to look back and recall what I expected. But whatever it was, it wasn't what I saw. Leviticus Perrault, looking shyly at me from behind those red velvet curtains, had the most engaging sorta smile I ever did see. His face was alive with boyish mischief, even though he was a full grown man and looked it for the most part.

"Well, don't just stand there drooling, come out and meet someone!!" Miss Wintermute commands harshly.

Slowly, he stepped out from behind the curtains and I would defy anyone to guess, just to look at him, that Leviticus Perrault was anything less than a normal man and a right handsome one at that. He stood looking at me and, Lord, his smile spread even wider.

He carefully walked forward and offered me his hand, which was soft and innocent-feeling when I shook it.

"Hi," he said, grinning and shaking my arm up and down like he was priming a old pump.

I replied, "Hi yourownself." It was impossible not to return his smile, but I have to confess, I was a little uncomfortable him holding onto my hand so long. And I thought it was sorta odd he couldn't keep his eyes in a direct line with mine for very long.

I looked over to Miss Wintermute and she said, like she could read my mind, "I know . . . he *looks* normal enough!! Ten minutes with him and you'll know he's crazier'n a March hare!! Let go his hand, Leviticus!! You two ain't married!!"

Well, he thought that was funny and he dropped my hand whilst he laughed awkwardly.

I disremember just exactly what we said next, but I'm sure it was all just easy talk. What I do remember, though, was this Leviticus was a real gentle and trusting looking

Then she huffed around, plopped herself down on the settee, and gave a mighty sigh. She crost her legs man-like and drummed her fingers on her knee.

Well, you couldn'ta hacked through the thick silence between us with a machete: she staring at me and me just trying to look as though everything was all right and going according to plan.

It was the longest ten-minute span of my life.

Finally, the kitchen door swung open and there stood Leviticus, grinning of course, and behind him stood three more of his kind. I knew I was in big trouble, 'cause each feller had a satchel in his hand.

Well, like she'd rehearsed this scene all her life, Miss Wintermute rose up, flailed her arms out over her head, and said to me, "There you are!! Now you've done it!! You had your chance, but no!! *You* had to ask him to say goodbye!! Now I'll have pandemonium with those other coconuts!!"

Her nostrils was flaring like a spent horse's and the spit kinda stuck in the corners of her mouth, and if I'da been any lesser a gentleman, I think I mighta winced to think of this woman loose and on the man-hunt.

Well, I approached Leviticus and said, "Sometime maybe we can have your friends down to visit, but let's just you and me go now, Leviticus."

I turned, hoping to high Heaven he would follow.

Miss Wintermute stood to one side, her arms folded, like as to say "this I gotta see!"

I heard footsteps follow me to the door, but when I turned 'round, alla them was in a tight little pack right behind Leviticus. I looked to Miss Wintermute for help, but she'd started to grin, like maybe she just won a major battle or something. I took Leviticus aside and said, "They can't come with us, son. They belong to other folks."

"What do you think they're doing here if they had kin could take care of 'em?!" she asked. "Nah, all they got is

feller and I reckon I liked him from that very first peep through those awful red, whore-like curtains.

# nine

*M*iss Wintermute took flight for the kitchen-lands, leaving me and Leviticus alone in the parlor, which made me even more squirrely. 'Course, mosta us, we only got stories about folks like Leviticus and no real work-a-day experience, so right off there's this element of suspicion and fear of not knowing what the feller will say or do next. Well, that's the way I felt and it seemed like the more I stumbled over my words, the wider his grin got.

"So," I began, like I was talking to a five-year-old, "how'd you like to live on a biiiiig ranch?"

He looked down and answered, "A pair a nently."

Slowly, his eyes returned to mine. I wasn't sure I caught his reply correctly, but I continued on. "I understand you can ride a horse. Is that right?" asks me, thinking I was doing real good so far.

"A pair a nently," he answered again, his face all aglow.

I didn't know what a pair of nentlies was, but talking about 'em sure brought a smile to his face.

"Well goooood. Because you can't run a ranch walking." I kinda smiled wider myself, wondering if he'd see the humor to that. But the silence that dropped between us indicated to me he didn't. "Well," I continued though my mouth was going dry, "you're coming with me, so I guess you better get your things together."

Well, he just stood there, grinned, and said, "A pair a nently."

It was then I started getting me a worn feeling. I thought I'd test him and see if I could get another kinda response outa him, so I asked, "Do you prefer Shakespeare to Longfellow?"

"A pair a nently."

A pair a nently, a pair a nently, I went over the words in my mind. What the hell was a pair of nentlies and what did they have to do with any of this? Then I thought I'd try something else. "Who you voting for for President?"

But he didn't say it that time and maybe I wisht he woulda. "Washington," he answered, and his face looked kinda proudful.

I could see right then what Miss Wintermute mighta been referring to. Well, at least he knew who the father of his country was. And hell, I could see as how they probably didn't discuss the political side of life in that house, so I gave him ol' Washington.

Miss Wintermute came back in and it was real amazing to see the smile disappear on Leviticus' face. Fact is, on seeing her, his face turned downright scourful, and I knew then at least the feller had some taste in women.

"I packed his things!!" she said, handing me a old carpetbagger that appeared real light. And then she asked me, "Is he gonna go peaceful or will you need a rope?!" She asked it plain as if she was asking about some maverick calf a-wandering through the yard.

My heart thunked onct at the very idea and then onct again, for maybe a rope might really be necessary. I looked at Leviticus and smiled as kindly as I could, and I think I found it hard to swallow. "No," I said. "We're gonna get on just fine, aren't we?" I knew he'd make his nently comment again.

His smile came back and he said it again, all right.

I sallied over to Miss Wintermute and asked outa the side of my mouth, keeping my smile on Leviticus, "What's a nently?"

She took a grandiose step back and asked with mucho gusto, "A nently?! What're you talking about?!"

"Well," stammers me, "when I ask him a question, instead of saying yes or no or get off my foot, all he says is 'a pair a nently.' "

Well, I didn't see anything funny in that, but you can be sure Miss Wintermute laughed out about as loud as any man I ever heard. I noticed she was missing several back teeth, which mighta contributed to her spinsterhood. Then I commenced to get a little nervous at her laughing the way she was, onaccounta I didn't want Leviticus to think I'd been defiling him. But he just laughed along with her.

"A pair a nently is his way of saying *apparently!!*" she finally choked out. And I think the tears of laughter creeping outa her narrow eye-slits was 99% steel-eating acid.

"Oh," I said intelligently, seeing no humor in it at all.

"It's a word he picked out of a sermon some sky pilot gave last year!!" she said. "It's a catch-all, that's sure!! He thinks using a big word makes him smarter!! *You* get him to say it right!!"

I looked at Leviticus. Onct he'd figured out Miss Wintermute was speaking ill of him, the light in his youthful face had gone out. I turned to him, looked as kindly as I could, and gently asked, "Is there some folks here you'd like to say goodbye to?"

"A pair a nently," he whispered back, hoping, I think, that Miss Wintermute wouldn't hear him. He began walking toward the kitchen, and you could tell then, watching him move along, that he wasn't no normal man.

When we was alone in the room, Miss Wintermute glared at me all impatient-like. "Well, that was a stupid move!! You almost had him out the door!!" she hollered.

the half-wits they was born with!!" Miss Wintermute adds, not adding any powder to my argument.

"Now I'd like to bring your friends," says I, "but. . ." I was working up to a good reason that he might understand. I'll tell you, all those eyes staring at me, I was beginning to sweat real hard. "It's . . . it's . . . well, it's just not legal. I'd get in real trouble."

At that bit of genius, Miss Wintermute walked to a desk, pulled out some papers, scratched some writing on 'em, and then handed 'em to me with the most evil kinda smile I think I ever saw. "Now it's legal!!" she humpfed.

I looked down at the papers with my mouth gaping wide enough to catch a buzzard, and I want to tell you it was so dry in there he woulda felt right at home.

"Well, you just take these back, Ma'am," said I, trying to hand the papers back. "I come for Leviticus Perrault and none other."

All the old war-bag did was gesture with a sorta girlish curtsy toward Leviticus and his friends. I reckon, by the grin of victory on her troublesome face, she musta been thinking this was the luckiest day of her life. I pitied all the single men in the county when I thoughta her on the prowl. But that was their problems. And as God was so cleverly pointing out, I had my own.

I was getting forceful mad, so I took Leviticus by the arm and said, "Just you, Leviticus. We can write your friends and see how they're doing."

"Write 'em in Olympia!!" Miss Wintermute taunted. "At the state asylum for the mad!! Ever visit an asylum, Mr. Leckner?!" She turned the knife a whole revolution.

Leviticus didn't move a inch. I tried to avoid his eyes, but I was drawn to 'em and I knew I was a goner. Sure, I'd heard all sorts of stories about mad houses and the like. So what? I asked myself. Stories, that's all. Hell, these folks ain't *my* responsibility! "Leviticus, you just gotta understand," I said, wondering if he could read the look on my face and realize my predicament.

"No!" he said right powerfully. Well, so much for understanding, I thought.

I stammered, "But I . . . can't," and I looked at the faces of the ones behind him. A right pitiful lot, you can be sure. But each one was silent and staring at me like what little there was to their lives was in my hands.

Well, remember what I told you 'bout loyalty and all? How I always prided myself on it? I suppose the way I looked at it was, there was something in this Leviticus feller that made him loyal too. So I thought to myself real quick, what was so bad about that? Maybe he wasn't as tetched as everyone seemed to think.

Oh hell, who can remember what I was thinking? I'd been pinned to the fence real good, that's sure. The room was all silent again, except for Ol' Man Perrault's chuckling, which I swore I heard in the treetops outside somewheres.


Stuffing four of 'em in the buggy took some doing. But the horse stood patient-like whilst they loaded in, and he looked at me like this was gonna cost me extra.

Miss Wintermute had been watching from the front porch, holding a check I'd written her to cover so-called unpaid expenses. No telling what was going through her mind, but I vowed to get even some day. She ripped the brass plaque off the siding with one powerful tug and tossed it at me, screws and all, shouting, "Here!! You'll be needing this!!"

I picked it up and I noticed how the edges had been altered by her strength. I glared at Miss Wintermute and figured maybe at least I'd get me a award for rescuing these poor fellers from the clutches of that woman. I took the horse's bridle, turned him, and began walking him back toward Pasco.

As I looked back to see if everyone was setting safe-like in the buggy, I noticed not one of 'em was looking back at the peaceful house or at Miss Wintermute, who was leaning against a porch pillar, waving the check goodbye to us, and calling out good riddance to her coconuts and to the head coconut leading the whole damn bunch.

Okay son, now stop writing. If I don't walk around some, I'll pull up lame for sure, and there ain't nothing crankier than a ol' cowpoke limping and feeling sorry for hisself.

## ten

Course, as any cow will tell you, there's safety in numbers, and I reckon that's what those friends of the Perrault boy thought too. They clung to each other in such a tight little remuda, I knew it was gonna be a tricky match getting 'em through the doorway of the hotel. In the lobby there was a round, velvet settee, and I placed the boys all 'round it. They was happy just to set there whilst I talked to the hotel clerk about where Jay was and what the possibilities was of putting up my little herd.

Well, after he'd taken just one look at my following I could tell the clerk was not real comeatable about things.

He said for me to set and he'd ring the cafe acrost the street for the manager to come over right away.

I took a seat acrost from the boys and, for the first time, made me a inventory of my latest Four Arrows predicament, but I knew at a glance I'd bitten off a little more Durham than I was used to working 'round my mouth. They was a right scrabbly looking lot, I want you to know.

I finally worked up the nerve to go over and introduce myownself and see just how deep the well was. I took out the papers Miss Wintermute had given me so's I could start putting the names to the faces.

"How do?" I said first to this shakey sorta feller. He was all kinda twisted up and looked like he'd be real hard to carry on a conversation with, so I thought I'd get him outa the way first. "My name's Royal Leckner," I said and I offered him my hand to shake, but his whole right arm was too busy shaking on its own accord to need any help from me. So he gave me his left hand to shake and I did, even though I thought it felt awkward.

He was Indian-dark, so I didn't have too hard a time deciding he was the one called Tommy Two Hearts. I had noticed this one had a hard time walking, and I reckoned it was onaccounta the terrible scar on his forehead. Factually, it was more like a dent. Anyway, the right side of his face was kinda helpless and his head leaned down on his right shoulder.

His dark eyes smiled up at me and I didn't even expect him to say nothing. Then, with a big contortion, he said, real slow-like, "My . . . name . . . is . . . Tommy : . . Two . . . Hearts. I'm . . . half . . . Indian. Spokane." You coulda parked a Studebaker Wagon between his words, but they *was* words. He paused to make another smile, which was real lop-sided and, well, to be honest, just a little drooly. "The . . . left . . . half . . . is . . . Indian. The . . . white . . . half . . . don't . . . work . . . too . . . good."

Well, you coulda knocked me down with a baby's

sneeze. The last thing I thought I'd find in this crew was a sensa humor. But there it was, grinning up at me.

"It's . . . good . . . of . . . you . . . to . . . take . . . me," he continued.

I looked down to his paper and read that his momma, the Spokane Indian half, had tried to smash his head against a rock to destroy the shame of bearing a white man's son without any matrimonial benefits. He was saved by some missionary folks, who took him back in '67, which made him just about 25 years old. The papers went on to make mention of the search for his relatives, but either a page was missing or whoever filled out the papers just quit writing. Well, I thought, searching real hard for the sunny side, half a brain is better than none, nine times outa ten.

Setting next to him and leaning into our conversation was the tiny one. A bittier thing I don't recall ever seeing. Must nota been over four-and-a-half feet and as thin as a bullwhip. I looked through the papers and, going by age alone, reckoned this one was Lou Beal, age: late teens. He looked real comical in clothes so much too big, like he was playing dress-up and still waiting to grow into his daddy's pants and shoes. He had big, sourful green eyes and looked just plain like the victim of not getting enough to eat.

His papers was lacking in information too, so I just jumped in. I offered him my hand and he looked at it kinda quizzical-like. So I asked, "Is your name Lou Beal?" I thought it was kind of a shame, him being so small and me being so tall, that he'd have to crane his neck up to me, so I knelt in front of him, waiting for his answer.

His green eyes coulda bored holes in me, and it pierced me additional to wonder what was behind those eyes. When he was done looking me over, a smile came acrost his tiny face and he said, "Lou Beal. Seven. Nice name. Short. Like me. You?"

Well, that feller spoke so fast it almost made up for the

Indian talking so slow. His voice was real high, like puberty had overlooked him, and all I could answer was, "It's a good name, Lou."

I noticed that when Lou blinked he blinked one eye at a time, which I figured could get to driving me crazy, if I let it.

"Sixty-two steps. Buggy to here," Lou continued, like onct he started talking, he couldn't stop.

"Lou . . . likes . . . numbers," Tommy explained for me.

"Sixty-two. Sixty-two," Lou said to Tommy, who nodded patiently in agreement.

Well, I thought I'd let 'em discuss sixty-two and I walked over to the next feller. This one had to be Thaddeus Wainwright. He just looked every inch a Thaddeus Wainwright. He was a older gentleman with a real ugly, worn face. He looked to me like he was seventy, but his papers said he wasn't quite fifty and that he'd—and here I shall quote from memory—"served in the Southern Rebellion whereupon he'd become two men." Unquote. That's what it said, sure as I'm setting right here and you're setting right there.

I looked him over real good and I sure was confused. 'Course I wasn't nearly as confused then as I was to become.

I said, "Howdy, Thaddeus, I'm Royal Leckner. How's yourownself?"

"We're fine," he started. Then he added in a voice altogether different from the one that had just said he was fine, "Speak for yourself, you no good, low-account Johnny Reb!" Before I could even register my befuddlement, he continued right on telling hisself how good *and* how rotten he felt.

"Toofer. Screw loose," Lou sputtered, like that was all I needed to know.

I felt kinda weak in my knees and I asked, "Toofer?"

"Toofer. Two . . . fer . . . one!" Tommy leaned over and

explained, half smiling, half drooling. "Miss . . . Winter-mute . . . named . . . him!"

Lou set his head back and laughed him a high-pitched ha-ha-ha-ha-ha. Five ha's exactly.

Well, I'd gone around the velvet settee and landed in front of Leviticus. I reckon he thought I liked him best. He had it all over those others as far as beauty goes, but I thought I'd let the jury stay out a little longer to decide just who was the looniest.

He broke out in smiles, but he couldn't hold my eyes. Come to think, not one of them fellers did look you right in the eye for very long. Well, I told myself, don't get too bamboozled about that. All in all, they seemed a real happy bunch and God knows I didn't have half a idea what to do with 'em all. But there I was, standing in the middle of that hotel lobby, casually a-circling the settee and wondering where the hell Jay was.

# eleven

*I* guess I was in shock or something about the whole pinch, 'cause I just sat down in the lobby, looking at my crew and trying to see where I went wrong. What in the name of Matthew, Mark, Luke, John, *and* Leviticus was I gonna do with these folks? I leaned back in my chair and placed my hand thoughtfully to my head like you see in pictures of great thinkers. Right off the top of my head, I thought onct I set Leviticus up at Four Arrows, I'd find some way to divert money and get the others into a home somewheres. Maybe Pendleton, Bend, or Walla Walla Wash—anywheres but Idlehour. Just how I was gonna cut Leviticus from the herd, why, I'd worry about that later.

Well, before I could furrow a proper row of thought on the matter, the hotel clerk walked over and I knew he had bad news for me. You know how you can tell bad news just by the way a man walks—a little bit tippy-toed, a little zig-zagged? Like the extra steps could put things off some?

He said, "I talked to our manager, Mr. Leckner, and, well, it seems we're all full up." He looked right apologetic, and we both knew why the manager was turning us away.

"Sign out front says 'vacancy,' " I says, kinda low and logical.

"That was my mistake. I forgot to put out the 'no.' I'm sorry. But you and Mr. Smyth are confirmed," says he, like that changed things.

"Confirmed what?" asks I. 'Course, I knew what he was talking about, but I sure did want to menace him a bit. I rose before he could answer and thought I'd use my height to my advantage.

He looked up at me and said, "Your room . . . it's confirmed."

I looked down at him and said, "No it ain't."

"Sir?"

"You ain't got rooms for my friends, you ain't got rooms for me," I said. I put my hat on, hoping real hard I'd called his bluff.

Well, the clerk set me aside and said, kinda low, "Well, truth is, Mr. Leckner . . . we've had some trouble with those . . . those kinda people before."

"How do you mean?" I asked.

"Well, they're crazy," the clerk explained as if I hadn't noticed.

"Different ain't crazy," I said. I had a feeling right there, that minute in that lobby on that day, that I would get real familiar with that bit of philosophy.

"I'm sorry," he said. "We just don't want any trouble." He ventured a little peek over his shoulder at the boys, and although I wouldn't've taken him for a timid man, he looked a bit edgy.

So I said, plain disgusted, "Then maybe you can recommend another hotel."

"You could try the Flanders Inn down the road," he suggested.

"Does your manager have any objections if we wait here for Mr. Smyth?" I asked, kinda looking down my nose at him.

The clerk took a glance at the clock over the desk. I suppose he was calculating when the manager was gonna be back. Then he asked, "Do you suppose Mr. Smyth'll be very long?"

"Well," I offered, "if you'll set with my friends, I'll go look for him."

As you might expect, he didn't want anything to do with

that, so he told me to go ahead and wait, but if we wanted to get a room somewheres else, we oughta get going.

I sat back down and looked out the window for Jay. It wasn't long before I spied him. I could tell by the grin on his face as he sashayed up the walk that he'd been doing 'everything' again, and I knew then I'd have to talk to him about the clap and all.

When I started outa the hotel door to intercept him, the four from Perrault's Home all stood up, like as to follow me. I smiled at Leviticus and motioned for him to set back down, and they all did, real dutiful-like. They'd been real patient, all to theirselves and smiling some, just happy to be out and about, I suspected.

Jay walked smack dab into me and said, "There you are. Well, what's he like?"

I turned Jay around so's he couldn't see the crew on the settee and I asked sternly, "Where the hell you been?"

His face lost its grin, but you could tell he was more interested in meeting Leviticus than discussing his new-found pasttime.

"Now you listen to me, boy," I went on. This time I used my augur's voice. "I got us a big problem. Leviticus wouldn't come without his. . ." I looked over Jay's shoulder to the boys on the settee, then looked back at Jay. "Without his buddies. We got us four to take back to Four Arrows."

"Four what?" he asked real loud, his eyebrows climbing up towards his floppy hair.

"Shhhh! No use letting the county know!"

"Four what?" he whispered, trying to gleen him a look inside the hotel.

I took another quick look inside and, to my horror, I saw the settee was empty. But before I could dive inside to round 'em up, Jay pulled my sleeve and asked, "Royal, are these the four of which you speak?"

There they was, all four of my nondescripts, staring out the window at me and Jay, smiling and fogging up the windowpanes some. The way them four stuck together was damned impressive, like they wasn't about to lose a single one of 'em along the way.

The cameras they have these days woulda done justice to Jay's expression whilst he just stared back at the four faces, but in those days all I had to register the moment was my memory, and to the day I die I'll never forget ol' Jay's face. His mouth dropped open and his face lost its boyish glow, and you'd need one of them microscopes to locate his eye-dots. Poor kid. I reckon it was the first time in his life that he'd seen a less than perfect human being. Well, he was old enough to know the chillier facts of life.

Slowly, he broke his stare through the window and he looked over to me, saying, "Royyyallll."

So I said, before he could up, quit, and punch the breeze on me, "I see now you can appreciate our problem."

"Four?"

"Count 'em."

He looked so shocked, I wondered if maybe I should slap him.

"Four . . . crazy. . . " he mumbled.

"They ain't crazy," I insisted, "just different! Now you listen to me, Jay! We gotta approach this logical-like. One problem at a time, hear? You go on in there and get our grip, and if you paid in advance for our room, you get the money back. They won't take us here. We gotta find some place that will. Now move!" I reckon it was decision-making and salty talk like that that had made me the foreman I was. Maybe it was the crack of my voice or the frothy look in my eyes, but Jay moved out real fast without anything like a hesitation.

I remember looking skywards, even though all I saw was the eaves of the hotel front, so I reckoned God didn't see the expression on my face. Sure as hell though, he heard the words I muttered, and I reckon He and me'll have to settle up on that someday.

Well, as the logical mind mighta ciphered, there wasn't any rooms available in all of Pasco that afternoon. So to hell with Pasco, I thought, and we commenced our journey back to Four Arrows.

*I*t's kinda too bad ol' Jay never wrote down *his* story, 'cause it would be real interesting to read about how he felt that first day, meeting the four from the Samuel J. Perrault Home for the Mentally Retarded, founded 1890. My memory serves me like a whore—here today and gone tomorrow—but when she's here, she's full of attentiveness. 'Course I didn't have a inkling that someday a President would send writers like you out looking for memories. Maybe if I'd known, I woulda made it a point not to forget so much.

Anyway, I told you Jay was shocked and horrified and, at first, he was real goosey around the boys, watching 'em real close and keeping conversation to a minimum, which probably suited alla us.

Well, we didn't have any bed rolls for the boys, so that let out setting up a camp that night. So we slept in a box car which was warm enough and private and, getting right down to the pith of the problem, the boxcar was a proper corral, which made my night watch on that herda strays about as easy as possible.

The boys was right cooperative. No one talked back or circled about me with a better idea, which is always the way it is with normal men. They seemed grateful for their dinner of beans, slab bacon, apples, and bread and, watching 'em eat, I knew we'd be butchering more cattle down to Four Arrows. But you know, it was good to watch 'em eat hearty, and they seemed all happy amongst theirselves. After dinner, we took a walk into the train yard, where we found a outhouse, and they stood in line, all patient-like. I thought back on how I'd seen fights break out amongst my ranch hands whilst standing in line for the outhouse. Now if only these boys could ride, rope, and develop some cow sense, I thought I mighta just stumbled onto a whole new breeda ranch hand. 'Course, I knew that woulda been too good to be true, but it served me as a good fantasy, just as well. No fights, no talkback, no griping, no fandangos.

Yes, we did have trouble with the journey back to Four Arrows, just as we did at the hotel in Pasco. Back in those days, hell, even now, so-called 'normal' folks have trouble accommodating folks like our crew. We had to wait for a ferry that didn't carry anybody else, onaccounta the ticket office didn't want to offend any passengers, so that took some extra time.

But Wallula . . . well, I already told you about that town. Things was better there. No one seemed to look twice at us as we trooped from the stage depot into the heart of town. The ladies that had showed Jay 'everything' proved good on their words and welcomed us back with empty arms, full corsets, and exact change. And right here I might just as well say, so you won't be guessing at it the rest of your life, the ladies looked at my crew as a whole new challenge. Most likely, they didn't get many challenges in their professions and, just about anyone will tell you, we alla us need challenges from time to time.

'Course, what it took to get them boys laid would be another whole other interview in itself, 'cept I sure as hell reckon no one would write it up, so with due respect to ol' FDR, I shall leave that scenario up to your imagination. Leave it go at what I told you, we alla us need challenges onct in a while.

The evening did not, though, come off without a imbroglio. No sooner had I settled down in the parlor with a glass of something fortifying, when one of the ladies brought me back the one called Lou Beal, the tiny one with the numbers vexation.

He was chanting, five dollars, ten dollars, twenty dollars, whilst the whore led him by the hand into the parlor. "Here, Royal, you can have this one back," said the soiled dove.

"Five dollars. Ten dollars. Twenty dollars," said Lou. I stood up and asked why she was returning him, thinking he might be only a slip of a feller but he sure as hell musta been old enough. Anyways, I didn't recollect age being a requirement at that particular establishment.

"Howdy Lou," I said whilst he kept tabulating five, ten, and twenty dollars. "What's the problem?"

The whore—I think she called herself Candy—sat him down real gentle-like, smiled at me through her thick, rose-painted lips, and said flat-like, "He's a girl."

Well I'll tell you, I'd had my share of surprises in my life, but I think that one topped 'em all. I looked at Lou real close and he, I mean she, looked back, smiling like inside she'd been planning this surprise all along.

Candy waltzed back upstairs, no doubt in a hurry to share the humor, the way she shared everything else. I reckon very likely it was her first case of mistaken identity too.

So now I perceived I had a whole new problem to work on whilst Lou was working on hers, which seemed to be nothing more complex than, "Five dollars. Ten dollars. Twenty dollars. . ."

# twelve

*W*ell, right off I added a 'ella' to Lou, but I always wrote it like this—Lou(ella)—onaccounta she·always said three handles was better'n one: Lou, Ella, and Louella.

Anyway, where was I? Oh, as long as we was on the go, the boys and Lou(ella) did just fine. They just seemed happy to look all about as we went, like they'd never seen sand or scrub, and they seemed to think it all went together kinda pretty-like. I could point out things as simple as a prairie flower and they all just ooed and awed and wanted to touch it. 'Course now that I look back on it, I think they was sorta trying to please me. They was no dummies. They knew I was the one holding their cards of fate. Even on the trainride over to Walla Walla Wash, where I expected the very terror of it all to sprangle 'em, they acted real organized and calm. It set me to thinking that they wasn't so bad a lot and that maybe ol' Miss Wintermute was the crazy one.

The train to Walla Walla Wash was the regular one, so we made better time, which was all right with me. I never liked being too far away from Four Arrows and I was getting a bit edgy. The boys and Lou(ella) took real good to train travel, even though they was asked to ride in a empty cattle car. You know why that was. Though it didn't seem to hurt their feelings none, I was damned if I was gonna enjoy human accommodations with my new crew clacking all about in that smelly cattle car. So Jay and me rode with 'em, and onct we opened the doors and rid us of the flies, it wasn't so bad. Jay was sore about it, I might add, onaccounta he'd been embarrassed in front of some feathered-out ladies, but onct he got over that, he seemed to enjoy setting in the doorway of the car, dangling his legs out, and watching the country roll by.

Onct we was in the train station, I nearly lost Lou(ella) onaccounta she was so enchanted by the numbers on all the train cars. All she had to do was take a gentle gander at 'em and the numbers rolled off her lips in proper order. Tommy Two Hearts told me she could repeat the numbers back to front or front to back, or she could pick out the exact middle number in the series and run 'em in either direction. All the boys thought Lou(ella)'s talent was a wonderful thing, and I have to admit I was amazed she could do it. But in the back of my mind and, admit it, yours too, what was the earthly good?

*F*olks in Walla Walla Wash, being like folks everywheres else, gave us suspicious stares as I led my crew single-file through the streets. It was getting late and I knew they was all hungry and would need a good night's rest. The idea of sleeping in a box car again made me cringe, so I left the crew in the park with Jay and started to look around for accommodations. I was smart, that time. I paid for the rooms and I told the hotel man that my ranch hands would be coming in later. I reckoned I'd sneak 'em upstairs a couple at a time.

Now dinner was a whole other quagmire entirely. I'd been a loyal customer to this one chow house called Sadie's and I took my crew there. It was no fancy place, just good, honest food served kinda bunkhouse style at a long table. Well, we sat down but I don't reckon any of my crew had ever eaten in a restaurant. Providing 'em with a choice of food was my first mistake. Toofer, the major-corporal Civil War problem, had to fight amongst hisself as to whether he would eat the Southern Fried Chicken or the Boston Boiled Dinner. He ended up having both, but not without a major skirmish between his Major Thaddeus North and his Corporal Billy Grey, which I quickly learned was his two inner fellers.

Leviticus, not to be outdone, ordered the same, and Tommy Two Hearts ordered a couple of steaks and, in his slow manner, liked to have taken six days to cut up the meat. Finally, Jay couldn't stand it any longer and grabbed the knife and fork from him and commenced to slicing away whilst Tommy just stared down at his plate.

Lou(ella), as bitty as she was, wanted to try everything and mumbled her way through a little of this and a little of that. I think she was counting her chews the whole time.

Jay, of course, was humiliated to be seen at the same table with my charges, and any attempts to build up a relationship with the waitress was tragically foiled.

We was there for two hours and built up a bill of six dollars and sixty-three cents, which don't seem like much nowadays, but was quite a blow to my account books then.

Jay and me worked the crew into the hotel just like I'd planned, a few at a time and kinda quick-like up the stairs. He took charge of Tommy Two Hearts in his room and I took the other three in mine.

I don't think Lou(ella) had any idea she was any different from the others, 'cause she commenced to get undressed in front of alla us. It worried me some, 'cause ever since that 'everything' night in Wallula, Leviticus seemed to sorta follow her 'round some. I don't know what made me think I was doing those boys a favor by getting 'em laid. I sure as hell had no idea I'd entirely change the way Leviticus smiled.

Well, I escorted Lou(ella) to the privy down the hall and told her to take her clothes off in there. When the door opened, she stepped out unshucked—swear to God— buck naked as a bluejay, and it was then I realized how literal she took things. I stuffed her back in the door, telling her to put on her night shirt. Then I looked 'round the hall to see if anybody had seen.

I got Lou(ella) back to our room and set her up on the divan, handing her a pillow and a blanket. Then I escorted Leviticus down the hall. I thought I'd let Toofer and Leviticus share the bed and I'd sleep in my bed roll on the floor.

But when Leviticus and me walked back into the room, he took one look at Lou(ella) on the divan, passed the bed, and commenced to try to bunk in with her.

When I protested, he smiled up at me and said, lamb-like, "We always sleep together."

Well, I could see right there that I had a whole other problem on my hands.

I looked over to Toofer as though I thought I could get the truth from him. He smiled back at me like he knowed why I was suspicious, though I'll never know exactly what he knowed.

"They do," he said, simple-like, which was immediately followed by his other voice with, "It's a sin, I told 'em from the beginning!" Then he turned on hisself and said, "They never *do* anything." Then the Major voice came back again with, "I don't care, it's still a sin! Now shuttup, Corporal, or I'll put you on report!"

Thinking that might be a good idea, I just looked back down at Lou(ella), who'd pulled the blanket up around her chin and seemed undisturbed by Leviticus bunking in on the opposite end of the divan. In fact, she let go of the blanket a little to allow him some warmth and then she rolled into the couch. Leviticus did the same, and I just stood there, confused.

I looked back at Toofer, who seemed as though he was fighting a invisible demon for the lion's share of the covers. Right then, I was beginning to side with Jay on the whole matter. I wanted to scream and flunk outa the whole damn situation. There was no logic to them folks whatsomever.

I grabbed my bed roll, threw it to the floor, and kicked it open. I turned out the lamps, not wanting to say anything 'cause I'd sure as hell say the wrong thing. I didn't even want to know how Jay was doing with Tommy Two Hearts. Damned if I didn't have a tough time pulling off to sleep that night!

*T*he remainder of the trip was about as eventful as it was interesting, which warn't very. Jay and me was getting used to life 'round Leviticus and his crew and some of the nervousness was beginning to wear off. Onct we got to Milton and settled everyone into the buckboard, they all seemed to know we was on our last leg of the journey. 'Course, they was tired of the excitement and they dozed like babies. Jay, onct he got hisself back in the saddle of Hero the Harelipped Horse, was more and more his ol' self and not so much the critic he'd been previously.

All along, I knew folks over to Idlehour was probably getting real curious about my new charge, and I spent more'n several hours staring at the landscape and imagining the looks on their faces when they saw I'd brought us back not one but, count 'em, four mentally out-of-sorts. But whilst I was thinking about it, a flash came to me that said, damn Idlehour! The less that town knew about Four Arrows' business, the better. I guess it was one of those rare occasions when Providence takes you gently by the hand, bashes you up against the nearest wall, and slaps you 'round your head a little till you agree to do something that ain't normally in your nature. You see, normally I woulda trooped my crew into Idlehour, had a few welcome-home-Royal drinks at the Glass, and introduced my crew all 'round. Well, you know how that woulda gone over.

So with Providence booting me down the road, we avoided Idlehour altogether and kept on the road to Four Arrows. As always, the ride was a healing one. The Walla Walla sparkled a welcome at us, and the cows grazing along the trail looked over at the buckboard as we passed and they sorta smiled as they chewed their cuds.

When we pulled into the long drive to the ranch house and passed under the Four Arrows sign, the crew seemed real interested. And although they hadn't said much amongst theirselves the whole trip from Milton, there was something even more quiet about 'em as the ranch house grew larger ahead of us. Although it wasn't fancy and pretty as their house up to Pasco, it was big and friendly looking.

A few of the hands working 'round the place rode over to greet us and escort us in. But after saying howdy, then figuring out the numbers of my predicament, they just kinda slacked off and followed behind the buckboard all silent-like.

I pulled the team to a halt and kinda made a general sigh—just glad to be back home—then looked around to my new crew and announced, "Well, here it is: Four Arrows."

The smile on Leviticus' face was wide, like he'd discovered gold or something, and the others stretched their necks to get a better glimpse of all the buildings, animals, and activity that was surrounding us.

Well, I reckoned they knew they was home.

And that's when I have to figure that the second part of my story began.

Hell, you look tired, son. Wanna stop for tonight? I don't mind telling you, I'd be happy to share some whiskey with you. Got any?

# Part Two

## o n e

*I* figured there was about nine, maybe ten hands that followed us into the yard. I knew right off that the sorta silence I was hearing from them boys meant they was looking over my crew with pretty slanted eyes. 'Course, Hardy had told 'em about the will and Perrault's boy and all, and that I'd left to fetch the heir. I have to admit, it disappointed me a bit to see the way some of the hands was reacting to the looks of my buckboard-load of newcomers. But hell, I don't know how I allowed as Four Arrows men would react different than any other men when looking on my crew.

"Howdy Bill, Jimmy, Luke. . ." I said, giving 'em my best whatznew grin. I looked 'round and didn't see Hardy, which concerned me some onaccounta I always liked having him close at hand.

The boys nodded back a welcome, but their eyes naturally was pulled toward my crew of nondescripts.

"Where's Hardy?" I asked, standing up in the buckboard like as to get down and stretch my legs. Well, I shoulda known, for the moment I stood up so did the other four, making the buckboard a little shaky. I guess that spooked someone's horse and there was a dusty little skirmish. I sat right back down and so did my crew, like they was playing monkey-see, monkey-do or something. Well, I hollered at someone for keeping such a skittish horse around, but I knew it wasn't the horse's fault.

"Hardy's up on the West Branch," someone answered. "Said he'd be back toward dusk."

"One of you boys ride up and fetch him back," I said, and I sure got the feeling I was just talking to the horses, for the hands was staring at the crew and trying to figure out what the hell I'd gotten us all into.

"Jay, help our guests outa the wagon," I said.

Jay pulled his right leg 'round his Hero's neck and slid down off his horse like young cowboys do when they's being the center of attention. He opened the buckboard hatch and, one by one, he helped them out.

By chance, one of the hands shot a wad of tobacco not far from Leviticus and it landed in the dust with a tidy wap! and Leviticus looked back up at the hand and grinned real big, like he was sure impressed. I could tell he was working up some good spit to try the trick hisself, but I caught his eye and his face darkened some and he gave a big swaller.

When the crew was all lined up like they was comfortable doing, I said, "Boys, these here are some guests we're having. Guests, meet the boys." At that, I marched the crew into the house where it was cool and dark and safe from eyeballing.

Jay hung back some, and I hadn't even walked through the doorway when I saw all the hands circling him for some information. "Get on in here, Jay!" I ordered real loud, and Jay hopped up onto the porch as fast as any jack rabbit and then eased hisself in through the screen door before it had even had a chance to swing back closed.

I guess I had always taken for granted the front room of the ranch house, onaccounta I been around it so long. But the crew from Pasco thought it was real interesting, for they was all around, looking and ooing and awing and reaching to touch things such as the chair Jay made outa that ol' Texas Longhorn, the mural of the cattle by the Walla Walla, the grandfather clock with his smiling, harvest moon face, the crystal inkwell on the desk and, oh, the agate rock fireplace and the wall of rifles, the spinet piano and all the rest.

Anita'd heard us walk in and she called out from the kitchen, "Is that chew, Mr. Leckner?" She walked in, wiping her hands on her apron, and she stopped short when she took in our guests. Maybe I'd gotten used to 'em or something, but I really didn't see anything so spectacular about 'em. Well, maybe Lou(ella) mighta looked a tiny bit strange, and maybe Tommy Two Hearts jerked about a little, but who would guess about Toofer except for maybe it was a little odd that he wore a Confederate hat with a Union coat. And Leviticus, well I already told you he looked right as rain, if you could get him to look directly at you, that is.

I knew I had to get the upper hand with Anita, even though she was usually pretty easy-going. I smiled at her like I was a fancy easterner talking to his cook and said, kinda formal-like, "We'll be seven for dinner, Anita."

"Any especial requests?" she asked, looking at me like seven was all right with her.

"No chili!" Jay boomed out before he could put a check on it. "That is, if I'm invited for dinner." He kinda looked shyly at me and I nodded yes.

I caught Anita's eye a-wandering to Lou(ella), who was counting the keys on the piano.

I said, "Whatever you can rustle up for us will be fine, Anita."

She took a diplomatic pause and asked, "And will chew be seven for breakfast?"

"Yes. Yes," I answered, nodding my head, like everything and everyone was hunky-dory.

She looked at the others with her black, Mexican eyes, and I knew her wheels was turning inside, so I planned on telling her just how things stood when I could get some time alone with her.

"The guest rooms. . ." she and I said, almost together. We just caught each other's eyes and I nodded and she nodded and she knew what was ahead for her.

"I thought Leviticus here should have his father's room," I went on, thinking I worked him into the situation real easy-like.

Anita nodded, giving him a half-smile.

So I went on, "And, a . . . and the Major-Corporal here could share a room with Tommy and let's see. . ." My eyes landed on Lou(ella). "And I guess Lou here can bunk, can. . ." I was calculating how many guest rooms we had and I thought I had run out. "Do we have a room for Lou?" I asked Anita.

She looked at Leviticus and said, "We can put a bunk in his room."

"No, no," said I. "This here is Lou*(ella)* and, well, that wouldn't do much. Oh, I know! Lou(ella) can put up in the small room in the back."

Anita gave me a long look like she was wondering when I was going to make any sense outa things. I wonder now, looking back on it all, if that poor, big, wonderful woman ever did figure things out.

$Z$ eb Hardy got back a short while later and he came a-bounding up the porch steps, grinning to beat the band and carrying a old flour sack. As the sack undulated to and fro, I knew at onct he'd been hunting king snakes.

He handed me the sack and said, "Welcome home, boss. I got you a present."

Well, I knew if I didn't give a peek into the sack and give out with a proper ooh or ahh, he'd be all hurt, and I reckoned with what I was about to spring on him, I oughta soap him a bit. I said it was one of the finest kingers ever and that I hoped it had the good sense it was born with to keep well outa Anita's way and that he'd have a long way to prove hisself to beat his predecessor's longevity.

"I got a surprise for you too, Hardy," I continued.

He stepped back a piece and got a looka suspicion on his face and said, "It's that Perrault boy, ain't it?"

"Well, you knew I was fetching him, Hardy," I said. "So that wouldn't be much of a surprise now, would it?"

"No, I guess you're right," he gave in.

Well, I didn't see why Hardy should suffer under the suspense any longer, so I went directly to the surprise part by saying, "I had to bring back three others."

'Course, you know he came right back with, "Three other what?"

Just about then, the pack entered the front room, all tight and together-like. They'd just been wandering from room to room exploring their new home. As you know, their appearance answered Hardy's question just about perfect.

Hardy made a quick head count, then looked at me and said, "Four? Are they all. . . ?" He stepped in to me and gave me a queer look with his eye. "All. . . ?" Then he kinda twirled his head around and I just nodded yes. "Crazy?" he whispered.

"Not crazy, just different," I whispered back.

"Enjoy your snake," Hardy said, turning to leave.

"Come back here," I warned. "I want you to meet my new crew."

I pulled Hardy back by the arm, thinking to myself that if I lost his loyalty, I might just as well get on with selling Four Arrows so's Idlehour could fritter the money away on public betterments like tile outhouses, manure receptacles, and horsefly control and, of course, a paid board of managers to administer such new-fangled wonders.

"Now smile," I warned Hardy as I pulled him over to the crew, "so's they know you're a friend."

"What do I say?" he asked outa the corner of his mouth, whilst the other corner tried to hold up a smile.

"Tell how happy you are that you've been given this opportunity," says I. Well, that stopped ol' Hardy in his tracks.

"What opportunity?" he asked.

"To teach 'em cow handling," I replied.

He looked over the lot. "All of 'em?" he asked, looking mostly at Tommy Two Hearts, who was shaking in his natural way.

"Relax, Hardy," said I. "It's only till I can set 'em up in a home somewheres. Come on. They're nice fellers. You'll see."

*I* don't care what anyone tells me. Those four I brought back down from Pasco was about as friendly and trusting and forgiving a group as you could hope for and, right there, you can see why I was so concerned about 'em meeting up with those corpuscularians, Silas T. and Julius and the rest of the crowd in the greedy little town of Idlehour.

You can put that dictionary down, son. I reckon you won't find that corpuscularian word. But back in my day, it meant bloodsucker, and you know what that is, so now you know what I thoughta Silas T. and Julius.

# two

*T*hat night Anita pulled off dinner real good by sending to the barnyard for a few more chickens. Now, you already know how my crew ate and appreciated food and all, and I told you also how ol' Anita loved to have her cooking taken seriously. At mealtimes, I figured, things was gonna go real smooth, providing, of course, we didn't run outa food. 'Course, the cats and the dogs 'round the place would have to start relying on the ranch hands for leftovers from then on.

The best part of the meal, though, was after the four pies had disappeared, our guests took their own plates into the kitchen for Anita. Yes sir, that just set with her real good and I could see from then on I best be doing the same.

Well, we'd all had a long day and they all seemed happy to turn in early. I was tired too and I know Jay was hankering to get on over to the bunk house to tell the boys about his trip and how he'd finally done 'everything' and how he had the disappearing pimples to prove it. But being as how I was never one to waste time, I asked both Hardy and Jay to set a spell in the library so's I could tell 'em about what we at Four Arrows was about to undertake.

Well, to soften 'em up a bit, I poured 'em a shota fancy liquor. After we sat down and allowed the comforts of the room to relax us a bit, I looked at Hardy and asked, "Well, what do you think?"

He rubbed his knee like he always did to ease its ache.

He looked at me with his wise ol' eyes and answered, "I think Ol' Man Perrault got the last laugh on you."

To which I asked, "How do you mean?"

"By saddling you with a impossible chore," he answered.

"Hell, Hardy," Jay broke in like younguns will, "Royal gets that money no matter what!"

Hardy and me looked at each other, and I knew and he knew that this wasn't about my money.

"Now, let me get this straight," Hardy continued, ignoring Jay like he did so well. "According to the will, there's to be this sorta accountant to see how Leviticus—Lord, what a handle—how the boy is doing at running Four Arrows."

"In a manner of speaking," I answered. "Now, I've done all sortsa studying on the matter, and this is how I look at it: We teach the boy 'bout cattle, you know, how to drive and ride and all that. Now, since you and me make mosta the major decisions anyway, I don't see how this account-ant feller or anyone else could say Leviticus ain't capable of handling ranch affairs. After all, all the will says is we have to make money on cattle sales next year and the boy gets everything. Hell, this spread ain't ever lost money as long as I was foreman." I didn't say it conceited-like, just factual.

But Hardy comes back with, "Roy, now I'm sure Ol' Man Perrault didn't plan it this way, but you know how prices've been dropping. Why, here the year's barely half over and folks is already beginning to panic."

"That's all back east mostly," I assured him. "Sure, prices are down some, Hardy, but what with all the railroads coming and going and crews needing meat, I don't see how we can lose."

"Who's they and what're they panicking about?" Jay asked, setting up straight, like maybe he'd better be a little concerned.

"Nothing you need to worry your fuzzy little head about, boy," Hardy said, I suppose onaccounta he didn't want to explain stocks and bonds and wheat prices and such.

"Anyway, Hardy," I continued, hoping Jay and Hardy wouldn't tangle over words like they was sometimes fond of doing, "who's to say who's responsible for this outfit? The titular head or the foreman?" I'd heard that tit-word made in reference to ol' Queen Vic onct and thought I'd worked it into the conversation real good.

Ol' Jay, he picked up his ears, like I knew he would, but I just kept on talking. "All I have to do is get Leviticus to learn to trust me, master a horse, and maybe answer some ranching questions, and we'll have it all set up." I let my smile of confidence shine on ol' doubtful Hardy.

Hardy shook his head some and commenced to rubbing his knee again, and I knew he was putting some head work in on the matter. "I don't know, Royal," he said after a spell. "I mean, the boy is nice enough, but I don't know how smart it is to work on giving him the power of Four Arrows."

Now, I don't raise my voice very often, which I always figured was a real good trait, but I guess I was becoming crazy myself over things. "Damn it, Hardy!" says I. "That boy is Perrault's son! He's had too much taken away from him already in his life! This place is his and I'm gonna see to it nobody takes it away from him!"

"Whoa, son," he said, like only he could and not have it sound like he was talking down to you. "You're looking at the one who probably has the most to lose if this deal don't pull off."

Jay'd stopped drinking and was all eyes and ears. I knew what Hardy was talking about, but I let him explain it himself: "If Four Arrows gets sold out from under me, ain't no one gonna keep on a hand as old as me. Hell, it's a miracle I'm still alive to cuss about it!"

Yep, that was it and he was right. "So then," I said, my

voice back to its usual cracking calm, "it looks like I can count on your help."

Hardy, he just rubbed his knee hard like as to get it ready for the rough road ahead. I looked over at him, glad to have such a leathered ally.

Then we set forth some plans for the rest of the week, like how first thing next morning I'd ride into town and see what Silas T. was up to.

It was good to fall into my own bed that night, even though down the hall I could hear Lou(ella) counting more woollybacks than there are in Australia and New Zealand and Ireland put together. When she stopped, I reckoned she'd dozed off at last and I, like a she-wolf, didn't settle down to sleep till I knew all my less ones was safely asleep.

Say, just how much you getting paid to set there and cramp your hand like that? Yeah, I guess you're right. Something's better'n nothing.

# three

*T*hough he put up a snort about it, I pulled Jay awake early the next morning and asked him to eat in the ranch house and sorta act as overseer, onaccounta I knew I'd best get into Idlehour and make my report to Silas T. before word got to him that I'd returned and he came snooping 'round Four Arrows.

It was still dark when I rode outa Four Arrows, and even though my black gelding seemed happy to see me back, he wasn't real pleased with the hour either. He stepped real light and cautious, like as to say, "I put a foot in a hole, I'm sailing you into the next county, Leckner!"

Well, it finally got light and the horse didn't trip onct.

I could smell the bacon frying at Mrs. Morgan's Eathouse clear up the block as I rode down Main Street. You know how there's just something 'bout bacon aromas on the wind that yanks your stomach awake, even if it's still working on a breakfast you just ate? Smells do that, and I guess bacon and coffee is the worst offenders. Well, Silas T. wouldn't open the bank for a while yet, so I ate another breakfast at Mrs. Morgan's, promising myself that I wouldn't eat lunch onaccounta it.

Well, as you can guess, I was the most popular yap at the eathouse. Folks jumped on me the minute I walked through the door, wanting to know all about the Four Arrows heir and what he was like, and they hoped it wasn't so awful a experience that maybe I'd lost my endearing qualities, like my sensa humor or my patience or anything.

I almost considered taking my plate outside to eat with my less talkative horse, but like always I answered their questions politely. I said Leviticus was a real nice sort and we wouldn't have any problems at all, onct I could get the hatchet outa his hands. Then I laughed and added a ha-ha-ha, joke's on them. But the looks I got back surely bothered me and I stopped with that line.

'Course, I didn't say a word about the other three I'd brought back. That was my business and not theirs. Besides, in the backa my mind I knew everyone there in that town was secretly hoping I'd fall flat on my face, onaccounta they'd all get something outa my failure. So I said enough to tug on their imaginations, and when I left, I felt good about 'em not really knowing any more about the Four Arrows situation than they did before I walked in.

When the sun began to peep over the east hills, the town came to life as towns did back in those days. Even though we had a electrical line in Idlehour, not all folks subscribed to it, so we was still dependent on sunlight, and businesses usually opened the moment it hit their store fronts.

I led my gelding down the street to the bank, and whilst I walked I tried to suck in my belly, 'cause after two breakfasts that morning I was full as a tick and I hated to think I'd get me one of them paunches like you see on middle-aged gents . . . overhangs I call 'em and you know why.

As I rounded the corner, I saw Julius Armentrout's buggy tied up to the hitch in fronta the bank, and right there I knew I'd best be careful. Just the thought of a lawyer and a banker together at such a early hour turned my blood cold. I stopped and considered going back to Four Arrows. My gelding took the opportunity to scratch his forehead along my back and, even though I knew that was his habit, it sure seemed like he was pushing me onwards. I took his advice and kept on going.

I tied him off, leaving plenty of room between him and

Armentrout's horse, onaccounta I didn't want my horse nose to nose with a lawyer's horse. That's just exercising good common sense. The horses looked at each other casual-like, then my gelding took his glance away and heaved him a heavy sigh, like as to tell me to hurry things up.

Now, it'd been a hot night, like all nights was in our corner during the summer. I need to tell you right away that the bank windows was open wide. No doubt Silas T. wanted to air the place out some before commencing work that morning. Anyway, I want you to know it ain't normally in my nature to drop a eave on anyone, it just sorta happened. 'Course, I hadn't planned on setting down, but when I heard Silas T. say my name as I approached the window, well, you better know I ducked and wisely instructed myself to set a spell after such a larruping breakfast. And what I overheard there curled my nosehairs.

I heard Silas T. say, "I received a wire from the accountants in Portland. Their man—a E.M. Gallucci—should arrive sometime this morning."

Then Julius asked, "Are the books ready?" And you can be sure I pricked my ears up.

"So perfectly in balance it brings tears to my eyes," Silas T. replied.

To which Julius said, "Not too flawless, I hope. After all, we're just small-town hayseeds to a Portland accountant." I had to nod in agreement.

"Don't worry, Julius," said Silas T. "I've left a few things for this guy to find fault with, just so we look innocent and in need of his modern techniques. Believe me, after I finish with Mr. Gallucci he'll be on our side."

There was a long pause, and I had one of 'em awful feelings they was both staring at me through the window as I slouched down even lower in the bench. Then I heard Julius ask, "Do you have the cash?" and the feeling of being stared at stopped.

"Only in the case of emergency," Silas T. replied, and I heard the shuffling of papers and thought he was probably straightening out his desk, which was a habit of his. I held my breath as I listened for more.

Then Julius asked, "How high are you prepared to go?"

"Hard to say," Silas T. answered. "It's been my experience that some men come very, very cheap."

I wisht to hell I coulda peeped in the window to see which one was winning the staredown. By the way ol' Silas T. worded things, it sounded to me like he was referring to Julius Armentrout as one of them men that came cheap, which didn't make no sense to me onaccounta, after all, 'lawyer' and 'cheap' just don't belong in the same sentence.

"And some men have no price," Julius replied back, kinda cool-like, getting back on his courtroom feet.

"Well, let's not get into that now," Silas T. said, which I was glad for. "Now here's the plan: I'll meet the stage, you present a copy of the will, do your legal holy holies, and leave. Then I'll convince Gallucci that Leckner is bound to fail and that he oughta start thinking about divesting Four Arrows. You'll buy us lunch and we'll have him back on the six o'clock to Pendleton. No muss, no fuss."

I'm sure my eyes was popping out as I listened. Now, I'd always suspected ol' Silas T. of slickery practices, but to hear him plan Four Arrows' demise made my mouth go dry and my heart beat a funeral dirge. I had to think fast, that was sure. I eased outa the bench as quiet as I could and tippey-toed over to my horse. I led him a few steps away, leaped aboard him, and headed for the stage company.

The stage's arrival was listed on the chalkboard for 8 a.m. I reckoned I had just a coupla hours to come up with a plan to foil up Silas T. and Julius Armentrout. Before I'd even had a chance to range things 'round in my mind, I found myself on the road to Pendleton. The only thing I could think of was to cut the stage off and meet this Gallucci feller first.

*W*ell, like you know, life is full of surprises and it wouldn't be very kindly of me to lead you on up to the point where you can guess what happens. So I figure I'll get the jump on you and tell you right now that E.M. Gallucci, accountant from the firm of Howell, Powell and Gallucci in Portland, Oregon, was a woman.

When I called for Albert, the stage driver, to pull over, he did so willingly, being as how we was friends. I explained I had to talk to his passenger and, well, you know me good enough now to know just what my face looked like when I opened the stage door to meet Mr.Gallucci and I saw a woman setting there, giving me a how-rude look.

A woman-accountant. I never in my whole life had hearda such a thing, even though I had heard that some women was getting damn uppity and wanting to vote and all.

It wasn't hard for her to dominate the conversation, though, onaccounta I was speechless at first. "E.M. Gallucci," she said, offering me her gloved hand—I suppose to shake—even though you hardly ever saw a woman shake hands. "And you are?"

"A . . . a. . . ." I elocuted, "Royal Leckner . . . I . . ." I gave her hand a wee shake, but she wrapped her fingers 'round my hand and she surely did let me know she had some strength.

There was a silence. She musta recognized my flustration, standing there half in and half outa the coach. "Was there any particular reason you stopped the stage?"

If I was staring at her, which I guess I was, it wasn't 'cause she had exceptional beauty. But then again, you gotta know this E.M. Gallucci was a damn sight easier to gaze upon than any other woman I ever met.

"A . . . do you mind if I just tie off my horse and ride into town with you?" I finally asked, although it seemed like six years that I'd been staring at her.

"What for?" she asked bluntly.

I tethered my horse to the side handle of the coach and said, "Well, I know this sounds strange, but, well, maybe I'd best tell you who I am." I pulled myself in, closed the door, and told Albert he could start up his team.

"You already have told me who you are," she replied, cool-like. Her voice was cool, all right. But them eyes . . . pure fire.

I mumbled, "Oh, so I did." And I wisht to hell I could pull my eyes offa her and babble something intelligent.

"You're foreman at Four Arrows," she continued. "I recognized your name from the files." She tapped a satchel next to her.

Like I said, I watched her real close and wondered what God musta been up to, placing a woman in the middle of the Four Arrows pickle.

Well, by my staring I reckon she felt like she had some explaining to do, and when she spoke it was real school-like and almost memorized. "All right, you don't see a woman accountant very often. As you've no doubt figured out, my last name is the same as the name on the business stationery. Well, my father, Emilio Gallucci, didn't plan it that way. He's the accountant, I'm the daughter. Notice I didn't say son. According to most people, I am unmanageable and, therefore, unmarriageable. Father had no place he could put me except in his business. Italians have a strong loyalty about family and business, you know. I detest numbers, I have nothing but the utmost contempt for most men, up to and including my father, and since I cannot possibly add a simple column of numbers and get the same answer twice, I am routinely sent out of the office at month end which, you will notice, is tomorrow."

I reckoned it musta been a full moon too.

She looked me straight in the eye, which I approve of in either man or woman or beast or any combination thereof. But damn, I hated not having the words at the draw and ready to fire back when someone speeches like she'd just done.

"May I speak frankly, Mr. Leckner?" she asked, leaning toward me some. Hell, if she hadn't been frank up to that point, I was a goner for what musta been coming next.

So I folded my arms in front of my chest with a protective-like instinct and mumbled, "Please do."

"When my father told me he was putting me in charge of the Four Arrows fiasco. . ."

"Fe-as-ko?" I asked, my voice cracking as usual.

"Italian for 'failure,' " she answered. "Anyway, when he said he was sending me to Idlehour, I considered killing him, but then I'd have to plug Howell and then Powell, and if there's one thing I'm not, it's a mass murderer."

"You sure?" I asked, weak-like.

She glanced me a look of that's-for-me-to-know and you-to-find-out and followed it with a sly smile which, I gotta tell you, I did find intriguing. She talked Snapdragon, but her smile was pure Morning Glory.

Finally, my mind started to work like it should when I remembered the severity of the Four Arrows—as she called it—fe-as-ko, which up to that point I'd been suffering under the misconception was a sauce of some kind.

"Well," I began, trying to remember if I'd brushed my teeth that morning, "since you've been frank with me I'll be frank with you."

She just Mona Lisa-smiled at me and rocked ever so gracefully with the motion of the coach.

I took a breath so's to get my ticker settled down, then said, "The reason I come out here to meet you was to warn you off about Silas T. Burnbaum." I tried not to let my eyes wander to her bodice, which appeared quite liberally cut.

"He'd be the banker," she said, knowing full well I was

getting nervous watching her rock and smile and hell, the heat in that damn coach didn't help.

"Yes, the banker," said I. "Well him and Julius Armentrout. . ."

"He'd be the late Perrault's lawyer," she interrupted.

"Yes, his lawyer," said I. "Now, I know you're to look things over regarding Perrault's will and all, but they've fixed things up some."

To which the Gallucci woman said, "Mr. Leckner, I can tell you, it doesn't matter one iota that they've fixed things up some. Banker, lawyer, woman: now, what word doesn't belong with the other two? Listen, Mr. Leckner, I'm only here for the outing. Like everyone else, they'll take one look at me and say, 'No woman's fit to audit *my* books,' that'll be the end of it, and I'll be sent packing back to Portland. That's the way it always happens. I'll return just in time to spend each day adding, re-adding, and telling my father to go to hell until. . ." and her half-smile returned as she added, ". . .until one day he does."

I sure was getting side-tracked by what she had to say and how she said it, but somehow I continued on with Four Arrows business and said, "Miss Gallucci, I got it on very good authority that they intend to bribe you if necessary to get you to turn your back on how they've set things up." There I was passing along to her the worst news I'd had since the will-reading, and she was just smiling at me like it was no news to her.

She said, "Mr. Leckner, it's a waste of time to tell me all this. I told you, since I've a difficult time disguising the fact that I'm a woman, they take one look at me and send me back."

To that I asked, "So where does that leave me and Four Arrows?" I was getting a little riled how this woman could just range along with things and not appreciate my predicament.

"Well," she answered, "my father and his partners will

have to make other account arrangements. But I will tell you this: whoever they send out in my place will be quite bribable, so if you have it in your mind to find an uncorruptible accountant, you better look elsewhere." She fanned herself with her hankie whilst she gazed out the window at the Walla Walla River.

I set back and forced my eyes off her whilst I thought things over. When it struck me, I almost laughed onaccounta it shoulda been obvious to me: the only accountants ol' Perrault woulda dealt with had to be crooked. But revelations could wait, for we was fast approaching Idlehour and I had to quickly pull together a plan.

"Miss Gallucci," I began, giving her my smile of opportunity, which everyone said was damn near irresistible. She looked over to me and—Lord, if them I-talian eyes of hers wasn't dazzling—her eyes met my smile and my smile met her eyes and I almost forgot what I was about to say.

"Yes?" she asked.

"I think you've been pushed 'round by men long enough," is what I did say at last. Considering who I was and what I thoughta most women and all, that was a damn radical statement. But I meant it, honest and true.

She leaned in to me a tad more and said, "Go on."

Says I, "Why don't you, just this onct, stand up to 'em, tell 'em *you're* the accountant and, hell or high water, they're stuck with you. Tell 'em Perrault's estate is paying the retainer, not them, and that I, as executioner of the will, demand that you stay on the job."

She listened very nicely, like probably her daddy taught her to do, then said, "You forget one thing, Mr. Leckner. I hate numbers in all sizes, shapes, and forms. I hate them and they hate me. The little black ones sneak around and trade places with the red ones until they all look pink to me. I'm trained, but I'm not good."

Whereupon I only smiled wider and said, "*They* don't know that."

"What possible advantage could I have in that?" she asked. Then her face softened a little as maybe the possibilities was coming to her.

Our eyes did some talking, you know, the kinda talk that can't be described onaccounta there just ain't the words available. Finally, I grinned at her and replied, "You'd have the advantage of knowing you was helping out some real nice folks. And them that know say that sorta thing comes in real handy on Judgment Day, when we alla us need every advantage we can get. Especially those of us that goes 'round planning on massacring the whole accountant firm of Howell, Powell and Gallucci."

When I smiled at her with that line, she laughed a real gutsy laugh and said, "And why should *you* care about all of this? After all, as I understand it, you're just a cowboy who is about to become very, very rich for babysitting some half-wit for five-hundred days." She didn't say any of it mean-like, just matter of fact-like.

My eyes looked down to the floorboards as alla Four Arrows flashed into my mind in the accompaniment of that trusting smile on Leviticus' face. I know my voice turned softer when I said, "Well, how things seem and how things is, well, they're two entirely different things."

Then Albert called down that we was pulling into Idlehour. "Well?" I asked Miss Gallucci. "You up to taking 'em on?"

She kinda twitched her mouth as she thought. "Well, it would throw a fine wrench into Daddy's machinery." Then she sat silent and chewed a little on her lip, like deciding to stand up to Silas T. and Julius Armentrout and her daddy to boot was the biggest decision of her life. "Oh hell! Why not?"

Well, in the period of just a few days I'd heard one woman say 'Piss!' and another say 'Hell!' and I'll tell you one thing, it was a new world coming, one that I wouldn't of missed for alla Four Arrows and the counties touching it thrown in to boot!

# four

*A*s we approached the stage depot, I craned my neck outa the window to see if Silas T. and Julius was there to meet the stage like I heard 'em say they would. Well, no one was there, so I popped my watch and was relieved to learn we was fifteen minutes early. I told Albert he had hisself a new record.

I helped Miss Gallucci outa the coach, and when I set her down I was surprised how sturdy she was and also taller than she appeared setting in the coach. Anyway, she gave the town a onct-over and I could tell she wasn't impressed, but then hardly anyone was.

I told Albert to take her plunder over to the boarding house. As she commenced walking a few steps ahead of me, I took in her get-up. Portland fashions was surely getting strange, I remember thinking. She had the biggest damn sleeves a-billowing out from her shirtwaist I think I ever saw. And then all this fluffery was pulled in together to form the tiniest waistline, and I got me my first glimpse of what we'd only heard of: a hourglass figure. (And I'm here to tell you, her p.m. was just as nice as her a.m.!) How she could breathe, I'll never know. Women and fashion: I don't reckon I'll ever understand it, which don't mean I can't appreciate it.

Anyway, onct we got to the bank, she paused on the steps, tapped the point of her worthless-looking parasol on the boardwalk, turned, and looked me eye to eye. "Are you going in too?" she asked, taking her valise from me.

"Would a Indian miss Beef Issue Day?" I replied, thinking I was being right clever.

She frowned at me like what-the-hell-does-that-have-to-do-with-anything and right then I knew the Beef Issue wasn't so big a issue over to Portland, so I just said, "I wouldn't miss ol' Silas T.'s expression when he sees just what kind of accountant he got hisself!"

"You mean a woman?" she asked, getting a little ruffle to her feathers.

I came right back with, "No, no. A accountant who can't be bought." I smiled broadly, stepped aheada her, opened the bank door, and held it wide for her. Well, she walked in through that door with the damnedest gait of aggression I reckon I ever saw, including the day after Jay got hisself laid.


*S*ilas T. and Julius sure didn't let me down none when I introduced the lady to 'em. Silas T. and Julius both stared at me whilst I just said, "Howdy Silas T. Howdy, Julius. I ran into Miss Gallucci on the way over here. Now ain't she a pleasant surprise?"

I reckon I could hunt for a week and still never find the right words to describe their faces. Put it this way, if a man could be elected to office on his shocked expression, then both the President and Vice-President of the U.S. of A. was standing right there in front of me, gawking at Miss Gallucci.

I guess Miss Gallucci was used to these encounters,

onaccounta she just shook their hands politely, smiled coolly, and began taking off her gloves.

"I assume you have all the files ready for me to go over?" she asked, real aggressive-like, and even though I'd only known her a short while, I was proud the way she dug right in.

Miss Gallucci had noticed a ledger on the desk and began looking through it. When Silas T. saw that, he jumped over and closed the ledger shut. "I'm sorry, Miss. Those records are confidential."

Miss Gallucci looked at me, and I knew from what she'd told me she thought it was happening again. But she held tight, took the book in her arms like a momma would take her baby, and said, "The late Mr. Perrault had the confidence to retain my father's accountant firm and my father had the confidence to assign this account to me. Now I *will* audit these books and I will do so in my room at the boarding house, free from any distractions. Now gentlemen, the fact that I happen to be a woman has nothing to do with being an accountant! Do I make myself clear?"

Julius stepped toward Miss Gallucci and said, "Now see here, young woman."

Well, she turned on him and I could tell there was years of anger and resentment about this see-here-young-woman kinda treatment in her voice. "You don't call me young woman! You call me Miss Gallucci or you don't call me!"

Ol' Silas T. made a move toward the book and said, "That ledger is not to leave this office." But Miss Gallucci was clutching it tight to her bosoms like it was something Moses mighta brought down from the mountain.

Here comes the real test, I thought as I watched Miss Gallucci's expression whilst Silas T. approached her. She didn't say nothing and I just couldn't leave to chance what might happen next, so I said, "Now, as executioner of. . ."

"Executor," they all three corrected.

But without missing a beat, I continued, ". . .Perrault's will, I feel it is my duty, Silas T., to make sure Miss Gallucci here gets full cooperation." I opened the door, thinking the best thing all around was for me and Miss Gallucci and the ledger to take our leaves.

Taking her cue, Miss Gallucci picked up her valise and said, "Thank you, gentlemen. You may be assured that this ledger and any other documents I'll be needing will be in good hands."

I don't think I ever did see two men more dumbfounded. And I reckon it'll be a long time before I ever see a lawyer struck speechless again.

As we was nearly outa the door, Silas T. called out, "Royal! I need to talk to you about the Perrault boy. . ."

"Oh, he's fine," says I. "Thank you for asking. I'm walking Miss Gallucci to her room now, Silas T. We got plenty of time to discuss Leviticus. First things first. So long, boys."

Onct outside the bank, I thought I might have to help Miss Gallucci down the steps, for it seemed her knees was weakening.

"There now," I asked, "was that so difficult? Most men is pansies, onct a woman takes over."

"No, it's just now I have to audit this ledger," she said, almost like it was my fault. "And I hate doing that!" With that, she took a deep breath and allowed me to walk at her side all the way to the boarding house.

Folks we passed was real interested in who she was, and the looks she drew almost made folks forget who I was and where I'd just returned from and with who and why.

Onct she got herself situated, I told her, she could come on out to Four Arrows and inspect my account books. We agreed I'd bring a buggy for her in two days, which would give me time to write in all my Pasco expenses and to get Leviticus and his crew feeling a little more to home.

We said goodbye and I remember saying to myself as I unhitched my gelding for the ride back to Four Arrows, how curiouser and curiouser this whole fe-as-ko was getting.

# five

*N*ow son, I know you're gonna wanna bust a gut laughing at this, but you shouldn't; you gotta know I don't recall this with any cruel feelings or to make fun, 'cause I think I already made my stand clear regarding Leviticus and his gang. But if you should happen to grin or smile or even chuckle some, I reckon that's all right and sorta between you and God.

First, you gotta know that back in the early days of Four Arrows, before Idlehour got so high and mighty, we had us a ranch store. There we kept the usual cowboy necessities—boots, blankets, ropes, Levis, shirts, and such. A hand could charge out what he needed against his wages and we'd all make out pretty equitable, 'cept I think ol' Perrault maybe gouged the price a bit, when ranch etiquette called for passing the wholesale price he got right along to his crew. Well little by little, mosta the men started shopping in town or ordering through catalogues and such, but we still had us some old and mostly odd-sized supplies in the ranch store. And of course, when I'd asked Hardy and Jay to see about outfitting Leviticus and the rest for ranch work, that was where they set 'em loose.

I suppose to the day I die, I won't be forgetting what a

vision they made, coming into the kitchen where I was having my breakfast. I reckon it wasn't a gentlemanly thing to do, spitting out my coffee acrost the table like I did, but I sure wasn't ready for how they'd put theirselves together.

You know how you see younguns these days dressing up to play cowboy? Or did you ever see a Wild West Show or a Broncho Billy movie? Well, with bagging pants cinched up with ropes or reins, hats so big they had to be held up with ears and noses, with bright red bandanas fluffed 'round necks like the feathers of a riled rooster, with boots either too big or too small or, in one case, not even close to matching the other—with all this and grins of 'look-at-me!' my new crew tromped into the kitchen, each holding a saddle and a blanket and, by all appearances, ready to ride the range, brand baby calves, break wild horses, hang no-good horsethieves, and settle whatever was left of our wild west.

Hardy and Jay squeezed in last, although the kitchen was right full. You could tell they'd been laughing some and, whilst I mopped up my coffee, they tried to catch my eye to see if I could continue to keep a straight face.

Leviticus spoke up first. "I'm gonna be a cowboy," he said. Then he quickly looked down at his saddle blanket and he heaved him a sigh kinda like he was too excited to say anything else about his good fortune.

Jay and Hardy looked at each other, then quick-like turned their backs so's my new crew didn't see 'em laugh.

Maybe the most farcical of all was Lou(ella). You know how tiny she was and well, standing there with clothes all rolled up and tucked in, she was almost clear hid by the old Magellan saddle she was holding. I reckon it was the toe-ballast in those enormous boots she wore that kept her balanced and standing.

I looked over to Hardy. His eyes was wet with held-in laughter. He grinned back at me and asked, "Where do you want us to start, boss?"

Jay just started to shake and snicker through his nose till he was forced to pull out his crusty ol' kerchief.

Of all the business I had to attend to that day, being my first working day back and all, and with E.M. Gallucci in town, the last thing I had time for was ranching lessons. But I thought some and looked over the crew all fulla grins and good, hopeful-like intentions. Then I plugged down my coffee, stood up, and said with a determined kinda resolve, "Riding lessons."

I worked my way through the new hands and led 'em outa the kitchen. I figured with me leading the way and looking all serious-like, the other Four Arrows hands might not laugh so much. Most was still fishing their horses outa the remuda and saddling up and waiting for work assignments. I told Hardy to get the boys along with their work so's we could have the corral mostly to ourselves.

Then I told Jay to cut us two of the most gentle critters he had. Well, we was alla us experienced hands and so we didn't normally have any pilgrims around for beginners. Jay said he had a few mares which was too long in the tooth for real work and that he'd pulled their shoes, but he thought he knew where the old girls was holding up.

Whilst he was fetching the mares outa retirement, I got my horse outa the remuda and showed my crew how to saddle him. My gelding seemed glad to be getting back to normal work, but I could tell he was getting suspicious at all the saddling, unsaddling, and re-saddling going on whilst I had each new hand give him a try.

I was encouraged at how they took the matter real serious-like and paid good attention whilst I talked. Lou(ella) seemed like the most skittish 'round horses, so's I showed her how to pat a horse's face and talk good and friendly and low.

'Course, it was Leviticus I was paying most attention to. He was the one that counted most. I showed him how to lift a horse's foot and how to clean it out.

When my horse lifted his tail to let out some air, well, that started the whole crew to giggling. Leviticus carefully lifted the horse's tail and then he made a imitating vapor sound. The others thought that was real funny, but my horse looked like he'd plant his shoes on the face of the next greenhorn to try that trick.

So then I told 'em how careful you gotta be 'round a horse's hindquarters and how far they could kick out when they got tetched off about something and how, in some cases, it didn't take much of a spark to light 'em off.

Yep, Jay's ol' mares looked like they'd seen better days all right, but they didn't put up too much of a fuss to being brought in, groomed, and saddled. Nope, almost like my ol' granny—who always enjoyed being asked to do a favor—the mares seemed to think maybe they'd enjoy a little outing.

Toofer had claimed all along that he could set any horse and that, during that Unpleasant Misunderstanding Between the States, he'd done most of his soldiering from atopt a horse. Well, as I found out, his Major could ride, but his corporal was as scared of horsing as any new, city-slicking recruit might be. If only he'd let one of his characters stick around for a while, I coulda done my job, but that man sure did jump from personality to personality, and I made a mental note to study up on such disorders and find out how you'd go about getting one to see a project through without the other getting in the way.

Leviticus pulled hisself up into the saddle real good, then hung onto the horn and froze when the horse gave a snort. Jay walked him 'round and he had good balance, which sure was gonna be a benefit to him. Finally, he relaxed some, although he sure did bounce around when Jay started to bring the mare to a trot. That ol' mare's ears started to twitch back and forth like as to say, 'Either this yahoo learns to keep still or I'll ride him!'

I thought Tommy Two Hearts might work real good into

wrangling since he was half Indian and all. But his palsy sure did interfere with his reining, and I reckoned it would take some kinda special horse to figure out what all his shaking meant. But I'd seen a horse carry a blind man onct and so I knew it could be done.

Well, whilst all the riding was going on, I'd lost Lou(ella) to some fascination of counting. This time it was the fenceposts that captured her. It wasn't long before she reported back to me that she had tallied fifty-six posts in one direction, but only thirty-two in the other direction and was that something she should be concerned about? "Not equal. No sense," she muttered, looking one way, then the other, I guess to see if she'd counted right.

Just as I was wondering how I was ever gonna get her safely on a horse and keep her there, Anita came tromping outa the house. With her apron a-flapping in the breeze and a wooden spoon in her hands, she approached me with such a sensa purpose that I sorta swallered uneasy-like.

"Mr. Leckner, what chew have that girl out here for?" she asked, although I guess 'demanded' might be a better word.

"She wants to learn ranching," I replied, with a aw-shucks-Mom-smile.

Lou(ella) looked up, knowing we was discussing her, and said pleasantly, "Fifty-six, thirty-two," as though that was as good a explanation as any about her being there.

"A girl like that should be learning cooking and cleaning!" Anita wore on, waving her spoon and looking more I-talian than Mexican.

"But. . ." I explained. "I thought. . ."

Then Anita said, "Well you thought wrong, Mr. Leckner." She took Lou(ella) gently by the arm and stood between me and her.

Well, you know there wasn't a hand on Four Arrows land that I'd let talk to me like that, but ol' Anita, well she was different. And she kept right on: "All these extra men to look after and there's finally another girl to help out and what do chew do? Bring her out here to teach her man's work!"

Well, I reckoned she had a point; Anita was real good at pointing out the obvious. I guess I'd just supposed Lou(ella) would want to keep with her pack. So I said down to Lou(ella), "Maybe she's right. How'd you like to go with Anita here and work in the house?"

Lou(ella) understood my question, you can be sure. But she turned and looked at Leviticus and with what she said, you coulda blown me over with a hen's fart. "He's boss," said she, running her words kinda together in her very immediate fashion.

"A pair a nently," Leviticus said, grinning proudful-like.

The others stopped to hear the boy's first, bona fide Four Arrows decision. Well, you could tell he was giving the matter some thought. He thought so long, in fact, I wondered if he needed a little review of the situation.

Anita, having no time for overdone thinking, pulled Lou(ella) under her most generous wing and said, straight to Leviticus, "Ranching is no work for a young lady!"

Maybe it was the volume of her voice or the 'young lady' part, but a smile came to Lou(ella)'s face, like no one had ever equated her with any sorta ladyhood. It wasn't a elegant smile, mind you, but it was a smile of no small measure either.

I'd been watching Leviticus real careful with half a eye, so's I could see how he operated under the pressure of making a decision. He finally stepped a little forward like as to speak. Then he withdrew back and formed a little huddle with his pals, and together they discussed the matter. Then, at last, he turned back, smiled, and said, "Yes."

Anita asked, "Ches what?"

"Yes, this is no work for a lady," Leviticus decided.

"Of course not!" she barked. Then she said to Lou(ella), "Come with me, chica."

When they started to leave, Leviticus asked, "Where are you going?"

Anita said, "To the house." I could just see her Mexican temper take rise.

"Why?" Leviticus, of course, didn't know ol' Anita like I did.

"Didn't chew just say this was no work for a lady?" Anita asked.

"Yes," Leviticus agreed.

"Well?" She was glaring him down.

"She's not a lady," he explained, pointing to Lou(ella).

Well, that had alla us a little confused, and I thought the debate might go on for weeks, so I stepped in and said to Leviticus, "Now maybe Anita is right. I think the best place for Lou(ella) is the house, you know, where she can learn cooking and cleaning and all those womanfolk chores."

"A pair a nently," Leviticus started, looking real studious.

Then Tommy comes out with, "Aw . . . let . . . her . . . stay."

"No. Women and horses don't mix," Toofer said, followed immediately by, "Hell, down South women ride better than men, side-saddle no less!"

Well, Leviticus was getting real confused. I pulled him aside and spoke into his ear, then he said, grinning of course, "Let *her* decide!" He pointed to Lou(ella), who'd bored with the whole thing and was back to counting fenceposts.

Lou(ella) looked up, feeling all the eyeballs on her. I had a feeling it was the first time she had to decide anything that regarded her own fate, and she intended on giving the matter the thought it required.

Jay and Hardy had grown weary and was leaning up against the side of the barn, probably not believing the contents of our discussion, maybe even making a wager on its outcome.

Lou(ella) looked at Anita and the large house beyond. Then she looked at each one of us and gave the barnyard air around us a sniffa consideration. She counted the horses present with her tiny, little finger, then calculated how many of us there was standing around, ran the figures 'round in her head some, then said something about not wanting to be part of a uneven number.

Anita beamed me her pearly-whites. I reckon she didn't care what formula the girl based her decision on and said, "Chew come with me and, first of all, we'll do something with chour hair." She looked at a few pitiful strands hanging loose from the large cowboy hat and asked whilst she led her away, "Don't you ever brush this?"

"No brush," said Lou(ella).

To which Anita said, "Well, chew shall have one of mine and each night one-hundred strokes should do the trick."

Well, as soon as she mentioned one hundred, I reckoned we all knew we'd lost Lou(ella) to Anita. The girl smiled up at Anita and repeated the sacred number: "One hundred? Oooo. Lucky."

Well, I knew Anita'd be needing some of that and figured that all this was best for everyone. Anyway, I had one less to teach riding to that day. But back in the cluttered North Forty of my mind was if Leviticus'd taken almost half a hour deciding where little Lou(ella) was gonna work, then how in hell would he be able to make a snap decision? In fact, I wondered how he could make any decision that regarded the fate of someone else, when all the boy really wanted to do was to just make everyone happy. How was I gonna clue him in, that whether you're running a ranch or just your own life, you can never please everybody?

Cripes, I reckoned I kinda envied him for just thinking that, well, maybe you could.

# six

*W*ell, like we agreed, a few days later I drove on into Idlehour to pick up E.M. Gallucci so's she could take a check on the Four Arrows books, which I'd spent two nights slaving over. Knowing how she felt about numbers and all, I felt kinda bad that there was so many smudges and cross-outs and oh-what-the-hell-close-enough columns. I guess then I came 'round to thinking, hell, she's earning her pay, just like I was, even though it'd taken me two nights of restless sleep to come to terms with the whole Gallucci-woman issue.

I guess she'd stuck to her word about being in charge of going over the bank books, for just as I was tying off the buggy at the boarding house, ol' Silas T. came steaming outa the door. The screen door slammed with such a clap that I could tell right off, it'd had some extra help closing.

I smiled as I walked toward the door and said, "Morning, Silas T." Well, his face looked like it'd been taken off, pressed through the wringer, and then hung out to dry for a coupla days without the benefit of ironing.

"Hello Royal," he managed, wiping his brow with his nice hankie.

'Course, I had a pretty good idea what it was, but I asked anyway: "Something wrong, Silas T.?"

"That . . . that . . . *wo*man!" he said, and he ran his hankie acrost his brow.

"Well, now with all 'em daughters over to your place, Silas T., one would figure. . ." I tugged at him.

"Pardon me," said Silas T. "It was misleading for me to have referred to her as a woman! Any semblance between her and my seven daughters is . . . well let me put it this way: that one woman-accountant makes all my girls eligible for sainthood. And I'll tell you this, that woman's father oughta be shot for sending her out here!"

I was having a good time with him, I'll admit, so I asked, "Shot, Silas T.?"

"Only after he's been hung for raising that . . . that . . . sireen!" he answered.

Before I could ask Silas T. to expound on that a little more, a book came flying outa the upstairs window and, after damn near clipping Silas T.'s head, landed with a dusty wack! at our feet.

"Yoo hoo, Mr. Burnbaum!" We both looked up and there she was, the sireen, Miss E.M. Gallucci, leaning outa the window with what I have to call right good balance. "I spilled some water on that book. I'm sorry, but you'll have to go over those figures again. All the numbers have run together. *Always* use pencil! Really, one would think a banker would know that! Anyway, I marked the pages for you."

Then she sang out a 'thank you' in a key that well may have been, heretofore, unknown to musical science. And then she noticed me and added, "Oh, I'll be ready in a minute, Mr. Leckner."

Silas T. dusted off the book and asked me, "Ready for what?"

"Inspecting *my* books, Silas T.," I replied, looking back up to Miss Gallucci as she quite literally hung outa the window.

"Turn back *now,* Royal!" Silas T. urged. "While you still have time!" Now just where that 'I'll-handle-this!' banker attitude of his had disappeared to in the last two days, I couldn't say, but you can see how confused I was.

"I certainly hope your books are easier to read than his!"

Miss Gallucci added, before she ducked her head back into the window.

My stomach sorta flip-flopped and then I told myself, look what you created, Royal!

Silas T. had opened his book to one of the marked pages and I thought it was real funny how his face paled when he noticed what pages had been smeared. "This will take me days to reconstruct," he said, and he slammed the book shut. "And here I thought it was almost over."

I asked, "What was over?"

"*Her,* that's what!" he bellowed, louder than I ever recalled him bellowing on a public street. "No one can work with her. I've had it! I'm wiring her father this morning to lodge my complaint. I'm having Julius work up something legal to get rid of her!"

'Course, Silas T., in all his rage, musta forgotten who he was confiding in, onaccounta I knew several things he didn't and, whether or not this Gallucci woman would become our enemy in common, he and I was still on two different sides of the Four Arrows fence.

Starting for the boarding house door, I said, "Well, maybe a few days of ranch life will do her some good. You know, fresh air and all."

"Wait a minute!" Silas T. called, bringing me to a uh-oh halt. "You haven't told me anything about the Perrault boy." He took a pause, then asked, "What's he like?"

Well, I knew ol' Silas T. had had a coupla rough days, but I turned and said anyway, "Don't ask, Silas T., don't ask."

"Rumor has it. . ." he began.

"Ain't no rumor can have it half as bad as it really is," I broke in, looking downward. I could look real sad when I wanted. I wasn't sure at the time why I chose to mislead Silas T., but over the years I've come to think that one just naturally misleads the feller sitting in the enemy camp, especially when he's in the financial professions.

He stepped toward me, his eyes kind of alight with a gruesome curiosity. "How do you mean?" he asked.

Just as I was set to fill him in on the horns, the hideous face, the drooling and all, this E.M. Gallucci sprung open the screen door acrost my boot and there it lodged, unable to swing either way and causing a certain amounta discomfort to my toes, I might add.

Upon seeing her, Silas T. hurried off to his bank without any further questions about Leviticus or warnings regarding my fate in the hands of this Miss Gallucci. Although I admit I was worried about some things, handling Miss Gallucci wasn't one of 'em.

Our eyes met and I was instantly reminded why I'd thought of little else but her. Well, we got my boot unstuck and had a little chuckle over it, then I took her satchel and we boarded the buggy.

*W*e talked about this and that on the drive back out to Four Arrows. I pointed out things I thought might interest her, but mostly I was laying things out in my mind, and this is how I figured things stood:

Silas T. was sweating. That was good.

Miss E.M. Gallucci was keeping him honest. That was good.

Leviticus and his crew was slowly learning how to not spook a horse. That was good.

The cattle tallies was up and the prime beef was graining before the trail drive. That was good.

Did you get all that? Well, add to it that I didn't have the damnedest idea what I was doing, but I was gonna do it anyhow. And I didn't know if that was good or not.

# seven

*S*hortly before we pulled into the long drive leading to the ranch house, I thought I'd better fill Miss Gallucci in on just what, I mean who to expect. I told her about Leviticus and how he insisted on bringing his friends back with him and how that was good and intelligent and all onaccounta half-wits only think of theirselves and even then not too careful-like. I tried to flower the situation the best I could 'cause, like you know, this woman was to have quite a say in the outcome of our situation. I knew first impressions was gonna be important, so I'd left Hardy and Jay with the tightest instructions on how the place was to look and how Leviticus and the boys oughta be doing something ranch-like when we returned.

So if you think riding a ol' sow is ranch-like, then I reckon you'll be happy to know they was all following my orders. Now, I knew that ol' sow to be a gentle sort, and God knows she was big enough to be ridden, but there was just something a little lacking in elegance to the whole scene. There they was, all of 'em, even Lou(ella) and Anita, riding the corral fence and laughing their teeths out at the sight of Leviticus bullyragging ol' Miss Porkpie and putting her through more humiliation than I reckon any sow deserves. Even the horses and cows privileged enough to witness the fe-as-ko from nearby pens was chuckling amongst theirselves.

'Course, it was Jay laughing the most. I heard his howl clear above the rest of the foofaraw.

"What's that going on at the corral?" Miss Gallucci asked, peering over my shoulder as I lifted her down from the seat.

"Ride 'em, hogboy!" I heard someone holler.

Well, what could I say to her? "Oh, the boys musta finished all their chores and now they's just having some fun," I said, lying through my teeth onaccounta everyone knows chores is never finished on a spread the size of Four Arrows. "Shall we go inside where it's cool?" And I tried to usher Miss Gallucci toward the steps.

But she took it upon herself to head toward the corral. Well, I remember looking skyward so's I could catch God's eye should He be snickering down at me. So much for Miss Gallucci's first impression, I thought. Here I'd been flapping my gums the whole trip home on how civil-like Leviticus was and all and to prove it he was now riding that poor ol' sow.

When Jay and Hardy saw me approach, you can be sure they snapped to attention. "Didn't expect you back so soon, Royal," Hardy said, a tinge of embarrassment coming to his weathered cheeks.

"That I see," I said, not wanting to rip into him, onaccounta Miss Gallucci was laughing hard as the rest.

"We finished breaking in the last horse, Royal," Jay jumps in, like that was all the explanation I needed for the folderoll.

"So now you thought you'd start breaking in the sows?" says I. Well, you know my eyes was cool and my face wasn't smiling. Maybe, if I hadn't asked 'em specific to make sure things was looking real good for Miss Gallucci, I woulda been able to join in the laughter. Maybe, if that ol' damn sow hadn't been such a pet to alla us I coulda seen the humor to things. As it was, I was madder'n a bobcat in a sack.

When Leviticus brought his mount to a stop in front of the corral gate, a pair a nently for the finale, he caught my eye and a grin of triumph came acrost his face. He was holding up his long legs so's they didn't drag and he was waving a stick he was using to guide Miss Porkpie.

"Look at me, Royal!" he cried, like I hadn't noticed him perched atopt that sow.

Now that my presence was announced, the laughter stopped and all eyes pranced upon me. I knew that what I replied would set the tone for the rest of the day which, like I told you, was damn important. So I looked at Leviticus and smiled kindly and patiently and said, "Good for you, Leviticus. But Miss Porkpie looks a little tired, so why don't you groom her good and put her away?"

I walked into the corral and took the stick away from Leviticus. I'd hate to describe the look Miss Porkpie gave me, but I knew there and then I'd never be able to have her butchered. Maybe she thought she finally had me just where she wanted me. Anyway, I knew I owed her that much.

Leviticus put his legs down, stood up, and allowed the sow to walk away from under him. All in all, she was handling the situation pretty well, which I attributed to her maturity.

"Go on, now," I said to Leviticus, "take her inside and groom her till she shines." My voice got firmer and the boy wouldn't let me catch his eyes.

"Groom a pig!" he said, looking down and holding back a smile. "Stupid," he added, and he giggled so's only I could hear and he sounded a little too much like Jay for my liking.

Since I wasn't sure how Leviticus would operate under embarrassment, I walked closer to him and said, "Every creature has a right to its dignity, son." Leviticus was still laughing, so I knew I'd have to make my point stronger. I pointed to Miss Porkpie, way on the other side of the corral, leaning into the fence, her face turned from us humans in shame.

Says I, "I reckon you must know what she's feeling, Leviticus. You see, sows, they think they's better'n horses, and onaccounta that aren't for such things as riding. So you take that sow into the barn, apologize to her, and groom her fine. Then slop her and tell her you'll make it up to her what you did today. Then I want you to clean up and come into the house to meet someone."

Well, even though he was still trying to hold in his excited laughter, I reckon he understood he'd hurt a lesser and things wouldn't be right in his mind till he made it straight between Miss Porkpie and hisself.

He wanted his friends to help him, but I made him know this was between him and the sow. Hardy and Jay had joined the other hands in getting back to work, leaving me and Miss Gallucci eye to eye with Tommy, Lou(ella), and Toofer, who was all wondering who this woman was.

I introduced 'em the best I could, and Anita, knowing the importance of our visitor, herded the crew back into the house where, I hoped, she had something prepared in the way of lemonade and cakes and normalcy.

*W*ell, like you'd expect, Miss Gallucci was a little nervous and I reckon this was rightly so, onaccounta she'd had a coupla rough days being a accountant and all. After we'd freshed up a bit, I sent the crew back outside to find Hardy and Jay so's they could continue on with their riding lessons. Lou(ella) helped Anita clean up, leaving Miss Gallucci and me, like we seemed to always end up, eye to eye.

"I think I understand your problem," she said after a spell, real lady-like, a side to her I don't think I'd seen much of up to that point. But setting there acrost the room, with her lemonade glass in her gloved hand, she looked real good. Maybe she knew that and decided to act the part.

"I reckon it's partly your problem now too," I said, "since you've agreed to conduct the audit and all."

She gave a quick look 'round the room, then said, "I hope I won't live to regret it."

"Oh you won't, you won't. Regret it, that is," I said, and I gave a little laugh.

"Well, it's all in the numbers, Mr. Leckner. No matter how well you get along with these . . . people," she said.

I reckon one of the smarter things I ever did was to just nod in agreement with her statement instead of starting to debate the conditions of Perrault's damned will.

"I suppose you'd like to get started with the books," I said, polishing off my lemonade and standing. "I pulled out everything I think you'll be needing." I showed her Perrault's study and added, "I hope you'll be comfortable here."

She walked around the fine desk and I could tell she was impressed with the layouta things: the silver and crystal inkwell, the fine leather chair, and the assorted paintings and bronzeworks all about.

"You know, from the books Mr. Burnbaum keeps, one wouldn't think Mr. Perrault did so well for himself," she said, tinkling the crystal jingle-bobs hanging from a lamp ol' Perrault'd ordered hisself from Paris, France. Miss Gallucci picked up the electric cord on the lamp, saw it wasn't plugged in anywheres, and asked me, "Where do I plug this in?"

"Oh, we never got us a line out here," said I. "I reckon Perrault planned for that some day. No, he just liked the way that lamp looked in the sunlight. It's just to decorate. It don't do much else."

"No electricity?" she asked, like that was a little unheard of in her book.

I just shook my head and lifted my boney shoulderbones a little like that was as good a explanation as any. I handed her the satchel she'd brought out. 'Course, I'd hearda such things, but I'd never seen what she pulled out of it. The abacus was real good looking and, by the smooth shininess of it, I could tell she'd used it some.

"You know how to work this?" I asked like a idiot. I wapped the beads so they spun.

Whereupon she took it from me and said, "No, Mr. Leckner. Like you, I just like to play with the beads." Her voice was a little snappish and oh, them eyes! Then she added, "I told you how terrible I am with figures. The abacus helps me keep on track."

It sure seemed funny her setting at Perrault's desk and me setting at the chair opposite, a place I thought I'd risen above. But as I watched her settle down to the books, the careful pinks from the lamp reflected on her face and I saw how nice a face she had. Hell, I had a few lines around my eyes too, who didn't in those days? But her lashes was long and hid what I thought was the most mysterious brown eyes I ever did see. Her hair reflected glints of red, and she did a real good job of piling it up so's it tucked under here and over this way. I coulda done without some of her nose, but it was one that some folks mighta thought of as statue-like and most definitely bespeaking her I-talian heritage and, I want you to know here and now, I didn't even issue so much as a giggle when she clipped a pair of spectacles on it. In fact, I thought that was making real good use of the protrusion. But all in all, this Miss Gallucci was a fine bale of woman, nose, balloonie sleeves, abacus and all.

And when Leviticus walked in, all washed up and reconciled with Miss Porkpie, I reckon he thought this Miss Gallucci was the most beautiful parcel he'd ever set eyes on, which proved to me onct again he was damn near a regular man.

$\mathcal{M}$iss Gallucci stayed two days, looking over the books, getting to know us and, I prayed, becoming sympathetic to our problems.

Upon her departure, she shook my hand, allowed me to call her E.M., and told me she'd be back over New Year's, onaccounta this was a big time for Howell, Powell and Gallucci, and her daddy would want her well outa the way during the year-end numbers time.

Although I hated to see her leave, I sure had a lot to do at Four Arrows and, gnawing at my innerself, I feared ol' Silas T.'s wrath from his failure to wrangle this Miss Gallucci into his camp.

# eight

*W*ell young man, if you knew anything at all about ranching, then you mighta guessed it took the better part of the summer to get everyone squared away on their skills. An exceptional amount of credit goes to Anita, for in spite of all her hot blood, she kept a cool head and gave Lou(ella) the benefit of all her domestic know-how. And, I have to add, from the moment Lou(ella) began her household obligations, there was the best tract kept on goods, supplies, utensils and the like. Ol' Anita could turn to her teensie charge and ask, How many tins of tomatoes we have in the cellar? or What's the current counta spoons in the bunkhouse? and Lou(ella), well she'd know, and proudly too.

If Anita had it easy in the house, then it only stands to reason that I had it tough in the corral; according to all the great minds of the world, things are just supposed to work that way, I guess. Leviticus and the boys gradually learned, but they surely did put a whole new wing on the expression, 'slowly but surely.'

By summer's end, every able hand drove the cattle up to Walla Walla Wash. Hardy and Jay was anxious to leave and I woulda liked to go along too, but I saw my duty as staying at Four Arrows and honing the horsemanships of Leviticus and his crew. But as I was to discover later, it surely mighta changed things some if I had gone along.

At home, without the everyday bustle and noise of hands, horses, and groaning cattle, the real learning happened at least. I knew Leviticus and the others was used to normal folks gawking at 'em, but I don't think that made 'em like it. So without anyone to snicker into their kerchiefs, my new crew did a whole lot better.

It woulda been good to think that Four Arrows hands was a notch better'n others when it came to tolerance and restraint and such, but damn it, they'd been right ugly and it was a real good two weeks without having 'em *or* the cattle around. I remember telling myself to address the issue when the boys returned.

Sad fact was . . . only two came back at all, and you know which two they was: Hardy and Jay.

"What the hell you mean, they quit?" I demanded of Hardy, speaking low and forcing a smile, hopeful that Hardy and Jay was pulling my leg, like they was fond of doing on occasion.

"They . . . a . . ." Hardy began, looking towards his boots and swaying a little, reluctant-like.

"Quit! Just said they was done with us!" Jay broke in, always eager to register his indignation, like yearlings will. He slapped his knee with his dusty hat, like as to say he'd show those traitors what-for.

Well, I ignored Jay's snorting 'bout the room and asked what'd happened.

"They . . . a . . ." Hardy tried again, looking 'round the room. Then he caught my eye and whispered, "They said they thought Four Arrows was a lost effort, with Leviticus primed to take charge."

"What?" I bellowed.

"And . . . a . . . that it wouldn't be long before someone'd be kilt with *them* roaming the place," he got out.

I eased myself down into a chair and set thinking on all this. Jay paced and Hardy kept looking for the answer on his boots.

"I told you, Hardy, it was that new hand! That Harold

Somebody!" Jay broke in, pointing his hat at Hardy. "He did all this!"

I looked at 'em both and asked, "What new hand?"

"We picked up this rider second day out," Hardy said. "Well, you know how we can always use a extra hand. Don't forget, we had two-hundred and six more head this year than last."

"And?" *I*

"And, well, he was a good puncher, Roy. . ." Hardy's hand started working down towards his troubling knee and I could tell he felt real bad about what he was about to say. But I held silent and let him continue. "He seemed to know all about Leviticus and his friends. It seems like all he could talk about was what awful things happen when folks like them is around."

"Where was he from that he knew about Leviticus?" I asked, the gears of suspicion getting a little oiled.

"Pasco!" Jay said, pointing in the general direction. "He talked about disappeared kids, raped women, and axed-up people, Roy!" he continued. Then he added, losing a little of his steam, "It was awful, some of the stories he told! He said there's this woman back east, Lizzie Borden, who chopped up her momma and daddy, and he said that could happen right here on Four Arrows." Then his shoulders twitched some, like he was pushing down a shiver.

"And so this one stranger scared off my entire crew of twenty-two hands?" I asked, trying to keep my calm.

"Twenty," Jay corrected, smiling weakly and indicating that all was not lost, for he and Hardy remained loyal.

"And, of course, nobody told me they was quitting till I paid 'em all off in Walla Walla," Hardy added, maybe defending his loss a little.

Well, there ain't nothing more uppity than a trail-sore cowboy with money in his pocket. You talk about a man with them delusions of grandeur. And I might add, if you think sailors is a superstitious sort, then you haven't set around too many campfires on the trail. So money plus weariness plus a few high yarns and I wasn't at all surprised to learn they all added up to the whole kitankabootle upping and leaving Four Arrows undefended for the winter.

And I reckoned it didn't matter much who this Harold Somebody was; he was sent out to disband the boys sure as hell, and all I can really recall about that day was being damn glad my hands got the cattle to Walla Walla Wash before they broke for other outfits.

I think I let Jay rant and Hardy feel bad whilst I just set and thought good-riddance for a while. But, of course, I was going to pay ol' Silas T. a visit when I went in to deposit the herd money. I knew he was behind this Harold Somebody. I guess Silas T. saw that I intended on seeing Perrault's will through and, hell or high water, work Leviticus into his rightful place as heir to Four Arrows.

"Royal?" Hardy asked, pulling me outa my mental plateaus. "What are we gonna do?"

"'Bout what?" I asked, kinda faraway.

"Oh," Jay hollered, his hands on his hips, "I suppose Hardy here and me're gonna run this whole dang place all by our lonesomes!"

I looked at Hardy and he just looked toward the ceiling like he didn't have nothing to do with Jay's snorty outbursts.

"We'll hire more hands," I allowed, like that was that.

"Good hands are getting scarce, Roy. Times are changing," Hardy softly reminded me.

Lord Almighty, I'd begun to tire of that 'times are changing' routine. Well, looking back, I suppose they was. They always have been. I don't know what made me think 1892 was any different.

"Winter's coming. Won't be much work till March," I said, determined to keep my cool in the face of the crisis.

Jay said, "Oh no, just fence-mending, irrigation-digging,

moving herds around, ice-breaking, and riding circuit! 'Course, I suppose Leviticus and them other . . . coconuts . . . can pull their shares!" Then he twisted hisself up like Tommy Two Hearts and pretended he was riding a lopsided horse and then added, "Look at me, Hardy! Least I can ride *halfa* horse!"

Well, that about did it. I got up and snatched Jay by his shirt and pulled him to my face. "Now you listen to me, boy. I lost twenty good hands today and I reckon one more won't matter. I don't care how good a wrangler you are or how good your momma shoots, you make fun of 'em boys ever again and you'll be off Four Arrows land so fast your spurs'll spin for a week! You understand me?"

Well, we knew he did, but I held him nose to nose till he nodded, and I could tell by the flusha his face and the wettening in his eyes that he knew I was dead serious.

"I'm sorry, Roy," he kinda mumbled, like as to say it out loud and clear was too injurious to his swollen and youthful pride. "I was just so all-fired worked up about them softers quitting on us and all."

I let go his shirt and then looked over to Hardy. "When will you have your winterlist ready?"

Hardy's face wadded up kinda funny, and I knew I'd reminded him of his most dreaded yearly duty. "Oh no, Roy, you said I wasn't gonna have to. . ."

"Do you see anyone else on this spread able to do the winterlist?" I asked.

Just then Lou(ella) came wandering in, loaded to her tiny chin with just-pressed linens. A big smile came acrost Hardy's face, like he'd just been handed a stay of execution, and he said, "Well, yes, I do see someone else. . ."

*C*ripes, I have to admit, Lou(ella) did a right accurate job of ranch inventory, right down to the last fencepost that needed replacing. Two weeks later, the end of September, Hardy and Lou(ella) had completed the winterlist and I had me a good idea of what had to be done to keep Four Arrows in good stead for the winter.

'Course, in the meantime ol' Silas T. and me had it out regarding the Harold Somebody affair. Well, he just blinked his stale blue eyes at me like he had nothing to do with it. Then he proceeded to tell me losing so many hands was real sore luck and he woulda sent over some of his, but he hadn't a man to spare, what with seven unmarried daughters and all. Well, we jousted a little more and he ended by telling me he'd also heard vile rumors 'bout the crew at Four Arrows and suggested I not let any of 'em outa my sight.

You can be sure what he said about that was true, for every living, breathing soul, and even a few horses, had heard about my new charges, and I discovered the real truth about a rumor: ain't nothing more powerful than a rumor whose time has come.

I left Silas T.'s office, ruminating on what he'd said and wondering what the hell to do about it. Although I don't recollect thinking I'd been placed on the Four Arrows of God's land to teach the folks of Idlehour 'bout rumors, or running a ranch with only six men and two women, or differences between us all, or anything else for that matter. But I do remember thinking back then that you must never think things is as bad as they're gonna get, for sure as hell the moment you do, the mortgage will foreclose, the Indians will uprise, and your mother-in-law will arrive just in time for the first drought in recent memory.

# nine

$\mathcal{W}$ell, the thoughta facing the chill of fall without a full set of hands made me lie awake more'n one night, I'll tell you that. Even though I'd usually let the summer drifters go in October for lacka chores to cover 'em, I was a little nervous about not having anyone but Jay and Hardy who, though I trusted 'em with my life, was hardly enough to run Four Arrows. Leviticus and his crew was finally assuming a almost normal command of horses, although to look at 'em you'd laugh. 'Course, alota the credit had to go to the horses Jay picked out for them. Like I said before, horses know the condition of their riders and onct a level of confidence and friendship is struck between beast and man, then things commenced to be less comical and more ranch-like.

Well, to ease my mind a bit, I placed some ads for winter hands in the papers in Pendleton, Walla Walla Wash, and even down as far as Winnemucca, all places I'd hoped the rumors of Four Arrows hadn't reached. Well, I musta underestimated the power of Silas T.'s capabilities, for I had one helluva time getting any man to respond. I did get one letter from a joker who thought he was being funny, saying as soon as he was released from the state asylum he'd be happy to join our crew, and he didn't know nothing about them murders over to Tacoma.

I finally found four boys from a spread down south which had bellied-up. They kept mostly to theirselves at first, and even though I'd explained our entire Four Arrows situation before signing 'em on, I doubted any of 'em would become bosom buddies with Leviticus and the others. But they took to each other better'n I'd hoped, the new hands helping out with the lesser ones.

So I'd come to the conclusion that the place could run better with a handfula men who respected each other than with sixty men who'd call you names behind your back or laugh when you slip up or fall off your horse. Like we was fond of saying, a empty saddle's better'n a mean rider. And as we feasted that Thanksgiving, I remembered to thank the Top Hand Above for sending me Skippy, Greg, Chris, and hell, who was that other yap? It don't matter now what his name was, but I was thankful for him too.

$\mathcal{T}$he winter that year was coming in strong, and I have to admit I'd been a little concerned about what might be 'round the corner for us. All summer we'd been cutting, baling, and storing hay for our stock, so I wasn't worried about feed, but like you know, when the weather sets down hard, no telling what can go wrong. Like firinstance, it's a whole day's work for a man just to break up ice so's the stock can drink. Then just as soon as you're done, along comes nightfall and the damn holes just freeze up again. A cow's breath is hot, but I never seen one yet could melt him his own drinking hole. And when the snow comes in hard from the Nor'east, the drifts can alter the path of the fenceline, so with the first warm Chinook blow, the snow melts and half your stock steps easy over the fence and wanders onto the next spread, mixing it up with the neighbor's cattle. And I'll tell you this, winter coats sure makes brand-ciphering a chore.

Christmas at Four Arrows was always a special occasion onaccounta we'd almost always have snow. Jay had spent some time with his momma explaining hisself, but he brought us back lotsa cakes and cookies and the good news that his vengeful momma, in the spirit of the season, was gonna forgive alla us for anything evil we'd taught her sweet young dilling. He said she'd asked about his pimples clearing up and he said he just smiled back at her and she never suspected a thing.

Well, we'd put alota preparations in for the holiday; hell, we'd even draped the outhouses with fir boughs, giving 'em a real nice, festive scent. I could tell Leviticus and the others hadn't ever celebrated Christmas like it should be celebrated, and I'll tell you now, it was just like having a passel of younguns around, they was so excited. We was all sneaking 'round, making gifts and winding up stories to pull each other off the trail regarding who was getting what from who. Anita and Lou(ella) baked and baked, and there wasn't a table in alla Four Arrows that wasn't blessed with a plate of cookies or candy.

Yessir, I have to thinka that as one of the best times in my life and, on top of everything else, I had only a few days left anticipating the return of E.M. Gallucci. I have to admit, I'd spent more'n one sleepless night thinking over her strange attractiveness and how she dressed and her curious snappish manner and all.

I'd been working real careful-like on the ranch books so's when she arrived she wouldn't have too many errors to find . . . in the numbers *and* in me, I reckon. There was a New Year's Dance all set up in Idlehour, and even though I'd been keeping what them political men nowadays call a low profile, I was anxious to get into town and show off my new boots and squire this Miss Gallucci on my arm.

I don't reckon I'll be forgetting that Christmas Day, 1892, for as long as I'm permitted to live. Even though, at my age, I tend to pass over some things, the events of that day is pressed in my mind flatter than the rose petals in my family Bible.

We'd had all the cowhands in for our Christmas celebra- tion early that morning. It was cold and dark outside and warm and bright inside. Just the way early Christmas morning oughta be. The fire was a-blazing and the candles on the tree was lit. We passed gifts all 'round and we all made out right equitable. Even the new hands gave and received, and I don't remember the true spirit of Christmas ever being more touchable. Then Anita and Lou(ella) spread us a breakfast like you'd read about in Dickens. After we ate, we dismissed for our early chores, and we all agreed to meet back at the house at ten for carols and toddies and, of course, more food.

I told Leviticus to instruct his crew to get on with their chores, and just because it was Christmas, it didn't mean any of us got the day off. Well, none of us wanted to leave the warmth of the occasion and the fire and the food, but work was work and, besides, cattle didn't generally acknowledge Christmas as being different from any other day.

I'd like to say I remember that Christmas for its crisp brightness, or the brilliant blue sky kissing the blanket of white all around, but what really stands out in my mind is the smoke on the horizon: huge, white billows of smoke and a sweet, terrifying scent that always means disaster.

Hardy and Jay was standing on the porch looking around. A good cowboy will smell smoke miles away and, just by instinct, start thinking how to save his own spread and livestock.

"The Anderson place," Hardy said to me as I pulled my gloves on.

I looked south and agreed, relieved the smoke wasn't a Four Arrows concern.

"Smoke's too white for the house. Bet it's the hay barn," Hardy continued, displaying his years of knowledge.

Setting his hat on his head, Jay added, "Yeah, I'll bet so too. That new storage barn Anderson was so proud of."

"We better ride on over and see if we can help," I said, leading 'em to the barn where I knew my gelding would put up a fuss on wearing a cold saddle, and on Christmas no less. "Hardy, tell Leviticus to round his crew; they can come too. Fire's as much a parta ranching as anything else," I added, talking over my shoulder. "Jay, you tell Anita she better slow dinner down."

Within fifteen minutes, we was alla us off and hotfooting toward the Anderson spread. I reckoned that the threata fire was a universal fear, onaccounta Leviticus, Tommy Two Hearts, and Toofer all looked as worried as did us regulars. The closer we got, the more the smoke clouds filled the sky and the farther away the joy of the day was. Of all the things to fear back in those days—drought, floods, anthrax, snakes, and politicians—fire was the worst and so it was a pretty silent ride.

By the time we got there, there was little we coulda done. Jay was right: it was the new hay storage that went up along with what was probably enough hay to feed the entire Anderson stock for the winter. By the look on Elliott Anderson's face, I wondered if maybe he thought he was wiped out. His wife and kids was in the buckboard, bundled against the cold and staring at the smoldering rubble. I'll never forget his little girl holding tight onto a Christmas balloon.

Somehow, 'Merry Christmas' didn't seem appropriate, so I just said, "I'm sorry, Elliott." I unmounted my horse and stood next to my neighbor.

Well, you could tell he was shocked. He was holding a handful of hay and kinda twirling it between his fingers as he stared at his loss.

"I don't see how that hay was dry enough to go up so fast," he muttered to me. "But it sure as hell did." He looked at me and I thought I coulda cried for him. Then he said, "And I used green timber. Green timber ain't supposed to light up like that."

Well, I wanted to sooth him some, so I said, "You did right, Elliott."

"Then how'd it happen? There ain't been no lightning for weeks!" he said.

"Who can say, Elliott? It mighta been smoldering for days. You got other storage, don't you?" I asked. I was trying to go around the tragedy and get on to salvaging Anderson's life.

His face was worn and far more aged-looking than his years. He simply replied, "Some. I got some down by the river."

I asked him if he had enough.

He looked at me kinda vague-like, then said whilst he tightened the scarf that held his hat down, "Hell, the cattle'll freeze before they have a chance to starve to death! So I don't see what it matters."

I felt right bad for Anderson. He'd had a awful time trying to make his spread pay for the last several years, and to me it looked like he woulda jumped the first train for anywhere if there'd been a track close at hand.

Then he looked past me and saw Leviticus and his crew, who was all looking real dismal. Then Anderson pointed a thick finger and shouted, "Only a crazy man woulda done this!"

Well, that was downright lunacy, and I pulled him 'round and said to his face, "Elliott, I know you're upset."

But he pulled hisself away and approached Leviticus and shouted out "Pyromaniac!"

Now, 'maniac' I recognized, but I didn't know nothing about no 'pyro.' Anyways, I reckoned it had to be a insult and I have to admit I was a little riled thinking Anderson used a word I'd never heard.

I don't think Leviticus knew the word either, but he did know the incriminating tone and the hate in Anderson's voice.

"Now you just hold back, Elliott," I said, coming between him and Leviticus.

"Everyone knows the kinda crimes *those* people commit!" he continued. I heard his wife call him back, but he kept on pointing and accusing.

"Now you look here, Anderson!" I broke in. "We come out here to see if we could help. Now I'm real sorry about your hay. But I'm not going to tolerate you thinking one of my boys did this. First of all, you got no idea whatsomever about *those* kinda people! Second, they was all with me."

"Then how could this happen? Fires don't just start!" he shouted back, on the verge of tears, I think.

"They can," Toofer broke in. "Spontaneous combustion." Just when I thought he'd given a good, intelligent-like explanation, he turned his head and I knew his other self was about to emerge. "Not dry enough," Toofer continued, like that was God's word on it.

Well, I knew then it was best for all concerned that we get on outa there. I mounted my gelding and said back down to Elliott. "Look, Elliott, we're neighbors and onaccounta that I'll do what I can to help. You let me know what you need and I'll do my best."

"You've done enough already!" he continued. "Bringing the likes of *them* down here where decent folk can't sleep nights for fear of what might happen next!"

If he hadn'ta just lost his hay, and if it hadn'ta been Christmas, and if his wife and kids wasn't all watching, and if his daughter wasn't clinging so hopeful-like to that damn balloon, I woulda pulled his voicebox out through his nose and let the buzzards play a tune on it. As it was, I shot him a look of disgust and turned my gelding away from him.

The ride back to the ranch house was mighty quiet. I didn't know what to say to Leviticus. I'd hoped that maybe the talk had been too wordy and too fast for him to grasp what had transpired, but I could tell by the look on his face he had a pretty good idea.

It was difficult to get back in the Christmas spirit after that. Oh, the smells of cinnamon and bayberry and pine tried their best to pull us outa our moods, but it wasn't till we'd settled down to our goose feast that I took on a well-that's-human-nature attitude. We drank wine that night, which we normally never did, and I think our rosy attitudes returned onaccounta it.

Leviticus and his crew excused theirselves from the table early, and I thought it was odd how much they'd been keeping to theirselves since the ride back from Anderson's place. They kept their heads together, and I woulda worried 'cept they was whispering and giggling some too, so I just figured they was up to some sorta Christmas surprise for alla us.

When they all bundled up and piled outa the house, I again got suspicious and watched 'em walk toward the barn. As soon as they was outside, they started with the snowballs, and I guess I sorta envied their gifts to return to childhood so easy-like. But as they neared the barn they settled down, and I had to be content to speculate about their goings-on after that, for the barn door closed tight behind 'em.

I guess I'd allowed myself to doze off and I wasn't sure what time it was when I woke up—must've been about five o'clock, for it was pitch dark outside. Anyway, I heard a ruckus outside as I pulled awake. The dogs was barking and I could hear all the men shouting.

You can be sure I made for the door like a flash, thinking maybe one of my lessers *was* a firebug. But the sight I saw was the farthest thing from my mind. There in the front yard was Leviticus and Lou(ella) setting atopt the seat a one wagon, with Toofer and Tommy setting atopt another. They had lanterns decorating the wagons and had fashioned all sortsa ribbons hanging hither and yon. Each buckboard was loaded, and I mean to tell you *loaded,* with bales of hay. Then, in the center of each load was a

Christmas tree decorated with paper ornaments and strings of popcorn, stolen, I reckoned, from the bunkhouse tree.

I don't know whose looks to describe—mine or theirs or the looks on the faces of the Anderson family—when we, alla us making a grand foofaraw, escorted those two hay racks on over to their spread on that cold, snowy Christmas night, 1892. You know, the memory of that still sorta gets me right here.

Speaking of my ticker, hand me that little bottle, will you son? That one right there. Thanks.


# t e n


O n December 30th, I went into Idlehour to await the arrival of Miss E.M. Gallucci. In the hopes that she'd come out and stay with us at Four Arrows, I took the buggy and our best hack, which was all right with my gelding onaccounta the snow had melted some and he never enjoyed mucking around in the slush.

Like I'd expected, folks in Idlehour was naturally curious about the Elliott Anderson fire. I guess it wasn't no surprise to me that word of the disaster had preceded me into town. I found my hackles rising when folks suggested that the fire'd been set by one of my nondescripts, and right then I decided that a rumor left unattended should be shot outa its misery. Not one Idlehourian had heard anything about the two hay racks we took over to Anderson.

Now, I didn't blame Anderson—I knew he hardly ever got into town—but I did blame those invisible forces which carried only the bad and the speculative and then turned around and completely passed over the good and the true.

"Well, Royal," Silas T. said, soundly clapping me on the back, which was something I hate any man to do. "Was Santa good to you?"

I turned around and there he was, dressed in a fine, new woolen coat, but with seven colorful mufflers wrapped 'round his neck.

I eyed the mufflers, lifted one up ginger-like, and said, "You'd think them seven daughtersa yours would get together and discuss what they was making you for Christmas. Might cut down on the duplication."

"They never get together and discuss anything," he said, going for humor but being sadly truthful, I thought. And then he added, "I suppose you're here to meet Miss Gallucci."

I looked down Main Street for signs of the stage and said, "Yep."

There we stood, both looking down the street and keeping it silent till Silas T. finally said, "Say, how about that Anderson fire?"

"Yep, that was some fire," I released.

More silence.

Then ol' Silas T. mumbled, almost to hisself, "Wonder how it started."

"Spontaneous combustion," I replied, between my teeth.

More silence and no stage coming to break it.

"I've heard arson," Silas T. continued casual-like, and he kept looking down the street.

"Well," I said, "you oughta know, Silas T." Then I smiled coyotishly over at him.

Well, he finally cut to the hearta the matter and asked, "Just how many of those maniacs do you have over there?"

I looked him straight and spoke hard, "I don't got any maniacs, Silas T. Just good, hard-working men."

"Word is, you got a fire-starter out there." I didn't respond, but kept looking for the stage.

"Word is," Silas T. continued, "you got a murderer out there. Word is. . ."

I grabbed him by all seven mufflers and pulled him close to my face so's there was no mistaking my meaning. "Word is, shuttup, Silas T.!" says I. Well, I hated to talk to a elder that way, but I wanted him to know that I wasn't gonna let him or anyone else speak wrongly of Leviticus and his crew. I let go of him and he didn't seem too undone.

"I'm only repeating rumor," he said.

"Well don't," says I. "It ain't becoming a banker. Besides, if I was you, Silas T., and had me seven unmarried daughters, I'd do my best to squelch a rumor every time I got the chance."

Fortunately, the stage rounded Main Street and our jousting ended. I have to admit, my heart did a flipflop as the coach drew to a stop. You know how you know someone, then they leave and you try and try to pull together in your mind the way they look and act and all? Well, I'd damn near forgotten what I'd found attractive about this Miss Gallucci woman, but the moment our eyes met again, I was instantly reminded.

Now, the train and stage trip from Portland to Idlehour is a long and agonizing one at best, especially in the winter, and when I lifted her down onto the platform, I could tell she was wearing mosta the trip on her face.

"How do, Miss Gallucci," Silas T. said, doffing his hat. "I trust you had a good trip?"

Well, the look she threw him coulda knocked that hat right outa his hand. Then she looked at me, like did I have any stupid questions to ask.

"If you could bear just one more ride, Miss Gallucci, we'd be proud to have you stay at Four Arrows, where I've instructed Anita to prepare a hot bath for you," I said, taking her valise from Albert, the stage driver.

"Oh no, Mrs. Burnbaum instructed me to bring you out to our place or I'm simply not to return at all," Silas T. said, taking aholda the valise.

"Albert," I said, "Silas T. here will be needing a one-way ticket to Portland." I tightened my grip on the valise and Silas T. and I exchanged a silent challenge.

At that point, Miss Gallucci snapped the valise away from both of us with a mighty tug. "Thank you both, but I'm staying at the boarding house." She looked at Silas T. and said, "I'll need the year-end books by year-end. That's tomorrow."

I'd definitely detected a more business-like attitude in the woman and I knew who'd planted that seed, and I was kicking myself for it.

"Would one of you gentlemen get my other bag?" she asked, already heading for the boarding house.

Both Silas T. and me jumped at the chance to assist. But when Albert opened the back hatcha the stage and revealed the largest damn trunk I think I ever saw, Silas T. and me just looked at each other like as to say, go ahead, *you* do it.

Well, I reckon we was quite a sight, Silas T. and me, struggling down the walk after Miss Gallucci, each of us suffering under the weight of that trunk.

"You bring along a assistant, Miss Gallucci?" I asked, outa breath, when we reached the boarding house. We eased the trunk down and Silas T. had to set on it to catch his breath and rub his banking shoulder.

She turned and flashed me that smile I'd been trying so hard to hang onto those months she'd been gone. She said, "Oh, didn't I tell you? We at Howell, Powell and Gallucci all decided it would be best, under the awkward set of circumstances of this whole Perrault account, that I should stay here in Idlehour for the remainder of the specified

500-day period. Which is," and she worked some figures in the air with her finger, "exactly 304 days. No, wait a minute. . . 'Thirty days hath September, April, June. . .' " and she ranged that saying 'round in her mind, then proudly corrected herself to "302 days."

Silas T.'s face turned the color of the grey clouds above us and he said, sorta under his breath, "That long, eh?"

"Yes. That way, I'll be able to audit the books on a month-to-month basis and, of course," she went on, looking at me, "make sure the tenets of the Perrault will are being kept."

Well, back then I didn't know what tenets was, but I assured her I was keeping 'em.

Silas T. finally excused hisself, I suppose to scramble over to his office to get those books together. No doubt he and Julius wasn't prepared for the year-end audit to actually occur on the year-end.

*I* helped Miss Gallucci get set up at the boarding house, which included hauling her trunk upstairs without the benefit of anyone's help. When I reached the rooms which was hers, I was nearly dead from the strain. All the things I was fixing to ask Miss Gallucci seemed to disappear under the weight.

I finally caught my breath and my memory and, even though I noticed she kept the door open, we was alone in her rooms.

"So," I began, "how've you been?"

She was taking her gloves off and looking at me in the reflection of her dresser mirror. "Fine, fine," she replied. She turned, leaned back on the dresser, and took her bonnet off. "And you, Mr. Leckner, how've *you* been?"

I replied, "Fine. Fine. So, you're gonna be staying in Idlehour for some time."

She tossed her hat on the bed and said, "I may be stuck

142

here for now, but I'll tell you this, Portland hasn't seen the last of me!"

Not that I thought it had, but I did think that was a kinda rash statement, especially the way she clouted her words. So I asked her, "Why do you say that?"

Keep in mind now, this Miss Gallucci was a strange one and, after all, she'd already taken her gloves and hat off and boldly tossed 'em onto the bed and, well you know what sorta ideas was passing through my mind.

"Because of you, Mr. Leckner," was her reply.

"Me?"

"Why of course," she said. "After all, it was you who first suggested I stand up to men. Well, it worked with Burnbaum, it worked with Armentrout, it worked with Howell, it worked with Powell and, most delicious of all, it worked with Gallucci!"

There was something odd glowing from her spuzzy eyes that I don't think I ever did see coming from a woman back in those days. 'Course, those looks are common in the eyesa women these days. It was the look of 'I-have-seen-the-light!' and, believe you me, I've spent lotsa nights wondering to God if I was personally responsible for giving women the right to vote, which is a whole other story in itself.

But I think I managed to utter, "Excuse me, I seem to be a little confused."

"Of course you are! And that's just the way I like it," she triumphed, and she took off her long, grey coat. The dress she wore fit right equitable. "Well, I'll tell you this," she continued. "Daddy may have won this round, but I'll win the fight!" And she fluffed out her leg o' mutton sleeves.

"Ma'am?" I asked, clearly confused, thinking what round, what fight? Those infinite nostrils of hers was beginning to flare, and I was wondering why I'd spent so much time thinking about her lately.

"Of course, when I told Daddy how you'd taught me to

stand up to men, he wasn't too pleased." She kinda smiled when she said that, then her face got all serious again and she added, "You know, I think Daddy and Silas T. Burnbaum are up to something."

I felt my mouth drop open. So much for a independent accounting firm, which was the exact wording of the will. Poor Perrault, I could see him kicking his hat clear acrost heaven's foothills!

I was unable to swaller, but I coughed out: "A . . . would you care to take that thought a few steps further?"

"Oh," she said, "it's just a feeling I get. But you're not to worry, Mr. Leckner. I'm here to help. Just remember, you have E.M. Gallucci in your corner!"

Well, the real reason I was there in the first place was to ask her to the New Year's Dance, so I decided to stray from the conversation and get to the invitation.

"A . . . Miss Gallucci, E.M.," I corrected, clearing my throat some, "there's a do here in town tomorrow night, you know, a New Year's Dance, and I was wondering, if. . ."

"Oh, no, that's no good at all!" she said, aghast-like.

"Huh?"

"Well, we just can't be seen together, socially, I mean," she said. "Don't you see? Then they'll suspect complicity!"

I knew my face was fulla blanks and I asked, "How's that?"

"Complicity! Complicity!" was all she said.

Then I nodded wisely, like I understood, but you and I both know I was more confused than a spun-around cat, and just about as happy.

"So of course, the dance is out," she said, logical-like, whilst she checked the condition of her hair in the mirror. Well, I think the look on my face concerned her a little, and she added, "Now don't pout, Mr. Leckner, I'm sure there're plenty of other girls who'd die to have you escort them to the dance."

That was true.

I reached for my hat, just wanting outa there to round up my thoughts. "Well, if you'll excuse me. . ."

"Oh, Mr. Leckner," she called, just as I was reaching the door. I turned, almost afraid to look at her. "Don't forget, I'm in your corner." And I'll be damned if that woman didn't wink at me.

Well, the way she stood there, smiling cocky-like with her hands on the second halfa her hourglass, I can't rightly say if I was comforted or scared as hell that this Miss Gallucci woman was, as she said it, in my corner.

# Part Three

## one

*W*ell, 1893 arrived just about the same way 1892 left: all tuckered out, covered with slush, and complicated by Miss Gallucci. I never did go to the New Year's Dance onaccounta there was another fire. This time, it was the McNabb place, west of Four Arrows. It was the haybarn went up, same as Anderson's, and it lit up the sky for miles around. McNabb and Anderson didn't take much time comparing sorrow, anger, and theories about the fires. 'Course, back in those days there wasn't much in the way of detecting a man-made fire from a God-made one. Fingers pointed to my crew and, I have to admit, two fires, one on Christmas and one on New Year's Eve, both hay barns, both on neighboring spreads, was a little more'n even I could attribute to coincidence.

Words flew, fingers pointed, and we was visited by Sheriff Agnew regarding the situation. The damn part about no evidence was, you see, it all became circumstantial, and if japery was a parta his job, then hell, he did it just fine. Well, I stood by Leviticus and his crew, but deep in my innermosts I was more'n concerned. What if one of my boys *was* a firebug? If so, which one and how? It was seldom they was on their own and outa sight.

Somehow, we was able to dodge bullets and keep intact. I sent McNabb more hay than I shoulda spared. Not to cover up any guilt but just outa good, neighborly intentions. 'Course, Idlehour thought I was just covering up for Leviticus and the rest.

The more it snowed, the more I worried 'bout my own stock. Anderson's and McNabb's animals was all feeding fine on Four Arrows hay, but I was rationing by February.

You know, Valentine's Day was the next 'special day,' even though we in Idlehour never celebrated it openly and no one ever took time offa work for it. But you can be sure I was watching the horizon for any signs of fire.

Never onct did it crost my mind that the next inferno would be one of my own Four Arrows barns. Like the other two fires, onct it started, it went up so ferocious-like that not even Moses and his departed Red Sea coulda saved it.

Miss Gallucci came out soon as she heard, even though she'd been pretty much staying cleara me and Four Arrows for those reasons of complicity (which I'd learned was a state of cahoots).

There she stood at the front door, them marvelous brown eyesa hers almost tearful. She said, "Royal, I'm so sorry. This is terrible." She walked through the door and on past me without awaiting a invite, saying, "Something has to be done!"

No truer words was ever spoke. I said, "We got maybe two weeks' hay and grain from the outer barns coming in. Everyone, even Lou(ella), is working on bringing in all we can scrounge."

E.M. Gallucci sat herself down in her favorite chair—at the desk—drummed her fingers impatient-like on the desk pad, and asked, "When will the new shipment arrive?"

"Ma'am?" I asked. "Shipmenta what?"

"Why, hay, of course! You did order more hay, didn't you?" She sat straight as a school marm ready to pounce on the classroom rascal.

"You don't just *order* more hay, E.M.," I said, my voice squeaking a little more'n usual.

Whereupon she demanded, "Why not?"

"This ain't simple as ordering a—pardon me—corset from Montgomery Wards, you know," I said. "Hay has to be grown, harvested, stored, and fed out with all respect for the winter. Ranchers set aside their own in these parts. Any extra hay is long gone to the coast, bought up by agents for westside animals."

E.M. popped up outa her chair so fast I wondered if the kinger was crossing her feet. She asked, "Where's your telephone?"

"If we don't got a electric line, we sure as hell don't got a telephone line!" I snapped, sarcastic-like and sounding like Jay.

She started buttoning her coat back up and headed for the door. I know things is different nowadays, but back then folks just didn't just pop in and out as fast as E.M. Gallucci did, and I was beginning to wonder why I didn't fall for something in the way of a more traditional woman.

She took my coat from the rack and threw it at me like one of my hands woulda and said, "Come back into town with me, Royal."

"What for?" I asked. Riding to Idlehour in the snow with the eyesa town barreling through me was the last thing I wanted to do. I had thinking and sorting and planning to do.

But she just answered with, "Because you don't want me to drive alone."

"You got out here alone," I allowed.

"Well then," she flapped, "because I asked you!" and she tightened her scarf with a tug which I thought might be a little symbolic.

Well, you must have a feeling for the directions my mind was wandering that day, after watching our hay go up in smoke the night before . . . with the whole Four Arrows operation at stake. No feed, no cattle; no cattle, no cattle drive; no cattle drive, no profit; no profit, no inheritance for Leviticus, and no Four Arrows for anyone.

*M*iss Gallucci let me drive the buggy into town, but I had the feeling I wasn't going fast enough for her, and she even suggested I let her take the reins. Outa consideration for the horse and the conditions of the road and all, I held tight and got us there safe.

She told me to go straight to the stage depot, which had the nearest telephone. The clerk had the woodstove going strong, and it sure felt good to warm up some. But E.M., bless her I-talian blood, didn't seem bothered by the chill at all and went straight to the telephone. When she noticed the clerk, a harmless sort, standing around in the room with a pair a nently little better to do than to eavesdrop, she set the device back down and cleared her throat, and he left real fast. I guess maybe E.M. had made telephone calls there before.

She worked the operators 'round till she got her number. Now this took some time, and I was quite content to let the time pass whilst I ran my iced fingers over the stove, wondering what the hell this Gallucci woman was up to.

Finally, talking so close to the speaking piece that I wondered if she would kiss it, she called out loud, "Hello, Daddy?"

Pause.

"Yes, it's me! E.M.!"

Pause.

"Yes, I got your Valentine. Did you get mine?"

Pause.

"Oh well, I'll mail it tomorrow."

Pause.

"Fine. Oh, Daddy? Remember that Baldridge woman?"

Pause.

"You know, that clerk down at Corbett's? The redhead."

Pause.

"And did I tell you Momma found a black satin shawl in the buggy?"

Long pause.

"I told her I *thought* it was mine."

Pause.

"No Daddy, that's not why I called."

Pause.

"I need you to send me some hay, Daddy."

Pause.

"No, no, not pay! Hay!"

Pause.

"Yes hay! As in cows and horses!"

Pause.

"Don't ask me why, Daddy, just ship me. . ." At this point she put her hand over the speaking arrangement and asked me, "How much hay do you need?"

Dumb-struck, I answered, "Cripes, E.M., if I could get my hands on. . ."—and I ran some formulas 'round my head—". . .if we pulled in our slats we could get by on four-hundred tons."

She spoke into the telephone again. "Four-hundred and fifty tons, Daddy."

Pause, whilst she held the hearing apparatus far away from her ear. I could hear Daddy's voice from clear acrost the room.

"Too bad, Daddy. You should have thought of that before you started to associate with that woman."

I wasn't sure I was hearing what I was hearing.

"Now Daddy, remember your heart."

Pause.

"Why Daddy, this is *not* blackmail! This is shrewd business. Just like you taught me."

Pause.

A grin of devilment that woulda done ol' Scratch Hisself

proud came to her face as she leaned over and asked me, "Alfalfa, timothy, or mixed grass?"

"A . . . mixed grass, if he can get it."

"Mixed grass, Daddy. And not a straw less than four-hundred and fifty-five tons."

Pause.

"You know, Daddy, the telephone operators are so efficient these days. Why, the one in Portland got me the Baldridge number without any trouble at all. Now how do you suppose a clerk at Corbett's can afford a telephone?"

Pause.

"Good, good, Daddy. A week will be just fine. Give my love to Momma. Bye, Daddy."

She hung the telephone up and leaned back in the chair, and a sly, scary smile crost her lips. "I just love these new devices," she said, twisting the telephone wire around her finger. "That wouldn't have been nearly as easy by telegraph. And not even half as fun!"

I have to admit I was damn near speechless, but I think I managed to say, "Your poor, poor Momma."

But E.M. flashed me a big one and said, "You wouldn't say that if you saw the gentleman *she* sneaks out with."

Now I was speechless.

But just when I finally opened my mouth to speak, E.M. said, "Now as far as anyone else is concerned, this hay shipment is a gift."

"But E.M.," said I, "what about that complicity thing?"

Whereupon she looked up at me like I was feeble-minded as any other man she'd ever dealt with. "Not from me, you dope! This is a gift from . . . from, I know! Miss Clarice Baldridge! Let 'em track that one down."

At that, she called the frozen clerk back inside. She continued to take advantage of my tongue being hog-tied and said, "I think I'll walk back to my place. You can get a lift back out to Four Arrows, can't you?"

My God she was proud of herself. I don't remember

seeing a more pleased-with-herself strut on any woman ever. Her hourglass was damn fulla the sand of determination. And right there, watching her from behind as she disappeared into the snowy distance, I decided not only that I was good'n proud, but damn lucky as well. For this Gallucci woman was in my corner . . . and God help the man who decided to stand opposite.

## two

*Y*ou know that expression, never underestimate the power of a woman? Well, I'm going to do you a favor, son, and tell you a extension of that theory, which goes like this: Never underestimate the power of a woman who has the goods on a man, and never underestimate the speed in which a man can act under the power of such a woman. The hay, not a straw less than five-hundred tons, arrived at the train depot in Athena within six days of E.M.'s acidie-syrup telephone call.

This time I was smart, though. I divvied the hay up amongst my eight barns, so if any further fire-bugging was to occur, I still had resources elsewhere. Smarter even than that, E.M. convinced me that not Silas T., nor Julius Armentrout, nor anyone else needed to know how many wagons of hay we hauled in that winter; not to mention how we got it.

Lucky for us too, for the winter commenced right

through spring that year. I don't recall seeing mucha anything but snow, but you know how things can clog all together when you're trying to recall specifical events.

If the weather was grey, the news of the economy was downright black, meaning no sun could be seen nor was it expected to warm our purses soon. Every time I got close to town I'd check the prices of cattle back east. I kept telling myself not to worry, that east was east and west was west and just 'cause prices was falling one place, it didn't have to affect Four Arrows none. Don't you just love how optimistic youth is?

Well, all we could do was our best, and even Leviticus and his crew pulled together real good. Maybe they didn't understand the red and the black of it, but they knew we was alla us fighting for Four Arrows.

*I* remember setting back one day. It was middle March and even though there'd been a sign of spring earlier that week, we was all suddenly snowed in by a passing tempest. It was a rare day, maybe that's why I remember it so clearly.

We'd alla us been working real hard, taking advantage of the warming and bringing in calf-heavy cows from the winter pastures. Even though me and all the cattle hands knew this was regular, Leviticus had been downright maniacal about this chore, so concerned about these she-beeves was he. Well, like you know, they's no such thing as a hand who's too concerned about his stock. So I just let him take charge.

Well, he wouldn't rest till every damn one of them cows was in safe for the next process of their lifes. And when we came acrost a early calf, well Leviticus and his crew, they nearly fell apart for gladness and worry and all. He insisted all the younguns be pulled together and be put in the great barn just to the southa the ranch house. Even though I'd tried to tell him that wasn't necessary onaccounta cows get real used to the weather and all and besides, to look around us, spring was arrived.

"No," he insisted, "babies need protection." Well, hell, I didn't see the harm and as I set there, watching that unexpected storm whirl deadly snow about the place, I wondered if maybe God hadn't placed some swami-like power into Leviticus. He wasn't smug at all or I-told-you-so about it. He just acted smooth whilst he and his crew pulled out towards the barn to get to know the calves which, thanks to him, was warm, safe, and protected by their mommas in the great barn.

'Course, it worried me some wondering if Leviticus would have a part in actually selling the critters when we went to market. But he never onct winced at a steak, so I thought he might understand the unpleasant, but necessary side of running cattle. Just to be on the safe side though, I'd always placed Leviticus and his crew elsewhere when we was slaughtering things to eat.

So there I set, pondering things. My eyes would wander from the trance of the fire to the account books on the desk before me. Then I'd look outside and see if the snow was still pelting us. There was plenty of problems to occupy my mind in those days, and I wondered why I couldn't get my thinker to settle down on one problem till it was worked out. It seemed the more I was around Leviticus, I got like him and he got like me. 'Course, now that I have the luxury of looking back with the wisdoma Solomon, I know it was that woman accountant, E.M. Gallucci, that stole my concentration.

Since she'd arrived and saved our cattle from starvation, she'd been at a odd-like distance, keeping mostly to herself at the boarding house. Twice a month we'd get together to overlook the books, but I was damned if I could get past credit-debits with her. Just when she seemed comeatable, I'd pull in close to examine the rosewater smell in her black hair, and she'd pull back and talk about hardware charges in town or something just as stupid.

Yessir, she fooled me real good. Hell, when a woman risks disinheritance to blackmail her own daddy for the want of a few thousand cattle . . . well, if that wasn't love, what is?

So when she pulled back from my advances, I tried to tell myself, fine, I wasn't put on Earth to be twirled 'round like the pencil in her lovely hand! My most pressing concern was Four Arrows and Leviticus and the will and all. Well, that's what I told myself. Myself didn't listen real good, though. You know how that goes.

*W*ell, the snow kept me 'round Four Arrows for two days. Then the Chinooks blew through and all we had was slosh, mud, loblolly and, in general, a spring mess. Cattle and boots got stuck, Anita and Lou(ella) complained, Miss Porkpie smiled, and I headed to Idlehour for spring cleaning and the half-monthlies at the bank.

Now, as a kid I never did study too much on ol' Shakespeare. In fact, I think I was twenty or so before I ever hearda him and all those plays he wrote up. But like you know, I was a reader and ever since I'd seen a traveling set of actors put up *Julius Caesar,* I was hooked by that Englishman. Shakespeare being neither here nor there, it was the Ides of March on the day I traveled to Idlehour, and when I laid my head to rest that night, I commenced to wondering if there might be something to that soothsayer business. For things surely did take a turn for the worst that day, Wednesday, March 15, 1893.

I put my gelding in the stable and, even though it cost me ten cents, I thought he was worth the grooming. He was steaming through the rain, and mud was caked up to his knees, and I thought if I had the nerve to take him out on such a day, the least I could do was to have him cleaned up some whilst I did business. Besides, I never knew how long the half-monthlies would take and why should he wait outside knee-high in mud?

'Course, onct inside the bank, I found myself knee-deep in a entirely different substance.

The teller told me they was all waiting in Silas T.'s office and for me to go on in. Ever since the will-reading, I'd had me a dislike for walking into a room where they's all waiting for me, but I opened the door anyway, slowly.

Silas T. wore that half-smile of his, Julius looked legally concerned, and E.M. Gallucci was flipping through a stack of papers, too involved to even look up.

They say we alla us got this dofunny gland in our bodies, called this 'gun or run' thing, and I still feel it come on me when I thinka that woman, Miss Wintermute. And I knew as soon as I laid my eyes on her that morning, that somehow ol' Silas T. and Julius had had a hand at digging her up.

# three

*I*t'd all gone to hell in a hand basket that morning, and I'll tell you, I'd just as soon jumped in that basket and faced ol' Scratch as face that Miss Wintermute again.

"Oh, come in, my boy, come in," said Silas T., and he rose like maybe he thought he might need to steady me some. "I believe you remember Miss Wintermute here." He indicated her voluminous-like presence.

"Uh-oh," I think I uttered, taking my hat off.

Miss Wintermute half-turned to face me. Her cold, marble face gave me the jimjams inside, and before I turned into stone myownself, I pulled my eyes off her and smiled helplessly down to Miss Gallucci.

Silas T. said, "Sit down, Royal, I think we might have a little problem here."

A *little* problem? I asked myself whilst setting down. Well, a pair a nently he didn't know this Miss Wintermute like I did. But I kept my cool and just said, "Really? And what could that be?"

"Miss Wintermute has presented us with several outstanding bills regarding her custodial care of Leviticus Perrault," Julius began, leaning back in his chair to look more relaxed and stuffing his fingers into those damn, tiny vest pocketsa his.

I took a direct look at Miss Wintermute and said, "I thought you and I had settled all that."

She musta forgot there was a lawyer at her side, so she began, "Well . . . for one thing. . ."

Julius finished for her: "I've looked over her claims, Royal, and I'm afraid they're valid."

I ignored Julius and went right for Miss Wintermute. "I gave you a check for your past wages, Madam."

Cool as custard she corrected me with, "Miss!!" I noticed that Miss Gallucci looked over at that and gave her a stare. "And if you're referring to *this* trifling amount . . ." And then she produced the check I'd written her when I'd delivered Leviticus from her talons.

I said, "Yes, that! We agreed that brought you and Perrault free and clear." I looked over to Julius and said, "Look Julius, I don't know what this woman is trying to pull, but you see the check right there. I paid her way back last summer!"

Silas T. took the check from Miss Wintermute, put it in fronta my face, and then turned it over. "She never cashed this check," he said.

"That's impossible; it hasn't shown up outstanding," I said, looking down to Miss Gallucci for help.

Miss Gallucci slammed the Four Arrows ledger shut and snorted, "That's because you never recorded it anywhere, Mr. Leckner!"

Julius explained, "In other words, Royal, Miss Wintermute has not accepted payment for her claims, meaning, of course, they're still unpaid."

I fixes a glare at Miss Wintermute and asks, "Just what are these claims?"

Someone passed me a sheeta paper and I took a moment to read down the list. Well, I knew when I said it there would be some gasps, but I said it anyway as I tossed the paper back on the table: "That's bullshit, pure and in its simplest form!"

"Please, Royal, there are ladies present," said Silas T. His face was going a little pink. He picked the paper up and balanced his spectacles on his nose and began reading out loud: "Food, bedding, sundries . . . these all seem perfectly legitimate. I think the estate should honor these bills."

I pointed to the uncashed check and said, "She *has* payment for those things, right there."

At that, she took the check and, with her fat, stubby pinkies sticking out (I think in a effort to be dainty), she ripped it up into tiny little pieces.

"I don't accept this measly amount as payment!!" she said. Then she opened her hand and blew the pieces at me, a action which looked real rehearsed.

I flicked a piece of the check off my knee as I thought what I was going to do next. Knowing that I was setting ticklish on the horns of a dilemma, I tried to keep unriled. So I turned to Julius and asked, "How much?"

"I could get a lawyer and get nasty about this, you know!!" Miss Wintermute barked in, trying to straighten up her bulging body till her chair gave her a warning crack.

I gave Julius and his jurisprudence a shifty look and said, "Looks to me like you already got yourself a lawyer."

To which Julius said, "You don't have either the time or the resources to get tied up in court about this, Royal. I suggest you simply pay the woman what she's asking. I've already taken the liberty of drawing up the appropriate papers for her to sign as quit claim."

"Pay her what she's asking?!" I bellowed, and I snatched up her list of claims. There was no total and I was too heated up to add in my head, so I asked, "What's all this come to?"

At that, Silas T. handed me another paper. He said, "This is with interest calculated up to now. I took the liberty. . ."

My eyes went straight to the figure and I hollered, "Three-thousand, two-hundred thirteen dollars and eighty-five cents? I'll burn in hell first!"

Miss Wintermute pulled a hankie out from her sleeve and patted her forehead with it. It was cool in there, but she was sweating. She said, "Well, I'm willing to negotiate!!"

"Yes, there, you see?" Silas T. said, and then he smiled cordial-like at the woman, like she was Andrew Carnegie. "Miss Wintermute has generously consented to round the figure off to an even three thousand."

"Well, she better do a helluva lot more rounding," I ranted, "'cause I ain't paying her that three thousand!"

"Royal," Julius advised, "you certainly can't afford to ignore her claim."

Well, I turned on him, fixed him a glare, and asked, "Who the hell's side you on anyway?"

Silas T. smiled toward Miss Wintermute and said, "Royal, I really must ask that you curb your tongue."

I was wild, I reckon you know that. I felt like I had Apaches on my right flank, wolves on my left, and only Miss Gallucci and her damned abacus to fight 'em off with. So I turned to E.M., my chest heaving, and I growled, "All right, Miss Woman-Accountant, you been mighty quiet. What you do say to alla this?"

"I say that if you'd logged that check into the books in the first place, then I would have caught it and maybe we would have figured this woman was up to something before. . ."—she waved her pencil at Miss Wintermute— ". . .before this woman. . ." She paused, took a sigh, then added, "Oh, nevermind." She talked real snippet-like.

I looked 'round the table. My voice was a little scrabbly when I asked, "So you say I have to pay this?"

Julius nodded, Silas T. nodded, Miss Wintermute nodded, but Miss Gallucci shook her head.

"No?" I asked her, getting more and more confused.

Miss Gallucci opened a ledger, circled a figure, slid the book over to me, and awaited my response.

"That's all?" I asked. I sure felt the blood leave my head.

"Unless you have hidden cash somewhere, that's all," she said. I can still hear her fingernail tapping the amount.

I looked to Miss Wintermute and said, sorta relieved, "Well, there you are. I can't pay you. No money."

Julius, of course, was quick to correct me. He handed me still another legal-looking form and said, "This, Royal, is Miss Wintermute's *demand* for payment."

"She can demand all she wants," I said, "but if I don't have the money, I don't have the money." I could feel my anger keep rising like the heat in July.

Then, like he hadn't heard what I'd said, Julius continued, "And this is the sheriff's notice to auction Four Arrows to satisfy her claim."

I took the notice, saw the depth of the quagmire, and said, "And who says them wheels of justice grind so slow?" I think I musta had a sad smile by then. I handed the paper to Silas T. and said, "My, my. It sure as hell looks like you all did your homework real good. Julius, do you represent that woman or Four Arrows and me?"

"I'm only trying to keep you and Four Arrows out of court," he allowed, giving me just halfa eye, like he was doing me some big favor and I didn't appreciate it.

"Yeah. Outa court and outa business!" I snort back.

Miss Gallucci threw down her pencil, leaned back in her chair, and looked real disgusted.

Some silence passed amongst us, then finally Silas T. spoke up, bright and cheery: "Well now, there's really no need to go to court, Julius. I'm sure the bank board will be happy to authorize a loan to Four Arrows."

Now normally the word 'loan' brought me shivers, but by then, I have to admit, it surely did sound like a good idea. But the bank board . . . there was another laugh. On it sat Idlehourians, tried and true. And you know how much them folks wanted us to succeed. And it might interest you to know, the chairman was none other than *Mrs.* Burnbaum herself.

I looked to E.M. and she looked back with a sigh of

resignation. I reckoned we was all hobbled right proper, 'cept the only one that shoulda been, Miss Wintermute.

"Will the 'lady' kindly wait till I can borrow the money?" I asks, forcing a gritty smile on Miss Wintermute. Hell, thought I, if nothing else it would buy me some time. I reckon that's the only good thing about credit and such: it's the only currency that'll buy time.

Miss Wintermute looked at Silas T. and asked, "How long will it take?!"

"Well," Silas T. said as he walked over to his calendar, "the soonest I can get a quorum will be, oh . . . I think we can get together by, let's see. . ." He flipped through the pages and continued, "Well, how does May 4th sound?"

"May 4th!" I hollered. "That's. . ." I counted to myself, ". . .hell, that's seven weeks, Silas T.!" Inside I was quaking at the prospect of Miss Wintermute haunting me for seven weeks. That wasn't the kinda time I was hoping for.

Silas T. looked at me and said, "I realize it's seven weeks, Roy, but you know my wife is down south and without her there's no quorum."

Miss Gallucci, perhaps knowing of such things as boards and quorums, asked, "How many do you need for a quorum?"

Silas T. exchanged a quick look with Julius, smiled a little, and replied, "Just Mrs. Burnbaum. But I'm sure Miss Wintermute understands and will await due process."

We all looked at her, and she slowly returned, "All right, seven weeks!! But I warn you, if he don't get the loan, I'll file these papers!!"

"I'm sure we can all work together on this," Silas T. said, which gave me another shiver.

"Of course, of course," Julius agreed. "These little disagreements are bound to happen when dealing with an estate the size of Four Arrows. Why, I'll be surprised if we don't run into a few other little snags." He caught my eyes, then cleared his throat, nervous-like, and took his eyes elsewhere.

Miss Wintermute rose and the chair gave a sigh of relief. She said, "Well, gentlemen, you may be assured I'll be waiting right here in town for seven weeks!!" She worked real hard at giving a ladylike appearance, but her voice, her size, and her tight-bunned hair told me otherwise. She was nothing but a small-time, big-mouthed, over-sized opportunist, the likesa which I ain't never seen this side of manhood.

Well, as it so happened, the Board of Directors finally met when the Burnbaum Quorum returned on Thursday, May 4th at 10 a.m. By noon, our loan was approved at a whopping 10%, funds was transferred to our account by two, and at exactly 10:23 a.m. on the very next day, Friday, May 5th, 1893, the Bank of Idlehour was robbed.

# four

*W*ell, you gotta know that we'd, alla us, been looking forward to the loan day for a good many weeks. Fortune had finally smiled on us and we finished the spring on steady feet. That is to say, the spring calf count was buxom and we was all healthy and no more ghosts like Miss Wintermute showed up to haunt us.

Hardy, bless his soul, had convinced the hands that if they was paid as usual every month, they would only spend their money on flummadiddle and such, and being as it was looking worse and worse economically speaking, the boys all seemed to think that no cash in their pockets was money in the bank. Naturally, as it so turned out, they was all pleased as punch that their wages was in my I.O.U. columns rather than in the Bank of Idlehour.

I'd heard that the quorum, that is Mrs. Burnbaum, had returned from her winter pastures the first week in May, so I was holding high hopes about the loan processing on schedule. Well, like I told you previous, the loan was approved and things was just fine and dandy till early Friday morning.

We alla us, Leviticus, Lou(ella), Tommy, Toofer, Jay, Hardy, and me rode to Idlehour that Friday morning. There'd been this contest about guessing the number of gum drops in a jar over to Swenson's Drug and Sundries, the prize of which was, of course, the jar and all its contents. Like you figured, Lou(ella) had spent hours counting those gum drops. Sure enough, Mr. Swenson sent word out that she'd won the contest, so we dropped off Leviticus and the Countess, as she had come to be known at Four Arrows, whilst I met E.M. at the bank. Some long-awaited catalogue goods had arrived for Hardy and Jay, so they headed for the Post Office, taking Tommy and Toofer with 'em. Like I said, all things finally seemed to be working well for alla us.

Miss Wintermute, E.M., Julius, Silas T., and me was setting at Silas T.'s desk trading signatures all around, satisfying all the legal rigmarole. Just as I was handing Miss Wintermute her three-thousand-dollar check, the teller came busting in, white as a corpse.

"We've been robbed!" he hollered, supporting hisself with the backa E.M.'s chair.

"What do you mean we've been robbed?" Silas T. demanded, standing up so quick his chair fell out behind him.

The teller took several deep breaths, then said, "I mean two men came in, shoved a gun in my face, and said, 'Gimme all yer money or you get all my lead!' "

Looking back, I recall that teller sure did a good job of imitating that robber, and several times I've thought a movie director might want to have hired him.

"So you just *gave* it to them?" Silas T. howled, running into the front room, like maybe he could catch up with the blackguards.

"Every dollar, every dime, every cent. I even gave 'em my penny bags," the teller said, taking some deep breaths. "They shoved me over to the safe and forced me to open it. Gee, I'm real sorry, Mr. Burnbaum."

But Mr. Burnbaum, along with the rest of us, was almost outa his office. Julius ran for Sheriff Agnew, E.M. fanned the poor teller, and I tried to get some answers outa Leviticus, who was setting, shocked-like, on the bench outside the bank.

"Leviticus, are you all right?" I asked him. I set down gentle next to him so's not to startle him further.

"Lou(ella)," he mumbled. And he just shook his head.

I looked 'round and asked, "What about her? She got her gum drops, didn't she?"

"Those men! They took her! They took her, Royal. And I didn't do nothing!" He put his head into his lap and cried quietly, rocking hisself to and fro.

By then, Sheriff Agnew and witnesses had started to gather 'round us. Those who'd seen the getaway confirmed what Leviticus had said: two men, their faces covered with red bandanas, had run outa the bank, bumped into Leviticus and Lou(ella), struggled some, and then grabbed her and tossed her onto a saddle.

Jay and Hardy ran acrost the street and I left Leviticus in their hands, for I knew things was gonna happen damn fast. Whilst Sheriff Agnew pulled together a posse comitatus, I went back into the bank for more information.

Miss Wintermute met me at the door. She grabbed my hand, forced it open, placed the pieces of my three-thousand-dollar check in it, and closed it back up. Then, with a edge that woulda shaved bark off a tree, she said, "Here's your check back, Mr. Leckner!!"

I looked down at my hand as I slowly opened it back up again.

"According to Mr. Burnbaum, his bank can't make good on this check!!" she continued, a little twitch coming to her already twitched-up face.

I looked past her to Silas T., who was fanning hisself with a empty cash bag, looking like he was preparing to pass out.

"There's no money," he said. "I can't cash that check."

"But the loan. . ." says I.

Silas T., all innocent-like, says, "What about the loan? Ninety day, short term at ten percent."

"There ain't no loan if there ain't no money!" says I, feeling that familiar clutcha panic at my throat.

"Everything's on paper, Royal," says he. "Legally and technically, the funds had already been transferred into your account."

Miss Wintermute gave out one of her hearty laughs and said, "They stole *your* money, Mr. Leckner, not the bank's!!"

Then I pulled the money bag from Silas T.'s hand and asked him, low and easy, "You're insured for robbers, ain't you Silas T.?"

"Now Royal, calm yourself," he said. "We've just been robbed, for God's sake. We'll work all this out later." Just then, Sheriff Agnew walked in to inspect the scene and that was the last I talked with Silas T. for a while.

Miss Wintermute took the quit claim that she'd just signed, ripped it in half like I'd seen her do so many times before, and let the pages drift to the floor. "You know, I think I'll remove my lien on Four Arrows!!" she said, coy-like. Well, I knew her too good to fall for that, so I held silent.

"Yes," she continued sure enough, "instead, I think I'll just lay claim to Four Arrows itself!! I could use a good ranch!!"

"Go ahead and try," I challenged her and I wondered how good it would feel to give her one acrost the chops.

"I'll give you one more month, Mr. Leckner!!" she hollers. "Even *I* can be reasonable!! I realize these little robberies occur from time to time, but after a month . . . well, just don't go making any long-range plans without consulting with me first!!" She turned on her heels, a feat in itself, and strutted outa the bank.

*W*ell, I'd ridden in one of Sheriff Agnew's posses before and I'll tell you this, that man was elected on his looks, not his sheriffing qualities. Therefore, Hardy, Jay, and me decided to strike out on our own to find Lou(ella), the robbers, and my loaned money. Leviticus, onct he pulled hisself together, was damn insistent on bringing his crew and joining us and, hell, I figured he had the most at stake, so I agreed.

Since the witnesses couldn't all get together regarding which direction the robbers had ridden outa town, Sheriff Agnew (so help me God) flipped a coin; and tails, he and his posse went south. We went north, but not because the coin said to. It was Leviticus who pointed out that Lou(ella) had left us a traila gum drops to follow. And there ain't nothing cracked about that maneuver.

So right then I knew that with the posse yahoos riding south and us riding north we'd find 'em first, which was exactly the way I wanted it. You see, a witness said he heard one of the robbers call out the other robber's name: Harold. Harold Somebody.

# five

*I* should tell you, this is the part when things started happening pretty fast, so maybe we oughta take a rest or something and maybe not begin this part, unless you got enough time to finish, in which case I'll be happy to keep on yapping.

Well okay, here goes.

Spring had hit us smack dab in the face that fateful day, and Jay was hit hardest of all. I don't remember him going three paces without sneezing or wheezing, and Hero the Harelipped Horse began looking damn fed up with Jay onaccounta he'd jerk back the reins every time he sneezed. We alla us got a chuckle outa the fact that Hero, just tuckered outa the whole situation, would come to a abrupt halt every time ol' Jay started his aaa-aaa-choooooing.

But in spite of this, we pressed on and followed Lou(ella)'s traila gum drops. It wasn't long before the path narrowed and we started to climb. Leviticus led us single file, stopping at each gum drop. He'd unmount, pick up the gum drop, carefully dust it off and place it in his saddlebag, then mount back up and continue on.

About the time the trail got damn near unpassable, we alla us got nervous and excited that we was getting close to their hideout, the money and, of course, Lou(ella).

I finally gave the order to unmount and I told Toofer and Tommy to set with the horses whilst we continued on foot up the narrow path, which led to all sorts of rocky hideout possibilities.

Just as we was climbing and listening, Leviticus hollered out, "Lou(ella)!"

First of all, he scared the living daylights outa me, hollering like that and right next to my ear, I might add. I pulled him back and said, stern-like, "Shush, boy! Maybe it would be nice if they didn't know we was coming."

At that, Leviticus looked down the path at Jay, pointed a finger, and said, "A pair a nently he gets to sneeze, so why can't I call?"

As nature would have it, Jay sneezed just then, adding a certain amounta powder to Leviticus' question. I allowed as he had a good point and told Jay to go back and join Tommy, Toofer, and the horses. Well, you know how he took that, and we nearly came to loggerheads about it. Well, he finally caved in, but I knew it'd be a long time before he'd stop puckering about it.

When it came time to rest, Hardy, Leviticus, and me settled down under the shade of a giant boulder and pulled out the grub we'd snatched on our way outa town. Leviticus spread out his handkerchief on the ground, then carefully dumped out the gum drops from his saddle bag. Just as Hardy was thinking what a mighty fine kickshaw that would be and reached over to grab some, Leviticus slapped his hand.

"No!" he said, sharp-like. I remember thinking how good it woulda been to have one of 'em photographers riding with us, for I surely woulda liked to preserve the look on ol' Hardy's face.

"Why not?" he asked, rubbing his hand.

Leviticus took a sigh like as to say he hated explaining the obvious. "She counted five-hundert and twelve. And she was right, you know. So don't you touch these." Then he commenced to count the pile of gum drops before him, doing the numbers out loud.

Hardy looked at me and rolled his ol' eyes to the heavens. But I thought I saw what Leviticus was getting up to. "How many do you count there?" I asked him, after he'd built hisself several neat piles.

He counted out loud, then to hisself, then made a to-do about rolling the gum drops back up in his handkerchief.

He finally replied, "Four-hundert, ninety-six," He then smiled broad at me and added, "We're almost there."

Hardy looked us both over, then snapped, "Burro milk! How would she know they're almost there? How do we know there is a 'there,' anyway? How do we know there ain't just a hole in the dang jar? Maybe they're gonna just keep right on riding to Timbuktu."

To which I asked back, "Why would they take a hostage if they was only gonna ride? No, I think Leviticus is right. They'll hideout in these rocks someplace and'll use Lou(ella) to bargain their way out."

"You been reading too many Penny Dreadfuls, Royal!" Hardy said, and he looked at me like maybe my daddy woulda.

"You're just mad 'cause I wouldn't let you have any gum drops," Leviticus jumped in, and for a minute I thought I might have a small ballyhoo on my hands. "A pair a nently," he added as the last word.

Well, Hardy calmed down and Leviticus, well it just wasn't in him to set a grudge, so he smiled at Hardy and we set back in the shade to gather our wits and breaths.

After a bit, I decided I'd climb up further and see what I could see, though I have to admit I sure as hell didn't like the idea of being picked off from above and having it all end right there. The path narrowed and I was wondering how much further their horses coulda gone. Things finally leveled off some and the hillside was more trees and less rocks. It was here that the two riders split up, one going thisaway and the other going thataway.

I wisht I had my gelding and thought, since I didn't, I'd best turn back soon and join the others. I sat down against a large rock to catch my breath and study on the situation.

It was then I heard a little ping! on the rock against me. I looked 'round with a start, but I didn't see nothing 'cept the tree branches all 'round me gently swaying in the breeze. I looked skyward, thinking maybe a bird dropped a nut or something worse. But the sky was empty.

Then came another ping! This time, a gum drop landed right in my lap. I spun 'round and looked above me.

On the hill above me stood tiny Lou(ella), holding her near-empty jar of gum drops close to her.

I started to scramble up after her and called out, "Lou(ella)!"

But she put her tiny finger to her mouth and warned me with a long shhhhhhh and, "Stay. Bad men. Over there. Wee wee."

Well, I have to admit, she sure didn't look any worst for the kidnapping. "Do you know where you're heading?" I whispered up to her.

She pointed further up the hill and whispered back, "Cave. That way. Dark."

"Are you all right?" I asked.

"Count money. If I'm good," she said.

Her eyes was smiling sweeter'n any child's.

"Good, Lou(ella)." said I. "You count the money and be a good girl. We'll get you out. If you hear guns, lay on the ground, sweatheart! You better go back now. Don't worry. We're all just down here."

"Leviticus too? He saving me too?" she asked.

I was sweating blood and damn sure she was gonna give me away, but like I told you before, these gentler folks sometimes just never knew a bad strait when they was floundering in the middle of one. (I reckon I've spent the better part of a lifetime wishing I had that gift.)

I shushed her and replied, "A pair a nently. A pair a nently." And I urged her back up the hill to join her captors. She scrambled up the hill, clutching her gum drops, and I thought there and then how lucky them captors was to have captured her, onaccounta any other female woulda been hysterical and downright dangerous to alla us. I thought it was too bad they couldn't've hauled away that Miss Wintermute. That woulda served all three of 'em right and been almost worth loosing three-thousand dollars over.

But things happen the way they's supposed to, as I was soon to discover.

## six

*W*hen I calculated Lou(ella) was safely back up the hill, I climbed higher to find this cave of a hideout. Onct I had its location fixed in my mind, I hot-footed it back down the hill to inform the resta my crew what we was up against. Assaulting a cave fortress from the downhill disadvantage ain't always been one of my favorite pastimes, but none of 'em had much to say in the way of a argument.

By the time we'd joined back up with the rest of the boys and the horses, it was commencing to get dark. Jay was damn near sneezed to a frazzle, so he was the first to call my attention to the fact we had a supply shack just over the hill and he volunteered to raid the winter quarters for more supplies. I thought that was right good calculating, but I sent Hardy with him and told Jay to keep riding back to Four Arrows onaccounta his hay fever was too ferocious and he might end up sneezing us into a ambush or something.

Leviticus was firstly relieved, then outraged when I told him about Lou(ella). A lifetime of that righteous wrath was commencing to surface, only I don't believe he knew just what to do with it onct it stirred up the peaceful waters of his mind. I'd told him not to worry, that I'd been in deeper kettles before, and that all would end well. Just how, I had no idea, but why bother the kid with that.

'Course, the whole time, in the back of my mind, was the name Harold. Harold Somebody. If only Hardy or Jay had gotten a bead on this gump, then they mighta recognized him as the hoodlum they picked up on our cattle drive that scattered mosta my hands. All night long, I tossed awake trying to cipher why there should be any cahooting regarding the robbery of the bank. I thought since I'd read a few books in my day, that I'd be able to come up with a sizeable plot to satisfy all logical ends, but I was damned if I could come up with a thing. It roiled me, the whole convolution, my luck and all, keeping me awake till exactly five minutes before Hardy woke me for my watch.

Well, if I was the sort to make a long story short, I woulda stopped a long time ago and you'd be falling asleep to the next man's story. But take my word for it that we waited for damn near 36 uneasy-like hours outside that hideout before making any contact with the robbers.

Tommy and Leviticus spent much of those 36 hours heads together, worrying theirselves sick and comforting each other in our hour of crisis. I couldn't make either one of 'em understand that simply asking for Lou(ella) back wasn't gonna do it. I tried my best to calm 'em, but by noon Sunday we was alla us outa patience and I got to thinking maybe I wasn't so smart thinking they was gonna use Lou(ella) to bargain their ways out.

Then it occurred to me, hell, what if that cave had a backdoor and they was all setting pretty in Timbuktu by then? This bolta lightning having struck me between the eyes where I couldn't ignore it, inspired me to tell the boys to prepare theirselves. We was going in.

We hiked up the hill and hid behind some protections. Hardy drew his gun. Toofer had a stick and Leviticus . . . well, I told him he was to lay it low onaccounta if he got hisself killed, it was all over anyway and then Lou(ella) probably wouldn't even want to return.

Toofer, God bless his souls, half-wanted us to storm the cave, irregardless of the casualties, and half-wanted us to send for reinforcements. 'Course, I reckon he forgot all our reinforcements was probably hip-deep in the Gulfa Mexico by then, if they'd all followed Sheriff Agnew, that is.

Now, I know it sounds like movie-talk, but this is what I called up to the cave: "We know you're in there. We have forty men out here. Throw out your guns and walk out with your hands up." I turned back around and looked at my four hands, shrugged my shoulders like as to say, hell, it *might* work, and waited.

All the desperadoes did was toss a bucket fulla used-up water down the hillside, damn near sloshing me. Well, I knew right away the cave didn't have a backdoor.

"Let the girl go and I'll see things go lighter for you," I tried. And you know I was keeping my head low and my powder dry.

Then a voice comes from inside the cave and demands, "Who the hell are you?"

I fired back, "Royal Leckner."

"Who?"

I looked down at the boys a little hurt-like and Hardy just shrugged his shoulders like I shouldn't be insulted.

"Royal Leckner. Foreman of Four Arrows," I called. "A sizeable chunk of that money you stole was mine and I want it back!"

So he asked back, "You mean you ain't even a sheriff or a deputy or nothing?"

Onct again, I looked back down at Hardy. It hadn't occurred to me that, in the face of a possible shoot-out, credentials was all that important. But I guess they had their pride too.

"You want to me to get the sheriff?" I called up. "He'd be happy to accept your surrender."

"Surrender, hell! We'll give up the girl only for safe passage to the border," the voice called back down.

"I told you so!" I whispered down to Hardy. Then, up to the cave, I asked, "Which border would that be?"

There was a long pause, as they musta been discussing that one.

"None of your beeswax!" he called down.

I repeated, "Beeswax?"

"Business! None of your business!" he said, all impatient-like.

"Aw come on boys," said I, "if you won't tell me where you're heading, how can I barter safe passage there?"

There was a long pause, then he called down, "Canadian border!"

"That's quite some passage," I called back.

"Tell Sheriff Agnew that's our terms or the girl gets one through the heart," he threatened.

Well, you know, right there Hardy had to hold onto the boys some.

I then tried to slip 'em up a little by asking, "You local boys?" I hadn't referred to the sheriff by his name and I thought it was sorta curious they was familiar with him. Ol' Sheriff Agnew's reputation stopped about a block outa Idlehour, you see.

"None of your funeral!" another voice called back. Now there was another one I hadn't heard, but I got his meaning clear as a bell and figured beeswax and funerals was some-how the same thing.

I asked, "How do I know the girl is all right?"

There was a shuffling and some dust arose from the cave

entrance. Then I heard Lou(ella)'s tiny voice call down, "Twelve-thousand, two-hundred and sixty-five dollars!"

"You all right, Lou(ella)?" I hollered up.

"Yeah, she's all right," the voice said. "As long as she's got something to count." Well, the robbers was sounding real edgy, so I backed off and said I'd get back to 'em regarding their terms, the safe passage and all.

'Course, the last thing I wanted to see was them boys getting outa the country. Not only did they carry Four Arrows loot, but if there was, like E.M. put it, complicity going on, then I needed 'em to help prove my case. So you have my word I was thinking on it real hard.

Now that the robbers knew we was down there, I saw no reason why we couldn't have us a fire that night so's we could heat our airtights of beans and tomatoes. And of course, Hardy's trail coffee tasted like paradise.

The hot food felt real good in our insides and the fire warmed our outsides. Everyone pretty much went to their own corner to settle down. I said I'd tend the fire and for 'em all to get some sleep. Staring into the embers made me thoughtful and retrospectful. Just when I myownself was getting a little dozey, Leviticus crept over to my side.

I asked him, "You feeling better now?"

To which he replied, "A pair a nently." He stared into the fire, and I could tell he was struggling down deep with some words.

So I asked him, "What is it, son? Don't worry about Lou(ella). She'll be all right."

"I know," he replied. "Royal?" I nodded. "Can I ask you something?" I nodded again.

Even though he wouldn't look at me, I watched his face real close and I was a little worried. There was a pain there I didn't recollect ever seeing there before. Normally, Leviticus was a real easy-going sort, just about as unburdensome as a colt.

He asked, "Why did my father wait till he died?"

"To do what?" I asked back, worried what his answer was.

"To bring me here," he said.

Well, I reckon that was the question I'd always feared him asking. Like you might remember, it was the question that firstly crost my mind when the whole Four Arrows problem came up. And even though I'd prepared a hundred different answers, I swear I couldn't remember a one of 'em that night.

"Why, Royal?" he asked again, this time looking me straight in the eyes.

Well, I have to tell you, it nearly tore my heart out. "Well, you know, Leviticus," I began as soft as I could, but trying to remember this was Leviticus the man I was talking to, not the boy. "I been thinking on that for some time now."

"You have?"

"Yep," said I. "Your daddy and me, well, we wasn't great friends, not at all like you and me is, so I can't say as I knew his head real good."

"What do you mean?" he asked.

"Well, what I mean is, I can only guess," I said.

"What's your guess?" He looked back down into the fire. My, he was handsome with the firelight dancing on his face.

I replied, "I think he felt so bad about leaving you when you was a baby, that he couldn't face you as a man." I watched his face real close-like.

The fire reflected tears in his eyes, but he didn't let 'em escape. He just nodded his head, ever so slightly and said, "Yeah. I was thinking that too. You know, I only saw him onct." He looked into the blackness of the trees around us and a little smile came to his face as he was recalling. "I acted a little gooney in those days."

"Well, I bet that if he saw you now, he'd be proud as any papa could be," I said. And I meant it.

His smile broadened and, with it, the tears plopped out

without a smack of shame and he said, "Yeah, I bet that too."

With that, he rose and walked back over to his bed roll, crawled in, pulled the blanket up close 'round his chin, and fell asleep with a wonderful smile on his face. You know, whenever I felt inclined to pity him, well, almost like he sensed it, he had a way of setting my heart at ease so that I'd end up pitying only poor ol' Royal.

It musta been about a hour later when Tommy heard something from acrost the camp. He'd been serving as our watchdog of sorts, onaccounta him being half Indian and all.

He said, "Shh." Hardy and Leviticus pulled awake.

Then Toofer asked, "What is it?" But he turned on hisself and said, "He said shh! So shh!"

Tommy made a careful move toward the sound and, hearing it again, motioned to me the direction from whenct it came.

I strained, but was damned if I could hear anything more'n the usual night sounds: a breeze in the trees, a faraway coyote.

But our line of horses was looking 'round, and when they do that you know something is out there. One horse gave out a deep gruzzle, which nearly stopped our hearts.

I drew a gun and stepped light towards the trail downwards. There was a cracking of branches as the foe came closer and I reckon there wasn't a heartbeat amongst alla us.

# seven

"Step forward and be recognized!" I called out. I held my gun up higher, not that I woulda shot or nothing.

Well, you gotta know that the last person I expected to step forward and be recognized was Miss E.M. Gallucci. I was relieved, but I sure doubted my heart thumper would ever be the same. I put my gun down and asked, "What in the name of Matthew, Mark, Luke, and John are you doing out here?"

As she stepped into the arc of our firelight, I was a little dismayed to see that *she* had a gun trained on *me*. And somehow I had little doubt she woulda used it. She was wearing the damnedest outfit I ever saw a woman in—man's clothes, plain and simple—and her hair was down and long, longer than I had imagined it to be but not altogether displeasing.

She made a great to-do about uncocking her gun, then she handed it to me, saying, "Here, take this thing, will you."

I took the piece gladly and demanded onct again, "Will you tell me what you're doing here?" With Hardy and the rest watching me, I wanted to present a picture of being in control of the situation.

But she trotted right past my question, stepped toward the fire, and said, "I could smell your coffee for a mile. Any left?"

Hardy poured her a cup and she said her howdy-do's to Leviticus and his crew.

For the third time I asked her, "What in hell are you doing up here?" (I thought the 'hell' might bring a response.)

She plopped herself down on a log, and setting there, steaming coffee in hand, glorious black hair reflecting blue rays from the fire, and dressed most uncomely, I thought she was the most fascinating thing I'd ever seen. She looked up at me, spread her face with that know-it-all smile, and said, "I'd love some whiskey in my coffee." She held her cup out.

That did it! I stomped over to her, took her cup away, and hollered, "It's a long way to ride just for whiskey in your coffee, E.M.!"

Seeing the importance of the issue, she looked 'round and asked, "Can they be trusted?"

"You know they can!"

"Did you know Miss Wintermute has a drinking problem?" E.M. asked, like maybe her question and her pompous-like way of asking it explained everything.

"All the way up here for that handsome bit of gossip? So what?" I asked, probably with my hands on my hips.

To which she replied, "So, once I discovered that, the rest was easy."

"What was easy?" I asked. I was trying mighty hard not to lose my control, onaccounta Hardy and the crew was eyeballing us by then.

"Oh, it took half a bottle of sherry and a wire for four-thousand dollars, but oh, what I found out!" She pulled a brush outa her valise and began to brush her hair, another fine annoyance, I must admit.

I gave up on getting the story outa her in one gulp, so I poured myself a cup and sat down next to her. In her own good time, I reckoned, just like any other female. The other boys drew in closer to hear what she had to say and, I must add, she was purse-prouda herself, a attitude which she wore real fine. And up to that point, I'd thought only men was cocky.

Finally, E.M. began with, "Well, something told me that a woman like that Miss Wintermute doesn't have the gumption to come up with a scheme worth three thousand just on her own." She pointed her brush at me and commenced, "So, since she was staying at the boarding house last week, I asked her in for a glass of sherry. Why, she took my offer up just like that!" And she snapped her fingers to show us how quick 'that' was. "One glass led to another until I had her squawking like a dying duck!" She looked 'round and corrected herself to say, "I mean, she was pouring her heart out to me."

"What did she say?" Leviticus asked, his smile wide and curious. I figured he'd waited a long time to get some dirt smudged on ol' Miss Wintermute.

She took a pause, real theatrical-like, then announced, "She said Silas T. had come to her with the whole idea!"

"I knew it!" I said, spilling my coffee and not caring. "What else? Julius is in on it too, isn't he?"

"Julius, Sheriff Agnew, and that noodle of a teller in the bank!" E.M. said, her sly smile taking me in.

At that I straightened up, for I sure didn't see what the teller had to do with anything. So I asked, "The teller?"

E.M. looked at me like I was about as duncical as a post and replied, "Of course, the teller! How else would he have known to give the robbers the counterfeit money?"

Well, she'd lost me. Says I, "Back up there just a minute. You mean. . ."

"I mean those aren't real robbers, those are Silas T.'s men!" she said. "And that isn't *real* money they stole, that's counterfeit money."

It was Leviticus who asked, a notch more confused than me, "But it is Lou(ella) they have, isn't it?"

"Taking a hostage wasn't a part of their plan," she went

on. "I think they just stumbled onto that part. Is she all right?"

I replied that she seemed unruffled, then said, "Now go back some, E.M. I gotta get this straight."

She said, "Silas T. got Miss Wintermute to try to break Four Arrows. So he'd look clean, he arranged a loan to cover you. Then he robbed his own bank so you couldn't get your hands on enough cash to pay off Miss Wintermute. Don't you see? Textbook case, Royal. Textbook case."

"You mean those yaps up there is risking their lifes for counterfeit money?" I asked.

"Well," she answered, "I don't think they know it's counterfeit, but I'll bet you dollars to doughnuts that when it comes time to pay them off, Silas T. will use that worthless stuff."

I admit, I was downright flummoxed. I'd missed a chapter or two somewheres. I asked, "Miss Wintermute told you all this for just half a bottle of sherry?"

"*And* her three thousand, plus one thousand extra I had to throw in to make it worth her while, Royal." She pulled a few papers outa her shirt and handed 'em to me. "Here's her second quit claim and a signed document releasing her of all complicity."

"So where did you get four thousand?" I asked, narrow-eyed, but having a pretty good idea.

"Daddy," she replied a little southern-bellishly, whilst she dusted off her trouser knees.

"The redheaded lady at Corbett's?" I asked.

"No, no, Royal. Believe me, she was only worth a shipment of hay," she said. "No, this time I held out for bigger stakes: I told Daddy I knew everything, including the part about his commission cut when Four Arrows was to be auctioned."

I ran my hands through my hair to relax my brain and said, "Now let me get this straight. I only owed Miss Wintermute before, but now I owe you four thousand and the bank three thousand. How come I just doubled my liabilities?"

She said, "You don't owe the bank a dime. I mean you do, but you don't. That three thousand you borrowed is technically still in your account."

"No it's not. They have it," I said, pointing up the hill and getting a little flustered.

At this, E.M. drew herself up, like she was insulted or something. "Look. Who's the accountant here? You or me?"

"You, E.M., but. . ."

E.M. broke in with, "What they have is one, a vault-full of bogus money; two, a hostage; and three, more problems than they know what to do with." She used her fingers to make her point like I was some second-grader who was still using the finger-toe system.

I looked over to Hardy and asked, "You getting any of this?"

He shook his head and his face was blank as a slab of marble.

Tommy Two Hearts, of all people, struggled to say, "When . . . they . . . find . . . out . . . they . . . got . . . counterfeit . . . money . . . they'll . . . kill . . . Lou(ella)."

This brought Toofer to his feet, both of him ready to take on Grant and Lee. He said, "We better get her now."

But it was Leviticus who calmed 'em down, which I took a real interest in. "No, wait," he said, and he looked real thoughtful-like. "We always get in trouble when we go too fast." He turned to me and asked, "Royal? What do we do? I don't care about Four Arrows. All I want is Lou(ella). Safe and sound."

He was right. They all was. Here we'd been talking loans and traitors and payoffs, and none of us was thinking of Lou(ella) held up in that cave counting counterfeit money.

All through the night we worked on a plan. The best idea came from Toofer, who could pull together real good ideas when botha him thought along the same track. We all agreed the best thing to do was to convince the robbers that they was about to be had by Silas T. That he'd had 'em steal counterfeit and he was gonna have 'em arrested for the robbery instead of having Sheriff Agnew see that they got away clean, which, we reckoned, was their original plan. Just before dawn, everyone was finally getting some sleep. I'd offered to stand the watch remaining onaccounta I was foreman and was supposed to get by with less sleep. Besides, I sure admired the idea of talking to E.M. alone. She'd walked away from the fire to stretch her legs and, with those trousers on, I noticed how very long those legs was.

She sat on a large boulder and I joined her there. We both just looked down into the valley as the dawn was beginning to crack.

It was a powerful moment.

I boldly took a strand of her hair and ran it through my fingers which, as I recall, was beginning to tremble. Feeling the slight tug, she turned and faced me. I dropped the strand, a little embarrassed.

Now, I've never been the forward type, but I let the words escape before I could put a check on 'em. "You know, even in that get-up, you're sure alota woman, E.M. Gallucci."

Well, the words was out, so what could I do 'cept await her reply? Which was, word for word, which I'll never disremember: "About time you saw that, Royal. Now, if you're going to kiss me, would you do it now, so I can get some sleep?"

She leaned back and I obliged her best I could, which I think was pretty good. In fact, I think that kiss was the next turning point in my story.

Hell, I've talked long enough for one day. Let's have us a nightcap and we'll take up this story tomorrow. That okay with you, son?

# Part Four

## o n e

*N*ow, if I got too personal-like there last night talking 'bout my boldness regarding E.M. Gallucci, then I just hope you'll understand. You said to say things like they happened, and I did.

Well, after the sun rose and my heart had settled down some, I rekindled the campfire (which I coulda done by just breathing on it), reheated the coffee, and went up the hill to talk to the robbers.

I called out easy-like, "Hey, you up there!" I was trying to work down a dry, crumbly biscuit so I took a sip of my coffee before calling out louder, "You, robbers! Come on out! I gotta talk to you!"

One called back, "What for?"

"For your own good," said I. "We know all about the robbery and Silas T.'s part in it!"

One of the men slowly came to the mouth of the cave and asked, "Silas T. who?"

"Silas T. the one-who-hired-you-to-rob-his-bank, that's who!" I said.

Then the other man came into the light and, looking down on me, asked, "That coffee you drinking?"

I held up my cup and replied, cordial-like, "Yep! Real good and hot, too. Just the way I like it."

The two men talked amongst theirselves and I was

thinking wouldn't it be ironical if they'd come out for our coffee, but not because we knew the whole plan?

I called up, "It may interest you to know that that ain't real money you stole. It's counterfeit. See? Ol' Silas T. was letting you boys steal counterfeit so's your cut'd be a total zero. Now, don't feel bad, boys. He took me just as fair!"

"You're lying," one of them said. "That money's real as rain."

"Look at it!" I suggested.

There was a pause, followed by: "Looks good to me."

I rumpled around in my pants pocket for the dollar I knew I had there. I wrapped it and a rock up in my bandana and tossed it up to 'em. "Here, boys. Here's what the real thing looks like. Compare the numbers. Have Lou(ella) look at it. If anyone can tell real from fake, it's her."

It took some time and some shuffling about, but my bandana and the rock finally came back, minus the dollar bill, of course.

"So we been chiseled, that it?" a robber called down.

And I replied, "By the sharpest picks in the state! But I got a plan that can get you two off the hook and will help us out at Four Arrows. You willing to come on down and talk?"

More gab between 'em, then, "Okay. We'll talk. We're coming down."

"Hold off," I said. "Send the girl down first with your guns."

"I don't think I'd like to put a gun in her hands," one said. "She might wanna count the bullets."

But I held, knowing little Lou(ella) wouldn't discharge a firearm even if she knew how, so I called up, "Girl first with the guns."

My, she was quite a sight: picking her way down that path, two guns tucked into her belt, a holster slung 'round her neck, two bags of money under one arm and a near empty jar of gum drops under the other.

Following her was the two robbers, not at all bad-looking sorts. I mean, to brush elbows with 'em in a saloon or church or somewheres, you'd never be inclined to think of 'em as varmints. "She was beginning to drive us crazy," the first robber said to me. "Counting, counting, all day long, counting. Don't she know nothing but numbers?"

I took the guns from her and said, "She knows to keep her cool in the face of disaster."

We all walked down the path together. Lou(ella)'s reunion with Leviticus and the rest was heart-fetching, and you had to be cold as a dead rock to keep a tear from rising.

It was agreed that we'd all go back to Four Arrows by way of the river, in hopes that no one, especially Sheriff Agnew's bumbling posse comitatus, would see us. The two robbers, Harold Webster and Jerry Chesley, came along peaceful-like, and all the while I was wondering if maybe I could get some cow-hand work out of 'em, being as we was falling drastically behind on Four Arrows work.

$E M$ and I, we rode drag behind the pack, swallowing some dust but working out on how we was gonna pull Four Arrows back outa debt and work a profit with the cattle drive. But prices was pretty shaky and we was commencing to get mighty worried.

So I said, "My first job is Four Arrows, E.M. I don't know as I have the time and grit to take on Silas T. and the rest right now."

She rocked to and fro, graceful-like, in the saddle of her rented horse, and I was impressed and surprised how well she set the hack, 'cause hacks don't usually give accommodating rides.

I was beginning to work up a proper sweat about things.

My, onct I put my mind to it, I sure could worry about things in those days. You'll be happy to know that I finally stopped all forms of worry in October of 1929, just when most folks was beginning. But that day riding back to Four Arrows, I surely do recall the dust sticking to my forehead.

I looked down at my saddlebags, which was bulging with the counterfeit money. E.M. must've followed my glance downward, for she too was staring and thinking. The light of inspiration struck us just about the same time. We'd simply repay ol' Silas T. the money Four Arrows owed him with his own damn, counterfeit money!

E.M. hit her forehead like as to punish her brain for being so sluggish, and said, "Why didn't I think of that before?"

"You was too busy extorting money from your daddy," I replied, smiling over to her. I pulled my horse up for a rest and we worked out the details.

"What if Silas T. won't accept it as payment on your loan?" E.M. asked.

"Then I reckon we got us a obligation to tell the folks of Idlehour just what sorta banker they're trusting their money to," says I. "Silas T.'s gotta be close to tenderhook-ing anyhow. Hell, five banks have folded up in Spokane already this year."

E.M. gave me her slyish smile and said, "Maybe that's how he's managed to stay afloat."

"You saying what I think you're saying?" I asked, and I reached into the saddle bag and pulled out a few bills of the phony money. It surely did look real to me, and I could see how folks could be taken in proper.

E.M. took the bill and examined it. "There's a lot of this in circulation nowadays. Even if you knew this was counterfeit, wouldn't you be tempted to spend it anyway? Let the next poor fool get stuck with it?"

I surely did admire the thought-tracks that woman made. I took the bill, placed it back into the saddlebag, and said,

"Well, I think that's just what we should do with it. Pass it on to the next poor fool. Our friend, Silas T. Burnbaum! And ol' Silas T. daren't say one word onaccounta we got the goods."

We rode a little in silence, then E.M. said, "You know, Royal, there's a considerably larger amount of cash there than what you owe the bank. . ."

"Well," said I, "I only took a quick tally, but I reckon there's close to twelve thousand. 'Course, Lou(ella)'d have the exact amount." E.M.'s face had a queer cross of mischief and larceny and I-talian beauty on it, prompting me to add, a little shaky-like, "E.M., what're you thinking?"

Of course, she answered with a question: "Were you planning on giving the *whole* amount back?"

I hadn't thought that far, and I think my basically honest nature was shining through the dust and sweat. I answered, "Well, according to Miss Wintermute, Sheriff Agnew and Julius Armentrout are both in on this, which sure makes arresting a crook a tough job. So I was thinking, maybe we oughta tell a higher-up about this. After all, this is stolen goods."

E.M. pointed to the saddlebags, looked me straight, and said, "No Royal, that is stolen *bads*. An entirely different thing. Just think of the power you could have over Silas T. hanging onto that money."

Lord, I never knew a woman with such thoughts, and I had to admit, I wondered what sorta thoughts she came up with behind bedroom shades. Some accountant she was turning out to be.

So I asked, "Miss E.M. Gallucci, more blackmail?"

"Insurance, Mr. Leckner," she answered. "Think how Silas T.'s tried to foul up Four Arrows. You think he'll let a little thing like your financial solvency stop him? He wants Four Arrows' assets, and the whole town is behind him. Think, man! *I* think we ought to dangle that extra nine thousand just out of his reach! Insurance, that's all."

I tried to reply a coupla times, but each time her confident brown eyes brought me up speechless. She Mona-Lisa'd me till I thought I coulda fallen right outa my saddle.

After a spell, I pulled up my gelding and said, "Stop your horse a minute."

"What's the matter?" she asked.

I leaned over, put my hand behind her neck, and pulled her in for a kiss. If I'd caught her off her guard, she sure didn't show it. It was a long, bold kiss, as daring and sweet as any. And hell, she coulda leaned back and pulled me right offa my horse, but I didn't care. 'Cause, you see, Royal R. Leckner was in love.

## two

*T*he next day, Miss E.M. Gallucci rode back to town, keeping silent and to herself, all a part of our plan. The rest of us hid out low at Four Arrows for a few days, letting things whirl about in town. The robbers, Harold and Jerry, worked in real good with the rest of the hands, and I sure was grateful for the extra help. They was still so roiled about how Silas T. had used 'em, I swore they woulda sold their spurs to help me and Leviticus out. Hell, ol' Harold Somebody even apologized for scattering my hands on the cattle drive. And, of course, they had my word that I wasn't gonna turn 'em in or nothing.

On Friday, exactly one week after the Bank of Idlehour

was robbed, I drove the buckboard into town with Leviticus and Lou(ella) at my side and with Toofer and Tommy riding alongside. It was early, but already the heat was rising and I knew a dry spell was on its way. Well, you can be sure folks stopped and stared, then commenced to follow us to the Bank of Idlehour. When they asked us what'd happened, we just kept silent and smiled down, and Lou(ella), realizing her famousness, waved shyly at a few of the folks.

Hearing the commotion, Silas T. came outa his bank and it was hard to catalogue his expression. His handlebar seemed to have lost some of its umph and he wasted no time ushering us into his office, locking the door on the town of Idlehour.

He took Lou(ella) gently by the arm and set her down in his office, whilst he gushed, "Miss Lou(ella)! I can't tell you how glad I am to see you're all right! We'll have to let Sheriff Agnew know right away you're back and safe!" He turned to me and asked, "Have you seen the sheriff?"

"Oh, I don't see why we should spoil all his fun. You know how he loves a posse comitatus," I replied. I pulled up a chair and set myownself down.

Ol' Silas T. blubbered on with, "Tell me, tell me, what happened? Did you catch those scoundrels? Did you recover the money? Oh, but of course, the money means nothing." This he added towards Lou(ella).

"Not much," Lou(ella) agreed, nodding toward Leviticus, who let out a great big snicker. He put his hands to his mouth and tried to pull hisself together whilst I proceeded to unravel our plot.

"Would somebody tell me what happened?" Silas T. asked, staring right at me.

"Well, we, that is, Leviticus here and his friends, you know these folks, don't you Silas T.?" Silas T. hurriedly shook their hands all 'round, knowing I wasn't gonna continue till everyone was properly introduced.

"Go on, go on," said Silas T.

"Well," said I, "we tracked the robbers to their hideout up towards Blue Bluff and we held 'em there for awhile. I reckon they realized the bad straits they was in and that Leviticus here and his friends wasn't about to let 'em pass without they release Lou(ella)." I took a pause to give Leviticus a smile of recognition and continued, "Well, it was quite a ruckus, but the robbers finally released Lou(ella) and I'll be damned if they didn't also release. . ." —I walked to Toofer, who took out a money bag from his coat—". . .three-thousand dollars of the money! I guess as a showa good faith before moving on, or something." I held the bag up and added, "Now, Silas T., I believe we got some transacting to do."

I knew he wanted to reach out for the bag, you know, like one of them knee-jerk reactions, but he held back some and said, "You recovered some of the money? How wonderful, Royal. How wonderful!" Then his face darkened some and he added, "What sort of transacting?"

"You got my three-thousand note somewheres handy?" I asked, looking 'round his fine leather and mahogany office.

"Uub, uub . . . yes," Silas T. fumbled. "But there's no rush on that, Royal."

My grin shined with my secret as I said, "Get it out, will you!"

He pulled it outa his desk drawer.

"Stamp one of 'em 'Paids' on it, too, whilst you're at it," says I.

"I don't understand," says Silas T.

I dumped the bag of money out on his desk and said, "Here's the three thousand I borrowed last week, complete with interest up to ten o'clock this morning."

"But I don't understand, Royal. You need that money to pay off Miss Wintermute." Though he talked to me, he looked at the money.

"Oh, didn't I tell you?" I said. "Miss Wintermute and me came to a understanding. I thought she mighta stopped by to tell you she quit all her land-liening."

"For free?" he asked, his mouth wide open.

"Well, let's just say we came to a understanding. But anyway, I won't be needing the three thousand after all, so here," I said, pushing the pile toward him, "you can have it back."

Silas T. looked at me suspicious-like, examined a twenty-dollar bill, and said, "How convenient that you recovered just the amount you owed."

Leviticus and Lou(ella) started to giggle and I shot 'em a hush up look.

Silas T. stamped my note 'Paid' and slowly handed it to me and, by the way he looked at me, I think he was wondering if I was wondering what he was wondering.

So I said, "Thank you. Now then, I was wondering if maybe now my credit is good enough for you to authorize me another loan."

Now he was looking totally confused. "Say, what goes on here? If you didn't need the three thousand, why are you. . ."

I ran my hand through my hair like I was calculating things up, thoughtful-like, and said, "Yep, nine thousand oughta do it."

"Royal," he said, "as your banker I can't advise you. . ."

"Yes, nine thousand, don't you think?" I asked my crew. I got nods of agreement all around.

Then Silas T. began to bluster, "Well, I don't know. There's certainly not much cash around. You know how things are nowadays, Royal. Well, I'd have to consult the board."

At this, I walked past Silas T. and drew up the shade on his window. Several townsfolk was standing outside, straining to get a word or two of our conversation. As I recall, that's one of the things Idlehourians was famous for . . . hell, let's just be kind and call it curiosity.

"It's warm in here, Silas T. Do you mind if I open the window some?" I asked with my hand on the latch. I remember smiling nicely at the folks on the outside.

Silas T. rushed to the window, pulled down the shade, and said, "Nine thousand, Royal? But why?"

"Oh, this and that," I replied.

He sat at his desk, looked me over good, and pulled out some loan-making papers.

"Why don't you ask your teller to bring in the money, Silas T.? We're sorta in a hurry," I went on. I never remember my voice sounding so honey-like.

It sure gladdened my heart to see him work all the why-fors over in his mind. He stuck his head out the door, whispered a few words to his teller and, in no time, a tray of green was brought in and laid upon the table.

"Nine thousand?" I asked.

To which Silas T. replied, gruff-like, "Sign here."

"Just a minute." I motioned for Lou(ella) to inspect the money. She pulled a few bills out and after a brief study, she turned to me with a lemon-ball face and shook her head no.

"How 'bout you bring us another tray, Silas T.? Lou(ella) don't much like the looks of that stuff," I said. Well, if he had any doubts that we was on to him, they was gone then. But he held it up real good.

"What in hell are you talking about, she doesn't like the looks of that money?" he demanded, arms folded in fronta him, defiant-like.

I simply looked at Lou(ella) and she started to rattle off a series of serial numbers which Silas T. seemed immediately to recognize.

"I see," he said slowly, as he acknowledged the corn. "Well, we might have something a little more to the lady's liking." He wasn't too cordial, I'll tell you that. But he picked up the tray, left the room, and returned with another tray-full.

Again, Lou(ella) looked the bills over and, when I'd got her nod of approval, I asked, "You still got that paid stamp handy?"

He asked, "I beg your pardon?" I swear his handlebars dropped down to his belt.

"Well, I know how important keeping good credit is 'round here," I said. "That's something our independent accounting firm has taught me. So, mark that note paid and I'll pay you back right now."

I could tell he was beginning to heat up. He stared at me cold, leaned against his desk, folded his arms acrost his chest again, and asked, "And just how did you come up with an additional nine-thousand dollars?"

"Oh," said I, "didn't I tell you? Those robbers thought maybe things'd go better on 'em, if they was ever caught that is, if they just returned all the money they stole." I felt my grin creeping out and, try as I did, I couldn't keep it offa my mush.

Ol' Silas T. scoured me good with that banker glare of his and I said, "I *did* say they returned twelve-thousand dollars, didn't I?"

"No, Leckner, you said *three* thousand."

"Oh, well you know how I am with numbers," I said. "Anyway, they returned the whole load. Hell, that's why we let 'em go, Silas T. You know, for robbers they wasn't all that stupid." I walked to Toofer and he pulled out the other, heavier bag of money, and I unloaded it upon Silas T.'s desk. "There's all the money they stole. Every penny." I took the empty bag and handed it to Leviticus, who commenced to fill it with the good money from the tray.

"You wanna go ahead and stamp that note, too, Silas T.?" I asked as I signed the nine-thousand-dollar note.

Silas T. said, "I don't know what you think you're trying to pull, but you're crazier than they are!"

Well, I knew that wasn't the time or the place to get into a thing about who was the crazy ones in that office, so I just said, taking the nine thousand from Leviticus, "Always a pleasure doing business with you, Silas T."

"You can't do this, Royal!" Silas T. said, looking, I think for the first time in his life, like a desperate man.

"I can and I am."

"But you don't know what this means. . ." he said, pleadful-like.

"It means," I interrupted, "you oughta consider yourself lucky I don't go to the authorities—I mean the *real* authorities—about this!" I said, looking down on him some.

"But I'll be ruined. I'll fold." Silas T. sank into his leather chair and buried his head in his hands.

"Serves you right, pulling a stunt like that on the people of Idlehour," I said, tisking him proper.

He looked up at me, clean broke in half, and said, "I would have folded like a house of cards months ago if it hadn't been for that shinplaster money." The heat in the room was getting downright immense and he was sweating extra.

I sure didn't like the direction the conversation was taking, and with Silas T. looking so remorseful-like. So I motioned for us to leave. I handed Leviticus the money, which was my first mistake that day.

Just as we was almost out the door, nine-thousand, direly-needed dollars for the better, Leviticus stopped, exchanged a worried glance with Lou(ella), then held out the money bag for Silas T.

Leviticus said, "This is wrong."

I seized the bag, then said to Leviticus, "No, no, this is right, Leviticus. What he did was wrong. What we're doing is right. He was wrong. We was right. See?"

Silas T. looked up like his neck was in the noose and

the governor was on the telephone. Leviticus took the bag from me again and offered it back to Silas T.

"What're you doing?" I demanded, onct again seizing the bag.

"No," Leviticus said, "the good money's for the people." And he snatched that bag for a third time.

Well, that made no sense to me, so I hollered, "What people?"

"Them!" Leviticus said, pointing toward the window.

"That's right," Toofer broke in. "You should take the counterfeit money so the people can get good." And I'll be damned if he didn't, for onct and of all times, agree with hisself.

Well, you know the words I was thinking. "Listen, you don't owe them Idlehour people one damn thing!" I began, and my voice cracked like it does when I get righteous-like. "They been against us, alla us, the whole time. Don't you know they'd just as soon see us fail?" I knew, even as I was talking, that the words was falling on closed ears and open hearts.

"Hey . . . I . . . know!" Tommy said, stepping outa his usual silence.

I rolled my eyes to the heavens.

"What? What?" Silas T. asked, hope-like.

"Make . . . him . . . give . . . us . . . all . . . the . . . bad . . . money," he struggled out, his white-man half shaking here and there.

"Yes, yes?" Silas T. encouraged him, looking like that noose was loosening up some.

"And . . . you . . . give . . . back. . ." Tommy paused to gather the words.

"Yes? Yes? I give back?" Silas T. dug. I reckon if he coulda reached into ol' Tommy and pulled the words out, he woulda.

". . .the . . . good . . . money . . . so . . . the . . . town . . . people . . . can . . . have . . . it." It took a while to get it out and, when he did, he looked to Leviticus and the rest, who all looked like they'd heard brilliance. Even Lou(ella).

"Because if he has bad money, he'll give out bad money. A pair a nently," Leviticus concluded. They all patted Leviticus on the back like he'd just papa'd quintuplets or something.

"Jeemanee Christmas, you guys!" I wailed. "This ain't at all what I'd planned!"

"Give us all the bad money and we'll burn it," Leviticus said to Silas T. in words I thought sounded real parent-like. "Here's the good." He held up the bag. Then he looked back at me, made for the window, and asked, "Shall I give it to the people now?"

I don't think I ever saw a feller move out faster than Silas T. "No! No!" he said. He took the bag from Leviticus. "You may be assured I'll see to it everyone gets real cash from now on instead of counterfeit."

I'd lost control of the whole fe-as-ko and I surely didn't relish the idea of facing E.M. without nine-thousand dollars of good, operating cash, like we'd planned.

"You can't trust him to co-operate," I said to Leviticus and his crew. "You just don't understand how these things work." I know I was sounding almost as desperate as Silas T. had, but it was suddenly me against 'em all.

"Oh, you'll have my full co-operation. I've learned my lesson, Royal, I really have," Silas T. said. His handlebars was slowly creeping back up.

"See?" Leviticus said, like just hearing ol' Silas T. promise made it all okay with him.

After a few seconds of slapbang consideration, I said, "Wait a minute. I have a provision." You know I trusted Silas T.'s word like I trusted a rattler in my bedroll not to bite me goodnight.

"A provision?" Silas T. asked. His eyes was darkening

some and he clutched the money closer. No telling how many times his heart had stopped thunking that morning.

"Yes," says I. "Fire your man out there, what's his name? Fire that teller and hire Lou(ella) here. She's the only one who can tell counterfeit from real at a glance." Well, I thought that was a stroke of genius, considering how Perrault's ghost had been yanking on the rug under my feet.

"Oh, that won't be necessary, Royal. I'll get you all the counterfeit in the vault right now," Silas T. said, real agreeable-like.

"Yes," said I, "but what about all the counterfeit circulating throughout the town? No, my way or none other. Lou(ella) is your new teller. She'll keep you honest." I took a stance, you know the kind: feet apart like as to say, go ahead, try to knock me over.

Silas T., well, he recognized a box canyon when he was in one. He just set back down and held onto the money like it was all that separated him from death. He leaned back in his fine leather chair and stared up at me. Then he looked at all the crew about the room. Cripes, he looked real wrung-out. I reckon even his shadow considered walking out on him that morning. But at least he had the marbles to nod me a "All right, Royal, you win."

Lou(ella) was nearly busting for the pride of being talked about so. Leviticus and his crew patted her on the back to congratulate her on her latest triumph in life, and when I left that office I felt a odd lumpa pride myownself. For up to then, I really hadn't realized how honest Leviticus and folks like him was. And after all, they'd prevented this ol' cowhand from becoming a first-class extorter . . . and one extorter to a story is probably enough.

You better re-load that pen of yours, son, 'cause the fe-as-ko was still falling all around us that hot summer morning of '93.

# three

Y ou see, the way I figured it, I was only halfway outa the Alamo onaccounta I still had E.M. Gallucci to reconcile. Hell, son, I can tell by the way you wince, you yourownself have had some dealings with uppity women.

So anyway, I sent Lou(ella) and Leviticus and the others over to the drugstore for a soda whilst I rendezvoused with E.M. Gallucci at the boarding house, like we'd planned.

Well, you know I was walking ticklish and rehearsing speeches as I went. The sun was glaring off the dusty yellow of Idlehour, and I wisht to hell I could just wander into the Glass and have me a cold beer.

"Well? How'd it go?" she asked whilst I set down next to her in the parlor.

"Fine. Fine. Not all according to plan, perhaps, but. . ." I had to occupy my eyes away from hers.

"What do you mean, not all according to plan?" she interrupted, her lovely I-talian face going concerned. "You traded the nine thousand, didn't you? You let him know that you know, didn't you, Royal?"

I didn't reply, but found myself playing with a anti-macassar on the divan.

"Royal?" she asked again.

"Oh, he knows I know," I said. "And the nine thousand, well, we passed it back and forth some. Then Leviticus . . . well, he . . . got a better idea." I think I let my words trail some.

"Leviticus!" she boomed, like I somehow knew she

would. She sprang up so fast I wondered if a corset stay had had the sauce to stab her.

Well, I had that awkward feeling that these were the testing waters of which you hear tell that invariably come to every she-he relationship.

"Oh, but you'da been proud," I allowed, "how he stood up all honest and thinking only of the good of the community!" I decided to hand it to her that way, rather than come right out with the fact we was just as much on a financial flounder as we was before I walked into the bank.

"But you traded the money, didn't you, Royal?" There was a tinge of panic coming to her voice.

"Well, yes, we did trade it. Sorta," I said.

"Sorta?" she shouted, echoing me. "Sorta? Sorta for what?"

Well, she surely did rant whilst I explained what'd happened that morning. And at first, I have to tell you, I didn't like the side of Miss Gallucci that cropped up. Then, when all sides was explained in detail, she quieted down some and allowed as she was only thinking of the betterment of Four Arrows, certainly not of her own behalf.

Finally, she said, "Damn! We sure could have used that money!" She drummed her fingers as she thought the situation through.

"Now, E.M., don't swear," I remember saying, not sure if she would throw something more than her dagger-eyes. "Well, now according to the will," I continued, "we just have to turn a profit on the cattle drive, so I didn't see what good nine-thousand dollars cash in hand would be," I said.

"Are you kidding?" she said. "That cash would have paid bills all summer so we can realize more profit come fall!" Then she looked sternly at me and asked, "Have you forgotten who the independent accounting firm is?"

"You," I replied.

"Howell, Powell and Gallucci, Royal!" she corrected me. "Three men who don't have a very fond view of this whole thing. Believe me, I would have found a way to use that money to tip the scales. You may be sure that when this whole thing is over, everyone else'll have their fingers on the scales too."

"Now," said I, "the cattle are looking real fine, E.M. And the count's up. We're gonna do dandy come fall. You wait and see." I reckon I've always set optimistic in the saddle.

At that, she took a newspaper from her satchel and handed it to me. She'd circled a few headlines to draw my eyes: **CATTLE PRICES FALL ONCE AGAIN . . . CALVES BRING LOWEST PRICE IN TWENTY YEARS . . . PANIC . . . RANCHERS FORECASTING DOOM.**

I looked at her, then the masthead. The paper wasn't from Chicago, Denver, or even Spokane; it was right outa Portland.

My mouth went dry as I asked, "They talking 'bout Portland prices?"

E.M. nodded sober-like. "We have problems, Royal. Look at that. Beef is down three cents a pound in just two days. And there's nothing in that paper or any other in this country that indicates prices will go back up or even stabilize."

I coulda kicked myself for ignoring the problem for so long. 'Course, I knew things was getting bad, but I always thought Oregon was immune to economic problems. Hell, we'd had it so good for so long, I guess I'd thought God had intended for it to stay that way. And to salt my wounds, a woman had to bring it to my attention.

I got up and wandered the room, thinking hard. I guess, for the first time ever, I thought we might actually lose Four Arrows and I don't recall ever feeling any lower than I did at that moment.

Finally, I said, "Well, the first thing we gotta do is call a meeting."

"Between who?" E.M. asked, sarcastic-like. "You and God?"

I half-smiled at her. "I believe He's outa the country. No, we gotta get together with the rest of the ranchers and see what everybody else is doing about this."

"What good will that do?" she asked. "You don't need any of their problems, Royal. You have to think of Four Arrows cattle." She plopped her hourglass back down. A rise of dust rose outa the horsehair divan and looked kinda gold dust-like in the stream of sunlight.

Well that was true, but neighbors is neighbors and I insisted. So I took my leave, wondering how in hell I'd come to think I was such a big gun. I don't think I knew about batting averages in those days, but if I did, I'da been in the low two-hundreds.

I rounded up Leviticus and his crew, who was charging their third rounda sodas. On the ride back, I told 'em all just where things stood. I doubted they understood the part about prices and all, but they listened real good, like they always did when I talked about vital things, and it felt good knowing they was listening, even if they wasn't hearing.

When I was done explaining things, we alla us fell silent, which is easy to do when you got buckboard wheels rhyming with horses' hooves and tack a-jingling back to the comforting squeak of worn-in leather.

I reckon I'd ridden that road a million times . . . in all sortsa weather, in all sortsa spirits, and in all sortsa mind. There I was, not even thirty yet, thinking I was, onct again, ol' Atlas with the weight of the world, including all its unsold cattle, slipping off my shoulders.

Onct back to Four Arrows, I told Jay and Hardy how things stood and you can be sure they was as upset with me as E.M. regarding the fateful events of the morning. But I bit them off, saying I was tired and if they was so damn smart, they'd know to leave me alone. Then I sent Jay out to inform the neighboring ranchers that I was calling a meeting in Idlehour for the night after next, regarding the current state of affairs.

I and my dilemma retired to my room early. I tried to smoke a pipe—which I always thought helped the thinking processes—but I soon put it out as just another fabled hoax. Unable to sleep, I just laid on my bed, stared at the ceiling, and studied the matter. I think I was wishing ol' God would get on back to His favored corner and settle some things. Then I thought about Perrault: of all the times for him to die and leave such a fandangled will, he had to pick the early nineties, when we was all up to our nosehairs in economic straits. Damn Perrault! Never did think of anyone other than hisself.

# four

*W*ell, if I was worried not too many folks would show up at the town hall for the meeting, then I had worried needless-like, for the room was packed not only with ranchers, but with their wives, mothers-in-law, and some of their ranch hands as well. Nearly all my men had accompanied me, including Anita, Leviticus, and his crew. A pair a nently, they was just as concerned as I was and we wasted no time in getting down to matters.

"Hey, tell us about those bank robbers, Royal!" someone shouted as I took the stand to speak. All of a sudden, I felt like the main act at a Chautauqua and maybe they only turned out to hear a good yarn.

I cast a look to Leviticus and E.M., then to Silas T. "Well,

I'd like to tell you all about it, folks," I began, my voice shaky and cracky onaccounta public speaking wasn't ever one of my long suits. "But we're here to talk cattle, not robbers." At that, they all silenced. "Like you know, prices is plummeting [I stole that word from the paper] and the whole reason for this meeting is to discuss what plans any of you have come up with which might be of some help to us all." Well, that sounded pretty damn good, I told myownself.

I looked out over the room and everyone pretty much just exchanged glances. Then someone came up with, "What can we do, Royal? Best take what we can get and be grateful!"

Another rancher called out, "My missus figured up last night that with all I got into my herd this year, I'd do better to kill 'em all now, sell the hides, and bury the carcasses, before I pump any more money into 'em and take a shellacking at the market!" Well, he sure didn't chew any cud with his piece.

This comment brought gasps and I called out, "Well, now that's a little drastic, Archer, don't you think? But that's not far from what I was thinking. I think I'm gonna drive my cattle over to Pendleton as soon as I can."

Someone called out, "In this weather? You been hanging 'round your screwball foundlings a little too long, Leckner!"

Some other soothsayer said, "Nobody drives cattle in this heat! It ain't rained in three weeks! Too risky. You'll lose half your spring calves, anyway!"

"Well," said I, forceful-like, "like Mrs. Archer said, best get rid of 'em now, before prices drop to nothing. What happens when we *all* get to the point when it's cheaper to kill 'em than to keep 'em?"

There was more disgruntlements till someone else called out, "How you gonna move over 2500 head of cattle with just a handful of men, anyway, Royal? We all been a little curious about that."

"Well, that brings me around to my next idea," I went on, hell bent for leather on not losing them folks then. "What if we was, alla us, to pool our cattle together and, using all the men possible, drive 'em to Pendleton for one huge sale? If I can wrangle a contract at a reasonable price, then we'd all at least break even." I looked out over the room. I swear I could see the heat of the day and the situation rise like those wavy visions off a desert.

Well, that brought out another mob-discussion and it took some time before they all quieted down.

"Well, I'm waiting to hear some better ideas," I finally called out, leaning on the podium. There was more this-ing and that-ing, till it was clear that no one thought too much of my idea and a every-man-for-hisself attitude generally prevailed. So much for ol' Lincoln's divided-house spiel.

So again I called out, "Come on now. There must be a answer out there." I noticed, toward the back, there had been a slight commotion amongst Leviticus and his crew which, like you know, was common and I had come to mostly ignore.

"Hey, he wants to say something!" a man called out, standing up and pointing to Tommy Two Hearts. There was a tinge of mock in his voice and I was getting ready for a fight.

Someone else called back, "Yeah, let's hear what the twitching red man has to say!" Then there was some cruel japery amongst the crowd.

I knew my face was red with rilement, but when I looked at Tommy I hoped my eyes told him it was okay. "You take care who you're calling a twitching red man, Frank Meyers!" I called back over the crowd. "Who was the man got hisself drunk last Fourtha July and fell asleep in his birthday suit and couldn't stride a horse for six days for the sunburn?"

Well, that surely lightened things up some and silenced the fun-making toward my crew. But, to my shocked eyes, Tommy insisted throughout and kept his hand raised high to speak.

Finally, since I wasn't sure what else to do, I called on him. He rose, shaky-like of course, and he came forward, holding a envelope up above his head for all to see.

"Read . . . this . . . please," he said, casting me a half-smile, which was his full load.

I took the envelope, a little embarrassed, and said to him quietly, "Tommy, I'll read this to you later. This ain't the time to read to you." His face was bright red with a lively spirit I ain't never seen on him. I thought maybe his good side was going to creep on over and gobble up his bad side. His smile just broadened, like he didn't understand a word I said, which, I thought, mighta been the case.

"It's . . . a . . . telegram," he continued. "Can't . . . you . . . read?"

"Of course I can read, Tommy, you know that," says I. "Why don't you go back and set down and I promise I'll read this later." I often look back and still feel bad . . . how like a child I treated Tommy that night. But hell, the whole town of Idlehour set perched at my feet, ready to either follow me or hang me.

Well, by then Leviticus and Toofer and Lou(ella) had crowded 'round the podium and I'd lost whatever control I had over the crowd. I guess it all looked a little ridiculous and there was I, the center of it all.

"Here, Royal, why don't you let *me* take over while you . . . get things straightened out," Silas T. said, rising and pulling down his vest, him then treating myownself a little like a child. He took my place at the podium.

Under the critical circumstances, I thought that was best and I ushered my crew into the judge's chambers. I was steamed, you know that.

I snatched the telegram outa Tommy's hand and said,

"What's so damn urgent about this?" Only then did it occur to me: how would Tommy Two Hearts, of all people, get hisself a telegram? "How did you get this?" I asked as I ripped it open.

"He sent for it!" Leviticus said, with great excitement. "He just got it!"

"What? What?" Lou(ella) asked, jumping up and down and nearly beside herself with the anxiety of it all.

"Let him read it," Toofer said. "Yeah, let him read it," Toofer said.

They was all gathered so close to me I could hardly hold the telegram still. "Back off," I finally said, and they did.

They musta thrilled to watch my face, for they started hugging each other like I'd found the map to the Lost Blue Bucket Mine or something.

I read it again, then looked at 'em, narrowing my glance some. "How'd you do this?" I asked, suspicious-like.

The working side of Tommy's face gushed a smile so big it nearly pulled up his non-working side in spite of itself.

"I . . . got . . . conn . . . ections," he said, slowly of course, but mighty and proudful.

Well, I wasn't then, nor am I now, a touching man, but I threw my arms around him and gave him probably the first hug of his life. He stiffened up. I guess he didn't know enough to hug back, but that damn, cockeyed smile was still hanging on his face.

Well, I wasted no time in making it back to the podium, followed by my crew. I nudged Silas T. aside and called the room to attention.

"Alla you! Alla you!" I called out. "I think I have here the answer to everything. And before I read this, all you gotta know is, it was these folks here, these people you all been standing in line to take a pot shot at, that come up with the idea."

Now listen to this: I have it memorized, but here's the telegram so you can read along. "I hereby authorize Royal

Leckner, Idlehour, Oregon, to act as sole agent for all cattle purchases for the Spokane Indian Reservation. Minimum five-thousand head to be purchased at market value, this date, and to be delivered to Walla Walla, Washington by September 15th, 1893 latest, for railroad shipment to reservation. Acceptance of this post constitutes a U.S. Government Contract. Please respond this office by July 1, 1893."

There was a heated silence whilst that sunk in. Then all at onct there was a general whooping and hollering, mosta which came from my own boys.

When things had quieted down some, one man, renownst for his devil's advocating, asked, "Do you think we have five-thousand cattle between alla us?"

The consensus was yes.

"All right then," he continued, "then how do we get five-thousand cattle to Walla Walla? The most any of us has ever driven has been a couple of hundred head. Well, 'cept for you, Royal."

"We'll do it the way he said!" someone spoke up for me. "All together! Every available man and boy!"

"Yeah, we'll do it!"

"We have to do it!"

"It's our only chance!"

Folks was shouting all around the room.

Well, I wasn't sure I was hearing the voices of Idlehourians speaking so comradish, but I looked 'round and, sure enough, I was in the courthouse of Idlehour, the very same courthouse where I'd first learnt about Leviticus.

So it was decided there and then, with one-hundred percent agreement, that we'd all pull in together, pledge every head to the contract, and drive 'em all—come hell, come high water, and come September—to Walla Walla Wash. And with the sure sale promised, we alla us knew we had the grit to get them cows through anything, even the Grand Canyon, if we had to.

$\mathcal{N}$ow, I should tell you something I didn't tell the folks in the courthouse that day. There was a P.S. at the end of that telegram, which explained how Tommy Two Hearts had worked his magic:

"P.S. Tommy, look forward to visiting you in your new home at Four Arrows. So glad you found peace and love at last. Your Aunt Zelda sends her love. Regards, Uncle Burt."

Uncle Burt, it seemed, was the Purchasing Agent for the Bureau of Indian Affairs for the State of Washington, back then in 1893, and ol' Tommy, he'd never let on he had regular folks anywheres.

Like you must know, when I walked into the courthouse that night, I wasn't sure if I would be riding out on a rail or in a chariot of salvation. And not one man, nor woman, nor mother-in-law uttered even one ill comment toward me and Leviticus and our crew as we passed outa the courthouse.

Well, I knew there was more to Tommy's story, so later that night, after things had died down some, I cornered Tommy in the cool of the porch. We both knew he'd been magical that day and I won't ever be forgetting that half smile of his as I set down next to him.

I asked him, "How come you never told me 'bout your kin in Spokane?"

He looked down at his bad hand lying helpless in his good one and said, "I . . . don't . . . know."

"Yes you do. Why?" I prodded.

He took a long pause and looked out into the yard. The smile disappeared and, by the look on his face, I wondered if I was pressing into some sorry land. I rose, thinking he wasn't gonna answer me and I was a damn fool for prying.

"Royal," he said, when I was just about to the door, "I . . . I . . . I . . . lived . . . with . . . Uncle . . . Burt . . . and . . . Aunt . . . Zelda . . . onct."

I was kicking myself for salting his wound. Well, you gotta know the last thing I wanted was to put Tommy through any painful-like memories, so I ask, soft-like, "But they sound like real good folks, Tommy.".

"They . . . are . . . good . . . folks . . . but . . . a . . . man . . . like . . . me . . . needs . . . to . . . be . . . with . . . his . . . own . . . kind."

"But don't they live on the reservation?" I asked. "That's your own kind, Tommy."

Then Tommy's jagged smile returned up to me and he said, "No . . . no . . . Royal . . . you . . . should . . . know . . . my . . . own . . . kind . . . is . . . Leviticus . . . Lou(ella) . . . and . . . Toofer. I . . . am . . . a . . . normal . . . man . . . to . . . them. No . . . one . . . else . . . thinks . . . I . . . am . . . a . . . normal . . . man."

Well, just when you think you know all there is to know in life, along comes what you thought was a lesser to put you in your place.

I came acrost the porch, took his good hand, shook it, and said, "Well, you just saved our hash, Tommy. And as far as I'm concerned, that took better than just a normal man."

He nodded his head and stood up, and we walked into the house, slowly but surely and side by side.

# five

*W*ell, you've wrote down pages and pages, and I reckon you're happy to know we're almost to the end of this whole fe-as-ko. I'll bet you get rheumatism in your hands onaccounta me and my leaky mouth. I'll give you some Bag Balm before you leave.

Well, the summer, though it was hot, went well onct the pressure of the falling beef prices was taken away. We alla us set out to raise the best beef we could for the Spokane Indians Beef Issue. Our problems wasn't solved by any means, but for the first time I ever did recollect, folks in that area worked together for the same goal.

As I marked the calendar off, day by day, to the end of the five-hundred-day period of Perrault's will, I got more and more worried. Making the profit was still gonna be a chore.

E.M. and me worked side by side, every day, robbing Peter's account to pay off Paul's, counting each penny and allotting funds only where we had to. The hands was still standing by me, happy to have their pay at the end of the September drive. I carried their accounts in town which, up to the day of Tommy's telegram, I hadn't been able to do. Like I said, we was all working together then and even the merchants went along with us ranchers.

But you know what a worrier I was in those days, and I laid awake some nights wondering if, after all the cattle moved outa the valley and into the cattle cars, folks would turn again and work towards Four Arrows' failure, so's they could turn Idlehour into a place of modern science or something. Always, it was at the back of my mind, where it found company with the memory of fires and bank robberies and Miss Wintermutes and Philadelphia lawyers and dishonest independent accountants and prejudice.

"It'll be close, Roy, real close," E.M. said, looking over my shoulder the eve of the cattle drive. I had before me the latest set of figures E.M. had worked up and it all depended on how much weight my cattle took off on the short, but trying, trail to Walla Walla Wash.

She placed her hand on my shoulder and well, you know how love comes to bloom with the summer sun. I took her hand and kissed it. Before you knew it, we was in a embrace the likes of which you see on the labels of French perfume bottles. Yep, we had grown mighty close over the summer.

Then we unlocked, for we heard Anita's rustle in the dining room. E.M. quickly took a stance away from my embrace and asked if I was sure the sixty-three men who'd signed on could handle five-thousand heada cattle.

I slicked back my hair, just so's in case Anita came in we'd look innocent, and replied, "Hard to say, considering half those boys ain't never driven a cow further than to the nearest water hole. But as long as the cattle don't know that, we'll make it."

Well, like we knew she would, Anita came in and fixed us both with a 'got-ya' look and announced dinner. As I recall, E.M. and I could hardly keep our eyes offa each other that night, which didn't make it any easier for me to pull off to sleep.


*N*ow, I'm willing to wager that anyone who might see fit to read this story has most likely seen a cowboy movie and thinks they know all about cattle drives. Well, take away Hoot Gibson, rustlers, stampedes, snake bites, and sad tunes of stale love rendered to a full moon and sleeping cattle, and you got a taste of our drive.

No, lucky for us, our drive was mostly just dusty and uneventful, which maybe don't make for good story-telling, but sure was easier on the cattle and me.

We did good. Real good, all things considered. Especially Leviticus and his crew did good. They rode like top ranahans and their easy natures was soothing to the cows. Even Lou(ella) did good keeping tracka all the different brands and each rancher's head count. She was the best tallyman we ever any of us had, and we alla us knew ol' Silas T.'s teller cage was manned by a expert.

When we all arrived back to Idlehour, we was alla us trail-weary, but glad we'd pulled it off. All the owners paid off their hands, banked their profits, maybe got a snootful, then went home to share their good news with their families. I, of course, went straight to Four Arrows to prepare for the final accounting, the results of which would determine the fate of Four Arrows.

*EM* had arranged it all to take place three days after our arrival back from the drive. Leviticus and me rose extra early to fancy up some. I need to tell you, I felt like a proud papa, helping Leviticus slick up for that day. I loaned him my proudest bolo tie and he made a fine, handsome reflection in my bedroom mirror. His clothes was store-bought and cut him justice through his broad shoulders, and I knew women looked twice when he passed.

He knew, somewheres on some plateau, that this was the day we'd alla us waited for. And though he couldn't have told you so's you'd understand, he knew he had the lives of Tommy, Toofer, and Lou(ella) all in the palm of his gentle hand.

Just like the will-reading, the final accounting was to take place in the judge's chambers at the courthouse. And also like the will-reading, nearly the same crowd was assembled: Judge Blaylock (who looked like he took a bad year), Sheriff Agnew (who never did look me in the eye after that robbery episode), Julius Armentrout (in *another* new suit; two suits in less than 500 days, Good God!), Pastor Dennison (with his hands folded, God-like as usual), and Silas T. (who woulda been my personal slave over the summer if I'da let him).

When Leviticus and I entered the room, I was surprised not to see E.M. Gallucci, who had left my company the day prior to welcome a representative from Howell, Powell and Gallucci. I stated right off I wouldn't start till she arrived.

When she finally entered a few moments later, I knew at a glance that the representative was none other than Mr. Hello-Daddy Gallucci. She smiled coy-like as she introduced her daddy all 'round, and I thought the handshake he gave me was particularily gruff and, to this day, I think he woulda made a fine gangster. A man born too soon, you know what I mean?

Judge Blaylock started right off with, "My, my, five-hundred days surely goes by quickly."

"Well, it hasn't been exactly five-hundred days, Judge Blaylock," Silas T. corrected, already getting nervous.

"It hasn't? I thought we had to wait five-hundred days," the judge said, whilst spreading papers out in front of him.

"You see, Judge," Julius explained, "we determined that it was Perrault's will that the final judgment be made as soon after the cattle drive as possible and that the five-hundred-day figure represented a maximum time."

"Oh, you did, did you?" the Judge asked back. "Well, I guess it doesn't matter. So what's the verdict?" He looked at everyone like we was all members of a jury and had a yea or a nay to say about it.

Miss Gallucci took the Four Arrows account book from her daddy's hands and placed it in front of Judge Blaylock. "Your honor," she began, her voice strong and clear, "these are the figures which, in my estimation, show the accounts of Four Arrows to be in a solvent state. Three-hundred and sixty dollars in the black, to be exact. My father here has verified my figures."

She flashed him a look which I wouldn't want to be on the receiving end of, and he replied, "Everything seems to be in order." His voice didn't sound too much like a Gallucci, but at least he said the right words.

"And you, Mr. Burnbaum, do these figures concur with your records?" Judge Blaylock asked Silas T. as he passed the book over to him.

Silas T. pinched on his glasses and glanced up and down the columns. He held the room silent. Because he'd been groveling to me since the bank robbery, I was confident he would be agreeable.

He said, "Yes, yes. All this looks good and sound. Good and sound." He looked the columns over again, turned a page here and there, and nodded his head wisely. Then he looked up, took off his glasses, leaving little marks on his nose, and said, "But you know, there *is* one little item."

I knew it! I knew it! I knew it! I knew Silas T. had another card to play! Cripes, I still feel that sting in my chest when he glanced over to me and Leviticus and said, "Gosh, Royal, I wisht you'd budgeted for attorney's fees. You didn't think Julius was volunteering his time on this case, did you?"

With that, he handed me a bill which I didn't even glance at onaccounta I was halfway down his throat before they could pull me off. He was only a little ruffled and mighty gloaty. I took a hated glance to Julius, who was inspecting his fingernails like this was no fault of his.

"Why the hell didn't you bill me all along?" I demands. I know I don't have hackles, but they was standing on end anyhow.

To which Julius quietly replied, "Because the majority of the work was just done in the last week."

"Four-hundred and two dollars!" E.M. hollers, as good as any man. "An outrage! Your honor, don't you think the presentation of this bill is just a little too convenient?"

The judge looked at the bill and compared it to the final Four Arrows net. "If you pay this, you'll be in the red by forty-two bucks. I don't know. This one might be too close to call." He cast a judicial glance toward the others.

Julius stood up and began orating: "Your Honor, don't you see, it hardly matters. Breaking even is hardly a successful cattle drive. Face it, Leckner and his charge here have failed with Four Arrows and I demand that you fulfill the wishes of the late Samuel J. Perrault and liquidate Four Arrows. Here. Here's a copy of the will. Maybe you better refresh your memory regarding its tenets."

The judge tossed down the will with a snap. "You small town, stuffed pettyfogger, I don't need to refresh my memory with anything!" Judge Blaylock growled back. He stood up and said, "I'm calling a recess of one hour while I think all this over. Where's the nearest outhouse?"

Pastor Dennison pointed outside and, as soon as the judge left, we alla us started yelling at each other. With all the talking and shouting and accusing and calling outside for fistacuffs, I hadn't noticed that Leviticus had left the room.

"I still don't see why it matters any to you, Royal," Silas T. kept saying. "You're about to become the richest man in the county as it is. Twenty-five-thousand dollars is hardly anything to sniff at. By the way, have you given any thought at all as to where you might invest. . ."

Then Julius broke in with, "Really Royal, give it up. You might save Four Arrows for this kid and he'll bumble along okay until you leave. Then what? How do you think he'll do without you? And then what becomes of your beloved Four Arrows?"

"Yeah. Take your money and run, Royal," Sheriff Agnew said.

I felt like the room was closing in on me. I looked to E.M. for help, but she was deeply involved in adding and double-checking her figures, running beads all up and down that damned abacus of hers.

I surely didn't like the look on Judge Blaylock's face when he returned. We all set down again and leaned into the judge as he began to speak: "Gentlemen, and lady, I'm afraid . . . that is, I've read and reread Perrault's will. I've read between the lines, beside the lines, and behind the lines, but without personally knowing the deceased it is nearly impossible for me to interpret his wording. In cases like this, where there is only black and white and unfortunately, in this case, red. . ."

I couldn't believe I was hearing him correctly. All the work, the planning, the scheming, the luck . . . for this!

There then came a timid knock on the door, which hardly any of us heard. When it came again, I rushed to the door and called out, "Hold it! Hold it! Somebody's at the door." I didn't care who it was. It coulda been ol' Scratch Hisself and I woulda sold him my soul for forty-two bucks right then and there if he coulda changed the course of things.

I opened the door and there stood Leviticus, hat in hand. In his hat was two crisp twenty-dollar bills.

"Hi, Royal," he said, displaying his looney, loveable smile. "I been keeping this from you. I hope you're not mad." Then his face went grim, for his confession was, a pair a nently, a difficult one.

"You what?" I asked.

"I know it was wrong, to hide money," he said. "But I thought I might need it some day. Here." He handed me the hat and slowly set down in the corner.

Silas T. rose, pointed, and shouted, "No fair! That money is his personal assets, not Four Arrows money. It can't be counted!"

"No, it's Four Arrows money!" Leviticus shouted back,

and he stood up bravely to face the judge and Silas T. "That's where I got it. At Four Arrows."

I softened my face and voice and asked him, "How did you get this money?"

"It's only forty dollars. Lou(ella) said it was two of the nicest twenty-dollar bills she ever saw!" Leviticus replied.

He looked like he was ready to cry. Whereupon Silas T. boomed, "Lou(ella)! And just where did *she* get it, I'd like to know? Perhaps you should know, Your Honor, that this Lou(ella) person we're talking about works for me at the bank. Now I'm going to have to audit all my books. She probably embezzled it! Hell, she's only earned seven dollars so far!"

"Silas T.," Julius broke in, grabbing for the banker's sleeve. "Sit down."

But Silas T. continued with, "Well, it's downright idiotic to think that girl could. . ."

"Silas T., I said sit down! Please," Julius advised again.

Then Judge Blaylock broke in with, "Well, I hardly see that it matters where this Lou(ella) got the money."

"Oh yes, yes it does!" says I. My attack position was clear as day. "Silas T. is right. Maybe this money *is* stolen. Maybe he'd like to take a closer look at it."

That was the point Silas T. put it all together. He slowly set down and swallered hard as I passed one of the twenties in front of him.

"Lou(ella) said it was memory money," Leviticus added, defensive-like.

"But you're still not showing a profit. You're minus two dollars!" Judge Blaylock said, looking like he was ready to puff out some. "Why couldn't you folks have straightened all this out before I got here?" He sounded real weary and like the heat was getting to him.

Then Mr. Gallucci stood up and said, "Silas T., Julius, I give up. Now, I've been in on this from the beginning and I've watched it all go haywire. One hitch after another. And now I've apparently even lost a daughter to this whole confounded Four Arrows fiasco!"

We all stared at him, mouths catching flies.

"Mr. Gallucci, I'm sure I don't know what you're talking about," Silas T. mumbled, his handlebar onct again losing its spunk.

"Yes you do!" Mr. Gallucci corrected him. "Oh, it was a good idea and an honorable attempt. It's not worth it, though. Your Honor, I'd like to resign my responsibilities in this matter." Mr. Gallucci put on his hat like as to leave, then added, "Oh, by the way, it's come to my attention that we had previously incorrectly billed the Perrault account. Although the error occurred sometime in '91, we've just recently discovered it." He took out a five-dollar gold piece from his pocket, tossed it on the table and said as he left, "There. Three dollars profit." He turned, looked at me, then Leviticus, then took a long stare at his daughter and said, shaking his head, "What an operation! Well, maybe we'll see you at Christmas, Elijah Marie. In an odd way, I miss you. So does your mother."

With that he left.

I looked at E.M., aghast-like, my face full of a teasing kinda delight, and I whispered, "Elijah Marie?"

The judge picked up the five-dollar gold piece along with the two counterfeit 'keepsakes,' placed 'em in the Four Arrows account book, and slammed it shut.

"Done and done!" he said. Then he reached out his hand to Leviticus and said, "Congratulations, young man. You've just inherited Four Arrows and all the insanity that goes with it!"

Now, unless you was in that room that day, then I reckon you've really never seen a smile.

# the last word on it

*W*ell, you stuck with me this long, so I reckon I can wind up quick. Say, kid, are you getting paid by the hour or by the story? Hell, if it's by the story, you may as well stick around and I'll rattle off a few more tales. After all, least now you're used to my way of telling and all.

What's left? Oh yes, I thought you might want to know how we alla us ended up. Well, Leviticus and Lou(ella), like you was hoping, climbed up onto the altar and got theirselves hitched. Cripes, as far as I could figure, they'd been sharing a bed for three years, so what the hell? Lou(ella) continued to work as a teller-watchdog at the bank till Silas T. died, three years later. Although the coroner said he'd suffered a heart attack, alla us knew he'd fagged out to escape his wife's nagging and the hopelessness of maintaining seven unmarried daughters and, of course, never seeing a penny of my fortune.

Anyway, after Silas T. bowed out, Lou(ella), with all our help, bought the bank and there she worked, memorizing numbers and being real generous to the folks of Idlehour, giving out loans like they oughta been, which was how desperately the money was needed and not on folks' ability to pay her back. And if she ran outa money (which she did real regular-like), Leviticus was generous with alla his money and he'd send her to work with her pockets full.

Tommy Two Hearts, with the helpa alla us, learnt to write passable and started writing to his aunt and uncle in Spokane. He got regular visits from 'em and he finally became one of my cleverest hands although, you know, he always did set a horse sorta caddy wampas.

Toofer also stayed on with us and he even almost stopped fighting amongst hisself, 'cept come election time, when we could count on him getting into a royal snit, till we'd all give up and just let him vote twice.

Well, the folks of Idlehour did real good, even though they never did get any of Four Arrows' assets like they'd all planned on. But when I got my twenty-five-thousand dollars, I gave some of it to the town anyway. But, genius-like, I appointed Leviticus, Tommy, Toofer, and Lou(ella) as trustees of it and they surely had some wonderful improvements done, including one of the first cement pools put in anywhere that I know of.

Jay grew up real good and became ranahan at Four Arrows. And ol' Hardy, well, we all chipped in and built him his own house overlooking the Walla Walla and he lived to see the United States go to war in Europe which, he told me before he went over the jump, was long enough for any man to live.

And what ever happened to Miss E.M. Gallucci and me? Well, we got us hitched too. And if you think our first encounters was a challenge, then you shoulda seen the rest of our lives together, like firinstance, that hell-bent-for-leather time that E.M. got so dang uppity about getting the vote. And then there was that year in the South Seas; there's a whole other episode. Oh, and did I ever mention I met ol' Queen Vic? Cripes, this ol' cowpoke's been lotsa places, including Hollywood, California. Yep, twenty-five thou sure went a long piece in those days.

But look at you. You're all tuckered out and maybe my other wanderings'll have to wait for another day. Just let it rest with this: we worked hard together and, by and by, we pulled Four Arrows outa its slump, making it, by the turn of the century, one of the finest cattle ranches anywhere. 1900. What a time. You ain't never lived till you seen a whole new century waltz in.

Since the beginning of this century, Leviticus has done just fine with the help of Jay, Lou(ella), Tommy Two Hearts, and Toofer and, a pair a nently, the memory of all I taught him. And I know for a fact that Leviticus always carried with him that note his daddy left him.

Remember? The envelope ol' Perrault said was to be given to his son after the 500 days? Come hell or high water? Well, like Tommy Two Hearts' fateful telegram, I've memorized it: "Dear son, Many people would have you think I got more than my fair share in life. Many people would have you think I took more than my fair share. But of all the things I was given, of all the things I took, when I gave you away, I gave away everything. Your father, Samuel J. Perrault"

I'd like to know how you're gonna wrestle all that chicken scratching into typed-out words, but I reckon that's your problem, son. Yours and ol' FDR's. So, unless you got any more questions, I reckon I'm plumb talked out. Hell, I yapped more this week than I have my whole life. But you got you a good way about you and I know you'll go far. Maybe you could see your way clear to send me a copy of alla this. That way, I might have something besides money to pass on to my heirs.

Well, I guess now you know how things was back then, back when we was young, up-snorting, and fulla the future. I know you writers like morals and the like, so I'll tell you this: as I look back on Leviticus and his crew, I've come to know one thing: A pair a nently, God puts in our brainpans what we need for what we gotta do, no more and no less. That way, there ain't no waste.

There. If that's a moral, use it. If it ain't, scribble it out and put in one of your own. So that's all. Period. The end.

**Randall Beth Platt** lives in Gig Harbor, Washington. She works for the Tacoma Y and travels the country playing in hand-ball tournaments. This is her first novel to be published, and the first of what she hopes will be many Royal Leckner novels.